Zainab Takes New York

Ayesha Harruna Attah is a Ghanaian-born writer living in Senegal. She was educated at Mount Holyoke College, Columbia University, and New York University. She is the author of the Commonwealth Writers Prize-nominated *Harmattan Rain*, *Saturdays Shadows*, *The Hundred Wells of Salaga*, currently translated into four languages, and *The Deep Blue Between*, a book for young adults. Her writing has appeared in the *New York Times*, *New York Times Magazine*, *Elle Italia*, *Asymptote* and the 2010 Caine Prize Writers' Anthology.

ZAINAB TAKES NEW YORK

AYESHA HARRUNA ATTAH

First published in eBook in 2021 by
HEADLINE ACCENT
An imprint of HEADLINE PUBLISHING GROUP

First published in paperback in 2022 by
HEADLINE ACCENT
An imprint of HEADLINE PUBLISHING GROUP

3

Cataloguing in Publication Data is available from the British Library

ISBN 978 1 4722 8839 4

Typeset in 10.5/13pt Bembo Std by Jouve (UK), Milton Keynes

Printed and bound in Great Britain by Clays Ltd, Elcograf S.p.A.

Headline's policy is to use papers that are natural, renewable and recyclable
products and made from wood grown in well-managed forests and other
controlled sources. The logging and manufacturing processes are expected
to conform to the environmental regulations of the country of origin.

HEADLINE PUBLISHING GROUP
An Hachette UK Company
Carmelite House
50 Victoria Embankment
London
EC4Y 0DZ

www.headline.co.uk
www.hachette.co.uk

For my besties.

Part One
June

Chapter One

Entry

'Doesn't this city make you feel amorous?' I said to Mary Grace, who was nosing behind a pickup truck on the FDR.

Hot, heavy air enveloped us, but it didn't bother me. I was pleased with how I already sounded like a New Yorker. *The FDR*. I only knew it because it was the highway closest to Densua, my childhood best friend who was already living in New York.

'Wow, *amorous*,' said Mary Grace. 'A word! I'm supposed to be the writer here. But you are right, enamoured is the way I feel when I come here. One falls in love with the city and in love in the city . . . Or maybe it's just romantics like us.'

Cool Mary Grace considered herself kin with me? I caught my reflection in the car's side mirror. My twists were flat from the three-hour trip from New England, and I fluffed them up with my fingers.

It was the middle of 2006. I'd spent the last four years of my life in a sleepy college village, and had lain dormant for most of that experience. But now I felt like I was pushing through an embryonic sac and was being born again in New York City.

'Pinch me,' I said out loud. 'I am *actually* moving here?'

'Yes, we're in New York City, baby!' Then a beat later, she honked and yelled, 'Move! Sorry, people don't know how to drive. He's from Jersey. No wonder.'

I wanted to point out that Mary Grace's number plate made her an outsider too, but what did I know? Maybe people from New Jersey were worse drivers than people from Massachusetts?

'I could never drive here,' I said. 'Even back home in Ghana, I was too scared to drive. So yeah, I don't drive, period.'

'New York has nothing on cities in the Philippines,' Mary Grace said. 'Or even Italy. Drive in Italy, and you can drive anywhere.'

She has lived.

'Did you say something?' I asked Mary Grace.

'Just about driving anywhere . . .'

So what was that I heard? A voice, certainly. A bit different from my own thoughts. Like it had emerged from outside of me, but it must have been wedged very well within my mind, because Mary Grace hadn't said those words and she wouldn't talk about her own self in the third person, would she? I cleared my throat and massaged my temple as if that would also clear my head. The heat was getting to me now.

The first time I saw Mary Grace was outside my dorm that very morning, and my first thought was hoping she wouldn't find me boring. With her pretty round face, big eyes, plump lips and skin almost as dark as mine, she had arrived in a RAV4, deeply dented on both sides, its bumper tacked back on with duct tape. The car was bursting with boxes, and on the roof were two plastic storage bins, their contents a mix of colours, textures and shapes. I didn't know how my two suitcases would Lego in with all the nyama nyama in the car, but we made it happen. She'd answered my ad on the five-college list serve and told me she was moving to New York, just like me. She went to Smith and I went to Mount Holyoke. She was going to NYU to write; I was going to SVA to draw. It was her red hair or the fact that she owned a car or that she knew how to get to New York; something about all that told me she and I came from very different worlds. But she seemed friendly, and the ride had gone smoothly.

We were whizzing down the FDR, preparing to shed our old skins and lead new lives.

'Want to change the music?' said Mary Grace, when traffic thickened and we were forced to slow down. The air in the car grew still. The hair on my arms stuck to my skin. 'I think we've listened to all five discs now.'

She pointed to the back. Her suitcases, boxes, blankets were covered in swirled S's of her hair. 'My CD folder is under the seat somewhere.'

I reached back; my fingers grazed furry surfaces, rubbery stringy things, and I tried not to gag at what I could be touching.

She has no home training, said the voice that had intruded earlier.

Those words, I knew them well. Who often said them? Not my mother. But close. The answer was on the tip of my tongue . . .

I finally made contact with what had to be the CD wallet and pulled it out.

And that was when it came to me. My late grandmother, Fati! When somebody walked past and didn't greet her, she said they didn't have home training. Someone came to her house and didn't eat food she'd offered, they had no home training. If I went to visit and stayed out too long with a cousin, I had no home training. Over the years, she'd found a way of seeping into my thoughts, stopping me from trying what most people went to college to experiment with: sex, drugs and alcohol. But even in those moments when she'd intruded, it was more the lessons she'd shoved down my throat than her voice. This was different. It was as if the real person had woken up in my body and was speaking in my head. If it really was her, what was she doing there? Was it the sultry entry into New York messing with me?

I looked at the fat CD wallet now on my jeans. Mary Grace had stuck all sorts of stickers on it: the iconic bitten apple, Ludacris, Sleater-Kinney, Bob Dylan, Michael Jackson, Kiss, Alanis Morissette, Lauryn Hill. She had the most eclectic taste in music I'd ever seen. The CDs inside the folder were just as varied, and suddenly my armpits itched, as they did any time I got nervous. This felt like a test to see if I was cool or not. I went for Lauryn Hill. She was universal.

'Good choice,' said Mary Grace. 'I'd love to see her in concert.'

'Me too.' I was trying to sound normal, but the voice I'd heard was bothering me. What was happening to me?

'Well, we're in the right place. I left Northampton one Tuesday evening just because Dave Matthews Band was playing at Madison Square Garden. I had a poli sci test the next day.'

'I wish I'd been that brave in college,' I said.

'My friend, you're still young, and you're moving to a place that wants you to go wild. You can finally go wild. If you need help, just call.'

You better not follow this one. She's dangerous.

And then:

Just because she's wild doesn't make her dangerous.

'OK?' I said out loud, a long-drawn-out question, more than a reply. Mary Grace didn't respond. I looked at my reflection again. What was going on? That just felt like two strangers were having a conversation in my head. Why was my mind suddenly so loud? I wiped off the fat beads of sweat from my temple. It had to be the heat or the hunger. That was it! In my excitement at moving to New York, I'd nibbled on a cinnamon bagel and left most of it on my plate. I would just endure the voices till I could get some food.

'Is it hot or is it just me?' I said, pulling at my collar.

'Here, let's turn on the AC.'

When the air cooled down, I felt slightly better. I was waiting for the voices to come back, but maybe talking to Mary Grace would make them stay away.

'How come you did poli sci and you're going to writing school?' I asked.

'I did it to please the parents,' said Mary Grace. 'Now I can do what I want. Writing fiction. What was *your* major?'

'Biology.'

'Ha. And you're gonna be an illustrator?'

'I did my pre-med requirement, but I barely passed. I minored in art and spent more time in the art department than in bio. My mother says, "Your ancestors didn't suffer all they did for you to end up as a starving artist", and yet here I am.'

'Sounds like something mine would say, too. That's what I like about international students. We *get* each other. So how did you know you wanted to be an illustrator, or why is it that you want to draw?'

Her question threw me off. I didn't want to admit how much of a fraud I felt for going to art school. I couldn't believe that SVA – one of the most competitive programmes for illustrators – had accepted me.

'I feel the most eloquent when I draw,' I said, 'if that makes any sense. Sometimes words get stuck in my mouth and don't come out right, but if I draw how I'm feeling, everything is clearer.'

'I get it. Writing is my therapy, too. But I want to make people pay to read my words. Ha, that reads FAT BUM,' Mary Grace said, pointing to an orange number plate ahead of us.

The plate's numbers and letters were 4A7 3UM.

'My brain does things like that,' she said. It was the first time the whole ride she'd come down a few notches on her cool ladder. It made her seem a little more like me.

'Did you take student housing?' I asked.

'Four years of student housing at Smith was enough,' she said, her hair, tied in a top bun, radiating a deep burgundy. With her Catholic name, I'd thought she was from South America, but she'd told me Cebu City in the Philippines. 'No, I have a place in Bushwick.'

We approached midtown New York, and I craned my neck far back, trying to see that point where most buildings kissed the sky. Even with the air conditioning on, the air was charged with the cacophony of a thousand honks, sirens and the smell of hot tarmac. So far, the voices had stayed away. Maybe it *was* the heat. Wasn't it incredible how the body worked? Overheat a bit and things go out of whack.

'What's your address?' Mary Grace asked.

I reached for my sketchbook, which carried my doodles and all manner of lists, including subway directions to Mr Thomas's, where I would be staying for three months before moving into student housing. Although Mary Grace was now making me reconsider my plans.

'I'll drop you off,' she said.

I paid her twenty-five dollars for the trip. Most people asked for twenty, but because I was carrying two suitcases and hers was a bigger car, I didn't mind the extra five.

'Let's hang out,' she said, and I was glad.

She left me at my doorstep, on a wide street lined on both sides with similarly hued brown buildings. This was going to be home. The voices hadn't come back.

Chapter Two
Brooklyn Apartment

I stood before a brownstone. These townhouses with their giant brown slabs had held my imagination since I was a child and gorged on *The Cosby Show.* Down the block, purple and yellow flowers pushed proudly out of pots under windows; on this building, the one I was about to enter, the plants looked crisped by the sun. I carried up one suitcase and then the other, and knocked.

When the Huxtables climbed into their house, they were blessed with the perfect life – a big family, with the parents living together and lots of siblings, a spacious living room, a kitchen with all the goodies a West African child could dream of, and those bedrooms! How I had dreamt of having a room like Vanessa's, with enough space for a big bed and an armchair. My dreaming was cut short when a small man with powder-white hair on his head and chin answered.

'Mr Thomas? I'm Zainab, um, from the Craigslist posting.' He pushed his nose into the air to look at me. He studied me, and what he saw was a skinny, tallish girl with dark brown skin in jeans and a striped shirt.

After probably deciding that I was harmless, he nodded and opened the door wider for me to bring the suitcases in. Inside, I squeezed my eyes, as if that would make the dark room brighter. He led me past a musty entryway to a living room that was hardly brighter. If only he would push open the shutters to let in the blue skies outside. I sat on a blanket-covered sofa and a cat jumped on me, its nails digging into my jeans.

'Jangles, down,' said Mr Thomas.

He peeled the cat off my lap and apologised.

It smells in here.

'Can I please have some water?' It was hot at Mr Thomas's. My theory was being proved. The New York heat activated the voices.

The old man, shoulders draped with a cardigan, shuffled around the corner of the living room and came back with a brown mug shaped like a face.

He watched me until I'd finished drinking. Then he spoke.

'The room's upstairs. Five hundred dollars a month. But my daughter's back in September, so just the three months. People don't always understand. Three months only. Wanna take a look?'

I nodded. Just how long had his daughter been away? The place could do with a good dusting – no, a purging, then refurbishing. The cat's acrid urine was now in my nostrils, and my nose itched. Even if this was cheap and temporary, I was beginning to doubt that I could spend even an hour here.

We scaled the creaky stairs, where a small stream of light squeezed in through a dusty translucent plastic sheet. I wondered who had lived here when it was first built. A bourgeois black family, I wanted to believe. They had settled here in the roaring twenties and had thrown wild intellectual parties that led to jazzy soirées afterwards. This man must have descended from one of the original owners.

He cracked open a door. Inside was a metal-framed bed next to faded brown wallpaper. I sneezed.

'God bless you,' he said. 'You'd have to do some cleaning when you come. I'm no good at it.'

It's why the rent is so cheap.

She can clean it and save money.

No. I wouldn't live here.

The voices were back. And maybe there were three of them? Was I hearing other people's thoughts? I turned around and peered over the banister. It was just Mr Thomas and me in the house. And these were certainly not Mr Thomas's thoughts. They were my thoughts, very much related to what I was thinking. I needed to cool down. I had to stay focused. I needed a home. I had a room to appraise.

But I couldn't cross the threshold. I had a way of propelling myself into the future, in my mind, but my future refused to have anything to do with this room. I couldn't picture myself sleeping on the most likely mite-infested mattress. I couldn't imagine having to dust the wallpaper. I couldn't see being inspired one bit by the room to get any drawing done. I could not envision myself tangling legs with anyone in this room. Because what was the point of coming to this city of hot men if I wasn't going to tangle legs sooner or later?

It was decided when we got into the bathroom.

'We share this one bathroom, so we're gonna make some kinda timetable or something.'

From outside the bathroom, I could see a film of brown coating what should have been a white ceramic tub. The smell of mildew clogged my nostrils and I stepped towards the staircase so I wouldn't gag.

'If you can write me a cheque for the deposit,' he said as he led the way downstairs, 'it's yours whenever you're ready.'

I unclasped the snap on my bag, dipped in my hand and danced my fingers around my chequebook.

'I can't believe it!' I said, palming my forehead. 'I could have sworn I packed it this morning.' I had to think fast. What was I doing with two suitcases and without my chequebook? It didn't add up. 'I'm going to stay with my family tonight, but I'll get back to you and have the deposit then.'

'Just come back with it at the end of this week and it should be fine.'

After he gave me directions on how to get to the G train to eventually make my way to Manhattan, I walked out of my dream of living like the Huxtables. I dragged my suitcases onto the landing outside and drew in the biggest breath of air. The horror! I hoped his daughter could come back faster, because someone needed to take care of that poor man and that house.

I walked slowly, my suitcases trailing me like a toddler's soiled blanket. They were hand-me-downs from my parents' trips to Rome and Frankfurt, and their outdated leather and all-round lack of style surely made me look like a bag lady. As I walked by row after row of brownstone buildings and their accompanying majestic trees, I felt self-pity rise in my chest. It would have been nice to live here. I could see myself calling a place like this home and being friends with my neighbours. But that dream was now crushed into powder and was being blown away by a sudden gust of hot wind.

Where would I stay?

My childhood friend Densua was my number one choice, but she was working in her all-important job, and I couldn't call her just out of the blue. So I phoned my mother's cousin, Uncle Ali. He lived in the Bronx and had a big house. I really didn't want to stay up there, especially since I'd decided that coming to New York would be my time to grow up. But now I didn't have much of a choice.

He picked up after two rings. After pleasantries, I told him what was going on.

'Um, so the place turned out to be a disaster and I need somewhere to crash.'

'I hear you, Zainabou,' he said. 'You know, let me call your aunt and get back to you.'

I'd expected him to say, 'You shouldn't even have to ask. You're family. This is your home.' When that wasn't forthcoming, that should have been my first red flag.

I waited, sitting on one of my suitcases, my back to an empty playground, as I studied the lime-green orb around the G train sign at the Myrtle–Willoughby subway stop. Shifting my gaze between a lot with grass pushing out of concrete and the storefronts across the road, I waited for the voices to come back. I waited for Uncle Ali, watching people push shopping carts with all sorts of contraptions in them. Coming from Mr Thomas's pretty street with its stately trees and gorgeous buildings, this subway stop was seedy. The faster I was gone from here, the happier I would be. The voices stayed quiet. Finally, my uncle called me back.

'Your aunty is home and expecting you. Take the number 2 to Gunhill Road.'

'How do I get the 2?'

He gave me directions, which I scribbled as soon as we hung up.

I knew some of my way around – I had memorised the one route I'd thought would become my lifeline: G train to the A train into Manhattan for my internship and then, after the summer, grad school. I supposed New Yorkers didn't say 'G train'. I would take the G.

I went down the steps with one suitcase, then ran back up for the other, praying nobody had put their grubby hands on my property. I got on the G, plunked myself on its orange chairs that reminded me of an inside-out orange popsicle, and felt my whole self deflate.

Densua's first day in New York must not have looked like this. Mary Grace was probably at her destination, already ensconced in comfort. Since I wasn't born rich, why hadn't I followed the path of most of the foreign students in my graduating class? I could be working at Pfizer or some other big pharmaceutical company. Or I could have switched tracks and gone to Lehman Brothers or Goldman Sachs or any of those two-name investment banks, and could be already living in a nice studio in Manhattan. No, I had to be the artist, the one bird doing wild twisty circles on its own while everyone else was in a straight V.

I switched to a crowded A, where people eyed me and my suitcases, and got down at Port Authority, the place I knew best in Manhattan, because it had always been my entry point into the city. My last year of college, any time I couldn't stand the village living any more, I would pack a weekend bag and take the bus to Densua's. Because she worked late hours, I would spend the whole afternoon going in and out of shops, from 42nd Street down to 34th, from 8th Avenue across to Park Avenue, and would never get bored. Sometimes, I would just walk, fancying myself a *flâneuse*, of course minus the wealth that the typical idle city walker came with.

I settled on the 2 up to the Bronx, grateful for a seat. My

disappointment rose even more than I thought possible, and I considered Mr Thomas's place. It had seemed the most decent on Craigslist and was honestly all I could afford earning a thousand dollars a month at my internship. And yet . . . my mother had raised me to be stronger than the weakness I'd just displayed. When she and my father split up, we moved out of a comfortable home with a nice surrounding fence and garden into a house in the middle of a crowded compound with other people. I didn't hear her once whine. She decorated the new house so nicely that it began to feel like home. All I had to do was slide on some ultra-strong yellow gloves and give Mr Thomas's house a good scrubbing, and I would have a beautiful place to call home . . .

We don't like cats.

One voice was back.

How did it work? I was still hungry, yes, but they had calmed down after a while. The voice was right, though. Jangles the cat was not doing it for me. I really had an aversion to the creatures, because I considered myself cat-like: always watching, sneaky. I would call Mr Thomas and tell him I was allergic to cats. It wasn't a total lie. I didn't like them, and my nose hadn't stopped tingling since I walked in.

I had to think positively. It would be good to eat home cooking at Uncle Ali's and not pay any rent. Sorry for Mr Thomas.

Maybe being back with family would also make the voices go away.

Chapter Three

The BX

I arrived in the Bronx with my two suitcases, and my pinched face met Uncle Ali's wife's pinched face. Not only did they live at almost the last stop in the Bronx, they also lived up four urine-stenched flights. I carried my suitcases all the way up and arrived at an apartment that smelt like stale palm oil and fermented corn. Suddenly, Mr Thomas's lodgings weren't looking so bad. Was living in New York destined to be an exercise in whose apartment smelt or looked the worst?

My boy and girl cousins, aged twelve and thirteen, came sullenly to join their mother. I liked children when they were two or three and could be cuddled and manipulated. At this stage between childhood and adolescence, I didn't know what to do with them.

'Hello, Aunty Emefa. Hi, Dzifa. Hello, Ibrahim!' I said, summoning pep and positivity. Maybe we'd all get along, and I could even become their cool cousin staying with them for the summer.

Only two weeks before, they had come to congratulate me for joining the ranks of Bachelor of Science. My aunt had held her children's hands as my uncle wielded a giant bouquet of flowers, proud of their niece who had graduated from a *very good* school in Massachusetts. 'It's like the Ivy League of liberal arts colleges,' I heard Uncle Ali say to anyone who would listen. Maybe it was the make-up she'd worn, or the floral shift dress, and her children in what must have been their Friday best – that is if they went to the mosque – but they were a lot more welcoming at my graduation.

Uncle Ali and Aunty Emefa were the exact opposite of my parents: my father was the Christian and my mother Muslim. I wasn't sure if Uncle Ali still prayed five times a day, after being married to a Christian woman for so long. Aunty Emefa had seemed so radiant and warm, asking me to pose over and over as she snapped photos of me in my kente-decorated gown and cap. Now she stood before me, head wrapped in a scarf, a face mask she'd probably dabbed on in the morning caking at the edges, and in a T-shirt and too-tight shorts. A golden cross rested on top of the T-shirt.

She doesn't want you here, said one of the voices in my mind.

I thought the voices came when it was hot, but this apartment wasn't hot.

She let me in, and I saw a living room that made me think of oranges. The curtains were reddish, the sofas were brown leather, the wall-to-wall carpeting was salmon-coloured. Neither my aunt nor my uncle seemed to possess one design bone. This was a room of utility. They bought things because they could afford them, or maybe because they'd been given them. A black bookcase was stuffed with books – my uncle's – and gilded picture frames of my cousins in various stages of lost teeth. Dzifa and Ibrahim went through an ajar door; beyond it was a bunk bed and a dresser bursting with clothing.

My uncle did not live in a big house. Whenever I'd visited New York, we'd meet in the city, where he'd buy me lo mein in the Manhattan Mall. He'd never outright said, 'I have a big house.' But the idea lived in suggestion.

'Life is fantastic in the Bronx,' he often said. And the last thing he'd said at my graduation was 'You and your father should come and stay with us: we'll grill, take long walks, we'll show you a good time.'

Taking long walks brought to mind green space. Being able to grill suggested at least having a back yard. Having room for me *and* my father implied having enough space for two extra bodies, did it not?

'Ibrahim, put the suitcases in your room,' said my aunt, her shorts snug against her hips, her caramel skin glistening. From the face mask alone, I was sure Aunty Emefa spent hours moisturising her skin and taking care of her body, unlike me.

'Oh, I can do it,' I offered, dragging the suitcase that had been bought in Rome. Ibrahim, beginning to shoot up past his sister, even though he was the younger of the two, reached for the other suitcase. We lugged them, unyielding things, across the velveteen of the carpet, into their room. I pushed them next to the bulging dresser.

'Dzifa,' shouted her mother. 'Put new sheets on Ibrahim's bed for Zainabou.'

I *really* didn't like being called Zainabou. I didn't know why it was that extended family members stretched people's names unnecessarily. My cousin Ayesha, my aunties called Ayeshatu. My mother was Jamilatu to this uncle.

'Aunty, please, I'll make the bed. But where will Ibrahim sleep?'

'On the sofa,' Ibrahim said.

I had moved to New York to displace a twelve-year-old from his bunk bed. I had moved to New York to share a room with a thirteen-year-old, and for some reason I was reminded of my twin half-siblings. How was I going to have sex while living in this place? How would I create a comic book that would rock bestseller lists?

'I can sleep on the sofa,' I said. At least it would be like having my own room when everyone had gone to bed.

'Ah, it's your choice,' said my aunt.

Would my uncle be getting a bigger place, or were my boy and girl cousin destined to share a room through adolescence? That would not be comfortable. And now I was in the mix.

Call back the old man.

It's too late.

She should learn to see when it's going well for her.

Stop talking, I wanted to shout. Instead, I smiled at Aunty Emefa's face mask and tried to ignore the chatter in my mind.

Who were these voices?

Chapter Four

Webster Hall

I'd called Densua on speakerphone so my uncle and aunt would know exactly who I was meeting and spending my Friday night with. My uncle didn't object; my aunt looked at me like she had cracked open the skin and bone on my forehead and could see into my brain. I was going fishing.

Now that Densua and I were zooming in a taxi downtown, my headiness grew. The lights, the blinking lights, the traffic lights flashing stop or go, the yellows zipping by, the smell of night (candied peanuts, meat grilling, the seared-garlic aroma of takeout), the thrill of what could be, the promise of sweat and movement and maybe even more. I was so excited, I refused to talk to Densua about the voices in case she confirmed that I was losing my mind.

After years of living in South Hadley, I couldn't contain my delight at having constant access to New York's party scene. Yes, we had parties at the Betty Shabazz Center and the different cultural centres in the five colleges, but the closest we came to the magic and grit of New York was UMass's The X. Once, even, a rumour spread that someone had a gun, and we split, got into the school van we'd borrowed and hightailed it back to the warmth of our all-women's college.

But this was New York, the city that kept going and going – things didn't end abruptly, as they did in our little village. In Ghana, my paternal older cousins went out often, but because I'd left home so early for college, I hadn't gone out at night in Accra.

I was sure it paled in comparison to New York. The few times I had gone clubbing here in New York, I had danced till my body couldn't sweat any more. The music was bone-shakingly good. In the past, Densua's promoter contact had let us into these places without checking our IDs. Densua didn't explain why, but he was no longer an avenue, so since there was no other place we – or more like I – could get into, being under twenty-one, Webster Hall it was. It was one of the very few places in the city that allowed underage people like myself to get a taste of nightlife.

We started at the top floor, where the DJ spun dancehall tunes. Densua and I wasted no time pushing ourselves into the mass of bodies, soapy from grinding and winding. Densua's curves were quickly scooped into the skinny pelvic bones of a tall man, and she didn't push him away, so I danced across from them, feeling as if there weren't enough people to take away my sudden feeling of loneliness. I could dance alone in my room and feel the world was mine, but here, I felt rejected. I looked around to see if there would be any willing takers, and a man half the size of Densua's partner plastered himself to me. He would do.

This boy is playing with fire.

They are just dancing.

Imagine if they didn't have clothes on.

That last thought – if I could call it that – made me peel away from the man. My partner roped his arm around my waist and led me right back to where we started off.

The voice was on to something. For the sex-starved, this was the closest thing to getting any. Although in my case, it wasn't that I was sex-starved, it was that I didn't even know where sex began and ended. What it looked like: I'd watched enough movies. But what it smelt, tasted, felt like: not a single clue. And, of course, because I wasn't getting it, it was all I could think about. This was the closest thing for now, sticking body parts with total strangers, with music whose reason for existing was simply to encourage us to do exactly that. Maybe, I decided, the voices were just my subconscious suddenly amplified.

'Damn, skinny girl,' said the man, whose manhood was pressing into me.

It annoyed me that he was talking, but I didn't want him to leave. He smelt like lemon and cedar wood had had a baby in his aftershave. Pleasant enough to me. He grabbed my hips and pounded himself into my backside, because the song sounded like 'pum pumpum', so yes, he had to *pum pum pum* my bum bum. Sometimes I would step outside of my body and the whole thing seemed ridiculous, and other times I would be completely enraptured in the movement and the titillation that came with being so close to another body.

While Densua had changed partners a few times, I grew used to mine. His body was warm and soft, like a well-loved teddy bear. He wasn't like the men going after Densua – the ones who spent days toning their muscles, oozing sex appeal and virility. To be honest, those kind of men scared me; they could probably sniff my virginity and stayed away. This cuddly one was just fine by me.

'No, no, no. You don't love me and I know now,' crooned the voice from the speakers.

My partner spun me around and asked for my name. I told him. His was Seth. It was a round name, a boy from the neighbourhood, not intimidating. His name matched his appearance.

'Ei, who is this one?' said Densua, when she finally had no dance partner and had caught on to the fact that I'd stuck to the same person all evening. 'We go downstairs?'

'OK,' I said, and turned around to tell Seth I was going.

'Can I get your number?' he said.

'Sure,' I said, rattling it off.

Densua and I descended, going past the techno floor, where blue, green and orange lights poured out the open door, accompanied by an electronic buzzing. I liked house music, but Densua wouldn't even consider it.

'Watch out for men who pick up girls in an under-twenty-one club,' she warned. 'In fact, just watch out for men who look for women in a club, period.'

'I wouldn't call Seth a *man*,' I said.

'Well, they all want one thing. And I'm sure I don't have to spell it out.'

It was easy for Densua to be dismissive. She got into and held on to relationships easily, even though she never discussed them with me. Through secondary school, she'd had the same boyfriend, and in college, she'd had two. Even though she was currently single, I knew that wouldn't last long. In any case, who knew if Seth would even call? We'd barely exchanged any words.

I was mostly left on my own in the hip-hop section downstairs, so I wallflowered and watched, touching my afro to make sure it was still fluffy and hadn't shrunk too much. Some of the people who'd been up in the reggae dancehall room had filtered down, but there was a different flavour to the two places. It was as if people slid into other skins down here. It was gritty, too. Gone were the fluid, sinuous wines of upstairs. Here, shoulders squared, hands shot out and everything was choppier. Faster. Rougher. I was half amused when Seth and two of his friends appeared at the entrance. I wondered if I should hide. He was nice enough, but I also didn't want him to feel obliged to dance with me. I watched as he and his friends made the rounds, and tried to make myself invisible – just by thought power – but he found me.

'Yes, Zainab!' he said. He grabbed my hand, flipped me around and backed my hips into his. Juvenile's most famous track came on and the crowd went wild.

'Where do you live?' he asked me, after the crowd had dropped it like it was hot.

Don't tell him.

That's how people get killed in places like this.

Oh, he seems harmless.

'I'm homeless,' I said, not because of the voices, but because it was how I felt.

'La da dee la da da,' said Seth. I didn't get the reference. '"Gypsy Woman"? It's a classic.'

'I'm moving to the city. Staying with family.'

'Oh good, I can show you the spots.'

We were the same height. Maybe I was slightly taller. When given a second chance, he was not bad looking. He had a nice smile. The lights cast a red glow on his skin, and it seemed blemish-free. And because he hadn't gone looking for anyone else to dance with, he scored a few more points.

'We're going to a diner after this. You'll come with us?'

'I have to check with my friend,' I said, suddenly relishing the attention. Not bad for my first official New York move outing.

When I asked her, Densua waved at Seth but through teeth that looked like they had trapped a small animal behind them said no.

She's a smart girl.

So we caught a taxi back to her apartment. I hadn't paid for a thing all night and I felt a stab of guilt as she handed a crisp twenty-dollar bill to the taxi driver. Cab driver. I should start saying cab. That's what they said in this town, right?

Back in Densua's studio, as she peeled off her clothes, she said, 'That was fun! I can't believe it's already Sunday.'

'Which means I start work tomorrow.'

'You're lucky you work in an industry with godly hours. Can you believe that because of work I've gone clubbing more than I've gone to church since I moved to New York? It's like the job was designed to encourage debauchery.'

'You could go to evening church,' I said, pulling on my pyjama bottoms.

'I'd fall asleep. And no, I would be late even for that. Please shower before coming into bed. After that oily man you were dancing with.'

Her comment stung, but I wouldn't let her get to me.

'I'm sure if you *really* wanted to, you could get to church,' I said, pulling off the pyjama bottoms. It was my small way of getting back at her. Over the years, I'd tried different approaches to deal with Densua's brusqueness. The best response was not getting emotional. 'I'm sure your job will make room for people to practise their religion.'

At first, I didn't have to choose between my father's Christianity and my mother's Islam. But after my parents divorced, I chose to become a Muslim, like my mother. In my second year of college, I went through an awakening, after taking art history. The professor made us read texts like *The Shipwrecked Sailor*, which preceded *The Odyssey*, and my mind was blown, like sparks-flying-everywhere-above-my-head blown. I learnt that a lot of Hellenistic art and thought was influenced by ancient Egypt, the land inhabited by woolly-haired people, and how Judaism, Christianity and Islam had drunk from the same cup. After this revelation, going for prayers interested me less and I drowned myself in learning about ancient Egypt. I wasn't living at home, so nobody noticed. Then I stopped praying. It was a slow transition, one that was still ongoing, leading to moments in which I would wallow in fear and guilt for being apostate, but I had too many questions. Like if Christianity had pushed faster and higher into Ghana than Islam had, wouldn't my mother also be Christian?

'You're clueless papa, Zainab. Maybe one day you'll decide to work in a bank, then you'll see for yourself. Let me wash off this grease. Too many oily men at Webster Hall. Then it's your turn. I had fun tonight and I'm glad we're back in the same city.'

And just like that, after hurting my feelings, she made me feel better, as only she knew how to over the fourteen or so years we'd known each other.

Chapter Five

Comic Dreams

The next day, after the longest ride of my life, I got off the subway at 33rd Street and Park Avenue and stopped, like in the movies, to soak in the new world waiting for me. It was the first day of my big-city internship. I had slipped on a cropped jacket with puffed sleeves, the nicest pair of trousers I owned, and kitten heels. Throughout college, I'd worked in labs, so this was technically my first office job. I click-clacked my way up to the building and presented my passport to the security guard.

'You get this back on your way out,' he said, handing me a lanyard and a sheet with a barcode. 'They'll give you a permanent keycard up there.'

I didn't want to leave my passport behind. Granted, it was one of the most useless passports in the world – I needed a visa to get everywhere – but it was all I had. To me, it was precious.

I rode up in the elevator, packed with suited bodies, jeaned legs, cups of steaming coffee, cheap cologne, sweet-smelling expensive perfume, body odour.

Someone smells like they haven't showered in here.

The mind noise needed to go quiet, especially on my first day.

When I got off on the ninth floor into the world of Altogether Media, I anticipated a rush of people coming and going, drawings of comics printed out in bold, pencils tucked behind ears, illustrators tearing out and crumpling sheets in artistic frustration and dumping said sheets in the nearest trash can, editors peering over these artists and shaking their heads, a hub of Creatives, yes, with a capital C. I saw myself working next to a super illustrator, sketching out her ideas or colouring in her work. By the end of the summer, she would trust me with my very own drawing project.

Instead, I met quiet cubicles. Grey boxes in a brown room. A man in a T-shirt and jeans, ruffled hair, shuffled towards a cubicle as if he'd spent the night right there.

'Um, I'm looking for Mr Wallace, please.'

'Go round the bend, he's in the second big office with the glass windows. The one on the right.'

He entered his cubicle. It was so quiet, except for the occasional rustle of paper and a printer printing.

It's like other ghosts live here.

Other ghosts?! Was that what I was dealing with? Whose ghosts? This was insane. Focus. I needed to focus.

I walked to Mr Wallace's office and there found a man in jeans and a shirt that could have seen an iron. His skin was dark peach, and his hair was long and tied back in a ponytail. He smiled and welcomed me to have a seat. He had a face that invited a second or third look.

He has nice lips. Full.

Shh, the girl needs to focus.

'We're glad to have you on board, Zainab. Am I saying that correctly?'

I nodded. His windows were the only source of natural light in the space, although most of that light was blocked by the concrete of the building adjacent to ours.

'I'll start you off with HR to get logistics out of the way, then we'll get to the fun stuff.'

Fun stuff with those delicious lips?

I almost choked.

He walked me out and along a row of glass offices and into the middle of the cluster of cubicles.

'Here she is,' said a woman who reminded me of one of my aunts.

Yes, she looks like Habiba.

A name. I'd have to keep it in my head and ask Uncle Ali if he knew a Habiba in the family. I sure didn't. If there *was* a Habiba, maybe my theory about hearing my grandmother's voice was right. Who the others were would maybe become clear soon, too.

The woman's bob-length perm was silk smooth. 'People have been waiting for you to get here,' she said. 'I'll bring her back when I'm done, Sam.'

'Thanks, Donna.'

Mr Wallace turned on his heel and left me with Donna. I wondered where these people she mentioned were.

'I just have to tell you how much I love Ghana,' she said. 'I went there on vacation and didn't want to come back. I was so excited to hear our summer intern was Ghanaian.'

'Where did you visit?'

'Accra, the Elmina Castle, and the other one in Cape Coast. Kumasi. I went with my daughter.'

'Yes,' I said. I'd visited the castles when I was in secondary school, and at the Cape Coast castle, Densua and I went to the bathroom and got separated from the rest of our class. We ended up in the governor's lodgings, a large room overlooking an expansive grey of sea, and I started talking about what it would have been like living in that era, the ball gowns I'd have worn.

'You would have been in the cellar,' Densua had said. 'And if you were up in this room, you were getting raped, even if you wore a ball gown.'

I could still remember the way my heart paused. Talk of a reality check.

'That must have been a really difficult visit,' I now said to Donna.

'My daughter and I couldn't stop crying. I didn't want to see the other castle. One was enough for me, but she said we had to. We owed it to the ancestors. To let them know we came back. She's starting Smith in the fall. And I saw on your résumé you graduated from Mount Holyoke.'

'I'm so sorry,' I said. 'And yes, I just graduated.'

'Congratulations, hun! I hope you don't mind if I bother you with the questions she'll have. I can't believe my baby's heading off to college. All right then, down to business. I'll need your passport, I-94 card and OPT information, so we can process your ID papers and get you paid.'

'The guard kept my passport downstairs.' I opened up my bag to take out the folder containing my whole life since arriving in the USA: résumé, tax forms, school transcripts, even my admission letters into Mount Holyoke and SVA, should anyone have a reason to doubt where I'd been and where I was going. I had the artwork I had submitted to SVA in the mix, too.

'No worries, I'll get you your ID, and tomorrow bring me the passport. Ooh, you did these?' Donna picked up one of my drawings – a tall, skinny girl standing in a chemistry lab mixing the wrong solutions together and dreaming of tagging a wall with graffiti. On the next page, an explosion blasts the test tubes out of her hands and her hair is a giant blue afro. 'Girl, you can draw.'

'Thank you,' I said. These were the drawings that had admitted me into grad school, but they didn't convince me. It was cute when I was in college to be telling a story about a college student. Now that I was done with it? There had to be more. Yes, I could draw, but did I have a story to tell? If I was going to do well in the Illustration as Visual Essay programme, I needed to have a story.

'Let me show you to your desk,' said Donna, standing up, tall and floral.

'Hun, here you are,' she said. It was a cubicle right outside Mr Wallace's. My heart fluttered. I would see him every day. 'I believe Sam will give you your password and get you started. You have any questions, don't hesitate. And don't forget the passport tomorrow, now.' She turned to the sun-filled office and shouted, 'Sam, she's all yours . . .'

Donna was probably the only one who lit up this drab place. She was probably the only one who had been waiting for me to show up.

Mr Wallace came back, armed with a Post-it note.

'Please sit,' he said. He stuck the Post-it on the corner of my computer screen. 'Same password for getting your email.' He smelt like a nice bar of soap. He was maybe in his late thirties. With a haircut and an ironed shirt, he might turn heads.

He's already turning your head.

'First project – and this might be your biggest project over the summer – digitising our comics. We've had our comics run in different newspapers, some in books, and we need them all scanned, uploaded and saved to our database. I'll show you the storeroom where you can find the comics.'

I followed him around a kitchenette and to a grey door. When he opened it, I was sure a diehard fan of comics would have swooned and shouted *AAAH!* I loved drawing, but now I wasn't sure if I was truly a comic fan. It was beginning to dawn on me how much scanning this work would involve.

'This shelf, our spring intern started, so that's done. See how far you can get. Yeah, start with this one.' He reached to a beam bursting with thick folders and picked a book.

He switched off the light and herded me back to my desk and dropped the comic book on the table. *Big Augie*. A man looking like a hillbilly in overalls. Scanning his adventures was to be my main job for the next three months.

'Thank you, Mr Wallace,' I said.

'Sam, please.'

He smiled and pushed an errant hair back into his ponytail.

Sam with the lips.

This was far from the vision I'd had of a New York summer internship. Not to mention these pesky voices. Nothing was going right so far.

Chapter Six
Evil Cousins

Uncle Ali's jazz pulsed the walls of the orange living room. Although I wasn't exactly sure how he and my mother were related, I'd always liked him. There was some story about how my grandmother Fati had adopted all sorts of children, and Uncle Ali might have been one of them. When his wife and children went to bed, he was often crouched over his white Toshiba computer, searching all manner of obscure topics on the internet or reading the tomes he loved.

'So you say at Altogether Media they syndicate newspaper articles too?' He turned to me, peering above the lenses of his reading glasses.

'Yes, Uncle.'

'We are reviving a newspaper for Ghanaians in the Bronx. So where you are is interesting. I might reach out to you for content.'

'OK, Uncle.' I didn't let on that I was really too new in the job to be making any requests. Or that it was more like a cemetery than it was a creative space. What calmed me was that anything involving Ghanaians would take lots of willpower and prayers to pull through. By the time Uncle Ali and his associates performed their resurrection, I would long be in grad school.

'Like your Mma Fati used to say, "Use every single door that life gives you."'

'Mmm,' I said. 'Talking of her . . . Do we have a Habiba? Like in the family?'

He was quiet, and then said, 'I think we have two or three

Habibas. One of them was actually Abiba, you know, without the "h", but she's a distant relation. Why do you ask?'

What should I say? And what would he say if I told him I was hearing voices? These voices were teaching me to lie.

'The name just popped into my head,' I finally said. 'And seemed familiar.'

'Yes, the one called Abiba, she even moved to Nigeria, if I remember well.'

Even if Uncle Ali's answer wasn't conclusive, it didn't disprove my theory. Habiba *was* someone in the family.

'What was Mma Fati like when you were younger?' I asked. Maybe investigating my grandmother would tell me why she was now haunting me. 'She wouldn't let me out of her sight every time I visited the north.'

'How do I describe Mma Fati?' He held the skin under his beardless chin and looked up, as if that was where all answers lay. Even though he was clean-shaven, there was always something frazzled about Uncle Ali, and maybe that's why I liked him. Like me, he wasn't quite put together. 'Let's see. She was a no-nonsense person wrapped in warmth, if such a thing can exist. She single-handedly sent us all to school by making clothes. I've never seen anyone so determined to make sure her children, real and adopted, had a better life. You would hear her machine running from morning to evening. She would only stop to say her prayers and to chew kola. I think she only ate at night. And she ate like a bird. She wasn't happy if one of us wasn't eating. She was a wonderful woman.

'You won't believe it, but Mma Fati's grandmother was still alive when I was a little boy. Her mother, Zeina – who you're named after – she died young. But Mma Fati's grandmother, Jamila, she was really fantastic. You'd have loved her. Always had a pipe in her mouth. And full of stories.'

'What was she smoking?'

'Tobacco.'

I didn't think I would ever smoke cigarettes, but a pipe held a certain amount of sophistication in my imagination. My great-great-grandmother was cool.

'Do you know what happened to Zeina, my namesake?' I hoped I wasn't named after someone who had suffered a terrible tragedy. I hadn't heard much about her.

'I think it was sickle cell, but in those days they had no way of knowing. Your grandmother Fati often said she was lucky she still had *her* grandmother to spoil her. My own mother died young too.'

Jamila, Zeina, Fati and my mother, also Jamila. These were the women who had lived and toiled for me to be here. These were the women for whom I had to be successful. And I could hear at least one of them.

Uncle Ali got up, stretched and yawned.

'I'm going to turn in. Do you want the music?'

I shook my head, and he pressed a button on the sound system in the bookcase.

'Goodnight, Zainabou.'

'Goodnight, Uncle.'

I rummaged through my handbag and extracted my notebook and a pencil as he shut his bedroom door. I looked about the room and the orange ambience grew so saturated, I couldn't focus on anything to sketch. Even if I drew the bookcase, what story was it telling me? I needed a story. I shut the notebook and slid under the covers.

Uncle Ali's building had been around for a long time – I could tell from its ochre-coloured art moderne exterior. The ornate ceiling with its icing-like whorls, where my eyes were now trained, too. Who was the first person who'd lived here when the building first went up in the twenties or thirties? A woman living on her own, I wanted to imagine. A writerly type. When she'd stared at this embossed ceiling looking for inspiration, had it come? Could I transform these thoughts into a story for grad school?

I turned off the lights, sank into the rather comfortable sofa, and was glad I wasn't sharing a room with Dzifa.

I had learnt a trick that got me through my boyfriend-less secondary school and college years. I slid my hand under the elastic of my pyjama bottoms and into the wonderful centre of pleasure on my body. With every creak, flip of a light switch or cough, I would snap back my hand and lie still, even though I had the covers on and no one would be the wiser. I managed to get myself to my happy spot, after several starts and stops.

How sweet this would be, sharing it with another body.

You shouldn't be doing these things.

'Leave me alone,' I whispered in the dark.

I spent the next week and some mostly intrigued by Sam's ponytail at work. He had four hairstyles. Sometimes the hair was tied at the nape of his neck, sometimes it was a little high, sometimes right on top of his head, and occasionally he wore it down.

'You were an English major?' he asked me one afternoon, bun high on his head and tied with a pink rubber band. He didn't seem like the cologne-wearing kind, but when he came into my cubicle, there was a hint of citrus about him.

The voices wouldn't stop. They commented on Sam's arms and how even though he was skinny, he looked strong.

'Arms,' I said. 'Sorry, art. Art minor. But I took a lot of English classes for prerequisites.'

'Cool beans.'

I almost laughed. Did people still say that? This was 2006.

'How do you feel about doing some editorial work?'

'I helped on the college newspaper,' I said. My work was photos and illustrations, but I occasionally edited.

'I think I may have an additional project for you. Let me get it together and get back to you.'

After he left my office, I tried sketching his hair, which was silky black. My renditions were flat and limp. I went back to scanning comics, hopeful for whatever this new project was. It might have helped if there were other interns around to interact with or moan to. Or if the cubicles were arranged in an open plan and I could have heard some office gossip. No, it was just me, the computer and the scanner. I thought about Densua's work as a banker. It had to be more interesting than what I was doing. Would I cave like many ahead of me had? Although banking seemed the antithesis of the person I wanted to become: free.

After another of those uneventful days, I came back from work to find my aunt and her children accusing me of having clogged the toilet. The whole thing was petty and annoying and I didn't want to spend another day with them. I called Densua and asked her if I could stay at hers till I found a place.

'You shouldn't have to ask,' she said.

Densua, my saviour since the 1990s.

When my mother and father weren't speaking, the air was sucked out of our home, as if their words were some kind of leavening agent the house needed to rise, to make things feel normal. It got so unbearable that I burst out crying in class when the teacher asked me to do a simple sum on the board. Densua walked out with me.

'Ask them for sleepovers at my house,' she said, after I'd told her about the cold war at home. 'Every weekend.'

My parents were so wrapped in their problems, it was a solution for them too. Densua filled our weekends with so much fun that I didn't have time to mope. We watched movies recorded on tape and listened to Groove FM non-stop, and occasionally called the radio station when her parents were out. Maybe, I convinced myself, if I wasn't around, my parents would air out their differences and return to the way things were. It made no difference.

Chapter Seven

First Glances

The next day, I needed to find a way to tell my uncle I was leaving, even though I knew what I was doing was *not done.* I couldn't just walk out on my family, even if I was an adult.

Life is too short to do what everyone expects of you.

But if everyone thought that way, the world would be chaotic.

It's good she's telling him now, in either case.

My uncle had really committed no crime (except exaggerate about his living situation), so it made it even harder to approach him. I did my best not to use the cursed toilet and kept everything tucked in my innards, meanwhile imagining the toxic waste seeping back into my body. I took a shower and made sure my suitcases were packed. I would leave after work in the evening. It would save me time and energy to take the suitcases to work, but that would just raise too many questions, *and* I was trying to maintain an air of mystery at work, *and* the suitcases would swallow all the space in my cubicle.

My uncle was generally an early riser, so I woke up even earlier. I would have waited to tell him after work, but the voices had argued a whole debate in my head while I was trying to sleep. To finally shut them up, I decided to just get it over and done with as soon as I got up.

'Zainabou,' he said, when we crossed paths in the kitchen, 'I never see you in the mornings. Special presentation at work today?'

I shook my head.

'Uncle.' I swallowed. 'Thank you for letting me stay on such short notice. I'll be leaving this evening.'

He regarded me, his eyes bloodshot from one bout of malaria too many, his cheeks slack, mouth agape. His expression wouldn't have been different if I'd given him a slap.

'What's the matter?' he said. 'You don't like it here? You know this is your home.'

Your wife is not our family.

She has become family, but she's horrible.

This was supposed to be temporary.

I didn't repeat those conflicting thoughts. Instead, I said, 'My friend is closer to work and she barely lives at home. She's a banker and said I can use her space. And I can get out of your way.'

Because your house is too small.

'Zainabou, I feel responsible for you. I know I can't stop you from doing what your heart calls you to do, but reconsider. I think it's been good for your cousins to have you around.'

I was quiet and looked at my feet on the orange carpeting. I had to think fast and not say anything to hurt Uncle Ali.

'I'm always in the way,' I said. 'It'll give Dzifa and Ibrahim back their space. My friend's apartment is truly empty all the time.'

'Be careful in this city,' he said, as if he'd plunged into my heart and could feel I was looking for the freedom to do all the depraved things in the world. 'It is seductive. It will make you want to try everything. Don't forget that the women in your family are virtuous. Your grandmother Fati, she didn't let your mother and any of the girls she raised do just whatever they pleased. They were at her side until they married.'

It's true.

How miserable.

If Grandma Fati is probably the first thought, who was the one who contradicted her all the time? I wondered.

Then I thought of my cousin Dzifa, wondering if the poor thing would be stuck in this apartment with the pesky toilet before a marriage was arranged for her. Surely my uncle was not that old-fashioned. I remembered I'd been told that Jamila, my mother's great-grandmother, depending on who you were talking to, was sweet and a little batty, or revolutionary in her happiness. My mother said she was the freest spirit she'd ever met. There was something about how she'd had multiple husbands. But I wasn't about to start a debate with my uncle about virtuous women when I needed to get to work. What would Jamila have done? I was sure she would have stood her ground.

'Yes, Uncle,' I said. 'I'll come back and get my suitcases in the evening.'

'I won't stop you if this is what you want.'

My chest unclenched itself, my whole being glad that Uncle Ali hadn't overreacted, but he had opened a tap that didn't want to close. These virtuous women he spoke of: I was already hearing Fati's voice. Who were the others – her cousins? Would I ever know?

I thought of the women in my family as I caught the subway heading downtown. From what Uncle Ali had told me, Jamila was a badass. Zeina, my namesake, was an enigma. Fati, my grandmother, was strict and old school (the story was that her husband – if he even married her – had abandoned her). My mother was confident, but all she did was work, and when she wasn't working, a film of sadness coated itself around her. It seemed as if a giant sieve had been slipped between the generations, and what was taken out was the good stuff, the badassery, so that what was left was a woman who was only virtuous. Or sad. Well, I'd been that woman for the first twenty years of my life, and I didn't want to be her any more. New York was the perfect place to get rid of her.

The only problem was that the most virtuous of women had come full force into my head.

Maybe I had to channel Jamila's spirit. Whatever it was. And if I couldn't get Jamila, maybe Zeina was the next best thing, even though I knew nothing much about her. Maybe something had happened after Jamila that led us to where we were today.

Why was I thinking of these dead women so much? It was becoming obsessive. One of them was maybe lodged in my brain, but could such a thing truly happen? I looked around the packed subway car. People were in their own worlds, headphones on, heads bowed over books, eyes staring at flyers. Did any of them have such turbulent internal lives?

When we got overhead on 125th Street, I texted my mother, knowing it would cost me a pretty penny.

Hi Mma. Ur grandma. How'd she die, pls? 4 project.

It was 8 a.m. here, and in Accra it was noon.

Grandma? responded my mother. Do you mean Jamila or Zeina? Jamila's daughter was Zeina, and Zeina's daughter was Fati, and I am Fati's daughter.

Of course I knew who was who. Why couldn't she use contractions like everybody else? That way she (and I) would have at least one less word to pay for. I had explained to her, numerous times, that it cost when she texted me. In America, nothing was free, not even receiving messages. But it was my own fault for having texted her.

Grandmother Fati had combined two opposite philosophies: strictness and spoiling me rotten. Every time she'd visit us in Accra, after school she'd ask me who my boyfriend was.

'No one,' I'd say, scrunching up my nose. I hated the interrogation.

'Good. Don't let anyone stick anything, not even a finger, down there,' she'd respond. 'Especially not boys. They are no good.'

Her words had travelled through my pores, into the epithelium of my uterus, anchored their rigid roots into my womb and shut down the whole place.

I texted back, How did Zeina die?

Ah, what a morbid thing to ask me over text. I think it was in pregnancy. No one is really sure. By the way, how is New York treating you? I hope you're keeping safe. I hear you shouldn't look people in the eye over there. Take care of yourself.

Where did my mother get her information from? But back to

the subject of my namesake. Why would I be named after someone who had a short lifespan? It seemed to doom me. I shook off the thoughts and went into work.

Later that day, my phone buzzed with a strange international number. I usually didn't answer the phone at work, because it was so quiet. Everyone would hear your conversation. But it could be from Ghana; it could be important.

'Zain,' said my mother, when I answered the call.

'Mma. Hello!'

'What's going on?' Her voice had climbed into its stern register. 'Uncle Ali says you're moving out.'

'Um, yes,' I whispered. 'Densua is letting me stay at hers. She's never in her apartment. At Uncle Ali's I was sleeping on a couch. It was supposed to be a brief stay.'

'He probably didn't let on, but he's quite hurt. He's very sensitive, you know. Well, as long as nothing bad happened . . .'

'No, nothing bad,' I said. I wouldn't tell her about the toilet episode. It was sure to cause unnecessary drama.

'Anyway, I can hear you're using your official voice, so let me leave you. Get something nice to thank Uncle Ali for letting you stay at his. Love you.'

I hung up. In the quiet of the office, a throat cleared, the big fan at the end of our floor hawked out a cough-like whirr, Donna laughed. Thank goodness she was here. What a strange place to work – even my college labs had had more life. Still, if I could come up with an idea outside of scanning, I would be able to impress Sam and also give myself something exciting to do. Should I pitch him a comic strip idea? Was that too forward?

Do it.

Do what? I hadn't gone beyond sketching Sam's hair. Uncle Ali's apartment had not given me the space to do any drawing. Maybe Densua's apartment would inspire me.

Chapter Eight

Tudor City

By the time I got out of the station, into a bus across town and schlepped my suitcases up 1st Avenue and into Densua's building in Tudor City, I had resolved not to stay poor in New York. That *should* have been one cab ride.

Densua had given me a spare key to her place, so after the doorman allowed me in, I rode up in the elevator and let myself into her studio. Its white walls made the apartment much brighter and airier than Uncle Ali's, even though it was smaller. I tried to tuck my suitcases into her closet, but the space was bursting with her clothes and uncountable shoes. I shoved one case under the bed but the other wouldn't fit, killing my desire to be as inconspicuous as possible. I eventually placed it next to the heater – thanking heavens it was summertime and it wasn't going to be turned on. I dug out a silk wrapper that a Nepali friend had gifted me and covered the case with its red paisley softness.

I stood back and appraised the space. To the right of my suitcase was Densua's bed, covered with a polyester-cotton sheet and decorated with stuffed bears, probably from boyfriends past, and a white Bible with gold lettering; two armchairs stood across from it. I spun towards the kitchenette, where she made her killer jollof rice – Densua was one of the students who had fed us in college and kept homesickness at bay – and ended at the door to the bathroom. She was paying so much in rent to live here, but it allowed her to walk to work, and was shelter for me now. I knew two grown women sharing a full-sized bed would soon grow stale, so I would still search on Craigslist.

I opened the fridge and slapped a cut of cheese between two slices of sandwich bread. My phone buzzed three times. It was funny how you went from radio silence to everyone suddenly thinking of you. It was as if there were cosmic whispers that got louder as soon as someone said 'Zainab'. The word started as a whisper in the universe, and grew in shape and form and timbre: 'Zainab, ZAINAB, ZAAAIIINNNAAABBB'. Then everybody got in on it and sent messages. I was sure it was the way the universe worked.

Don't forget to buy Uncle Ali and Aunty Emefa a gift. With love from Accra, Mma was the first message.

Hi Z. Music show at Pianos, LES. Lauryn Hill vibes. COME! Mary Grace.

Hey. Had fun the other night. Seth. Nothing else. No call to action. I hated messages like that. Completely left the recipient to do the work of deciphering what the point of it was.

What could I get for my aunt and uncle? It had to be affordable. A bottle of wine? Uncle Ali didn't even drink. What was I thinking?

The Lower East Side music thing sounded promising.

Yes! What time? I texted Mary Grace.

Hey, I responded to Seth's message. Me too. How are you? At least I was a decent human being and a polite texter.

I wouldn't have responded.

Men should chase.

There'd be no fun in life if women just sat down waiting.

'Who are you?' I said out loud to the empty apartment. The voices said nothing. 'Oh, now you can't talk? I'm listening.'

All I heard was the hum of Densua's fridge.

'Mma Fati?'

Nothing. So far, they'd felt more like a distraction than anything else. As long as no one else could hear them, maybe I could learn to live with them and find out what it took to block them.

Why had they just appeared in my head? It had to be something in the New York air that heightened the unexplainable.

Look for a house.

'Yes,' I said. 'I was going to do that. Thank you very much. And leave me alone if you're going to be cowardly and not say who you are.'

Craigslist was overflowing with apartment listings, but after seeing what a dump Mr Thomas's place was, I was more circumspect. For one, I raised my lower limit. My ideal apartment was between five hundred and six hundred dollars a month. Once school started, I would have a fellowship to help with the rest. With my price range, the Bronx was the most interesting. But I wanted to be as far away from my family as possible. I bookmarked a few places, but couldn't concentrate. The orange rectangle of my phone kept lighting up.

8 p.m., wrote Mary Grace.

What u up to? asked Seth.

Oh, your father says hello, too. He says there is a documentary on architecture in the Islamic world you should watch. He saw it on the BBC. Maybe you can do architecture if the illustration thing doesn't pan out. Your father agrees with me.

My parents. No longer together, but still best friends. My father, not Muslim, but still heavily invested in the world. My mother, the longest texter in the world and a dream-killer. Neither of them knew I was no longer religious. Had I been *that* zealous about believing in Islam? If I was, it was their fault. Before and after their divorce, I needed somewhere to bury myself to make sense of the world crumbling around me. I found beauty in poets like Rumi. From his poems, I drew, I found belief and peace, until I got to college and learnt even more about the world, and all those protective walls came tumbling down.

I flung off the Nepali scarf and unbuckled the clasps of my suitcase. I was very excited about hanging out with Mary Grace. Maybe she knew cool New Yorkers already. As for Seth, my response to him could wait. I liked the attention, yes, but it felt like the wrong kind of attention.

Now, what did one wear to a music show in the Lower East Side? Densua would know, but I was not to disturb her at work unless there was an emergency. I pulled out a pair of jeans and a simple sleeveless blouse I'd bought on sale from Macy's at the Holyoke Mall. I held them against my body and studied myself in Densua's mirror. My hips were looking fuller than when I first arrived a week and some ago. I would rather die than tell her, but Aunty Emefa's okra stews were finger-tastingly good. I hoped the jeans would still fit.

It's in your head.

I whipped around to check behind me. No kidding. These voices definitely had a twisted sense of humour. But back to preparing for my evening. My hair looked flat. Untwist my twists, throw on hoops and I was sure I would look put together.

I poured myself a glass of orange juice and placed the white blouse on the countertop. Densua's iron was under the kitchen sink, and she even had an ironing board, but that was too fussy for me. I took my towel, folded it in half, spread it over the faux-marble counter and was just about to reach for the iron when the glass tipped over and spilt orange over my white blouse. Luckily it came out with a few rinses and some soap. I still had time. I took my wallet and the blouse, and headed for the basement. It was totally wasteful to spend so many quarters to dry one puny blouse, but I looked good and effortless in it. I threw it into the belly of the drying machine, slotted in three quarters and rode back upstairs. Hand on door handle. It wouldn't give.

I'd totally forgotten to push back the safety button on the lock. My phone was in there, the key was in there.

The doorman downstairs didn't have a spare key, and since I wasn't the person renting the space anyway, he couldn't help me out.

Luckily, I hadn't changed out of the clothes I was wearing and I had my wallet. This had to count as an emergency, especially since Densua might not come home until after midnight. Tucking my tail between my legs, I walked out of Tudor City and cut across to Lexington Avenue, taking my time to ogle the Chrysler Building and its art deco exterior, which always made me think of glamorous times past. I went up to 47th Street and ended up at 270 Park Avenue. Densua told me that a woman had designed her building, even though a man took most of the credit.

Our queens had to be called kings to be taken seriously.

I looked up and admired the steel and glass kissing the sky.

Usually when I arrived at her office to pick up keys, I met Densua in the lobby, with advance notice. This time I was in for a good tongue-lashing.

'Densua Mensah, please,' I said.

'Is she expecting you?'

'No. But we live together. It's a bit of an emergency.'

'Name?'

The receptionist scribbled down my details and picked up the phone. She called twice, but Densua didn't answer. The third time, she left a message. I wanted to be as painless a guest as possible, and this wasn't a good start.

After half an hour, Densua emerged from the open door of the elevator and stared at me wide-eyed. She didn't need to say any words.

'I'm so, so sorry. I locked myself out.'

'Oh my God, Zainab, you must be joking.'

She huffed and stormed into the elevator. What exactly could she be doing that made sleep and taking care of one's self minor next to impressing one's boss?

She came back down and handed me a key ringed with a J. P. Morgan key holder, then tugged the hem of her jacket and said sternly, 'Bring it back and leave it with the receptionist. And this is the last time.'

'Thank you, thank you,' I said, extending my prayer hands out to her.

Chapter Nine

Pianos

Mary Grace was late. I stood across from the place we were meeting, reading and rereading the sign, 'New & Used, Bought & Sold, PIANOS, Incredible Prices', until the words began to resemble a mismatch of crazy-looking characters. I unspooled myself out of the madness. Pianos *was* a clever name for a music venue. The signboard looked legit, and I wondered if they had prised it away from another shop, or if this really was a place where pianos were once sold. How old would it have been, and who could have bought a piano in those days? I took piano lessons for a minute, and then couldn't stand my teacher's breath, so I pretended to be bad at reading music and he told my mother he didn't think we should continue. It was a shame, because I could have been a celebrated pianist by now.

My eyes traced the zigzags of the outside fire escape stairs, above the Pianos signage. I imagined how decades before, families squeezed into windowless buildings like these in the Lower East Side used to be a diseased explosion waiting to happen. I could understand these people. Such places had provided comfort for many newcomers to New York, and even if they could make them sick, they were spaces for them to lay their heads. Shelter was not something to take lightly.

I looked back down to see if Mary Grace was any closer. Two men caught my eye as they approached from the left. One of them was tall and his gaze met mine. My heart sprinted. Would this be my New York story – that I just met my man randomly on the side of the road?

Remember your mother's message. Don't look people in the eye.

Oh, but this is a public place.

As they got closer, I shifted. Why were there two of them, and not just the one who was obviously staring back at me? OK, even if he didn't become my man, he could be the one who broke me into New York.

'Choco-late!' shouted the shorter one, drawing me out of my fantasy. 'Mmm-hmm!' He licked his lips. 'Chocolate, can I holler at you?'

Then the one I'd been eyeing grinned, revealing teeth capped in gold. That would be a no-no for me. Was I so desperate that now I was attracting men I couldn't even take to Densua, yet alone my mother?

What a waste of money.

But why judge? Gold teeth are not new on this earth.

See, it's good for her to learn her lessons all on her own.

I tried to picture the scene in which I introduced either of them to my parents, and it amused me so much that I couldn't help but smile, which the men probably interpreted as an invitation to proceed. Before the shorter man could holler what he wanted, I quickly crossed the street to join the small line that had sprung up in the time I'd been waiting. The two men continued on their way, and my heart – which had been sprinting – went back to its regular pace. The thrill of danger.

I lingered at the back, watching a hefty man sitting on a three-legged stool at the entrance inspecting IDs. I gulped – I hadn't thought I'd need to be twenty-one to get into a place like this. It would be disappointing if I were turned away, mostly because I wanted to get back to Densua's apartment as late as I possibly could. From the corner of the street, I caught the red blast of Mary Grace's hair, and I wondered why she chose to be so conspicuous. I waved at her and she crossed over to me.

'Oh hey,' she said. 'Sorry I'm late. I'm never driving into Manhattan again. Rookie mistake. But the show won't start till nine, so we're fine.'

She was dressed in black, just as she was the day I'd met her. A long-sleeved black shirt with a long black skirt. An easy uniform that probably only she could pull off. I would look funereal if I copied her. She came off as mysterious.

We joined the line, and my stomach churned. Getting turned away from here would be embarrassing. Maybe they wanted to make sure people were over eighteen was my optimistic thinking.

She handed over her ID, a flat plastic card. The big man peered at it through his glasses, studied Mary Grace, then nodded at her to go in. I handed him my passport. He looked at me, flipped through the passport, looked at me again. My armpits itched as if a thousand ants had suddenly climbed in there. Then he nodded and let me in. I was floored. What had happened?

'Is this an under-twenty-one club?' I asked Mary Grace as she pulled her hair into a bun.

'No. Why?'

'I'm not twenty-one. Not till September.'

'No way. Let me see.' She grabbed my passport. 'Brilliant! Look, the date is written the British way: 03/09/1985. To the bouncer outside, it reads March ninth, not September third!'

'Why didn't I think of that?'

'You're a baby! But yo, I'm glad we've found this hack, because there aren't many places I could get you into with your real age.'

I beamed. Mary Grace wanted to get me into places. I thought of a quick comeback.

'Yes, just Webster Hall,' I said.

'Yo! I used to come to New York just to party there. Now, you can't pay me to set foot in there.'

Why was she suddenly using 'yo' so much? I don't remember her peppering her sentences with the word as we drove down from Massachusetts. Maybe it was her way of feeling like a New Yorker. In any case, the evening was finally off to a promising start. Having entry into all of New York City's nightlife was a game-changer. I kissed my passport and put it in my bag.

The band, a group of white boys on string instruments, was

hardly soulful, and the farthest thing from Lauryn Hill I'd ever heard, but we sat through their wails and screaming and more wailing.

'Mercaaaay!' yelled the lead singer. Each time a scream poured out of him, Mary Grace and I pursed our lips at each other and broke out into peals of laughter.

'I am so sorry,' she whispered, her shoulders pulsing with laughter. 'I confused them with another band that have the same name. This night is a bust. Are you hungry? I know the best after-hours spot.'

I *was* hungry, but wasn't sure where we'd be going. I really had to save my coins. Mary Grace kept singing 'Mercy!' and holding her belly as she burst out laughing. She led the way, and we'd barely taken two steps when she said, 'We're here.'

We stood outside and peered in through a wide window. Inside, men in hats gobbled down slices of pizza, and I was sure we looked like something out of a Hopper painting. We walked in and Mary Grace waved at one of the men behind the counter.

'I live in this area.'

'I thought you lived in Brook—'

'I didn't mean it literally.'

Wit, puns and irony clearly were not my strong suit. I was just glad we weren't in an expensive eatery. Pizza by the slice I could do.

We both ordered slices of mozzarella and I was shocked to find Mary Grace shaking pepper flakes like a shekere over hers, powdering the cheese with red circles until the whole thing was a carpet of scarlet.

'The only way I eat anything.'

'And I thought only Ghanaians liked spice.'

'Ooh, you have to take me to a Ghanaian restaurant. Where do the Ghanaians live?'

'In the Bronx.'

I was not planning on returning to the Bronx any time soon. Uncle Ali and I would have to resume meeting in the Manhattan Mall.

'Is there a Filipino community in New York?'

'Of course. You know this city is the world in miniature. But I avoid my people.'

She voiced words that had been couched in my own heart for a long time, words I'd been too afraid to even think. It wasn't just about Uncle Ali. It was the whole Ghanaian community that intimidated me. In college, Densua had acted as my buffer, and when she left, I stopped going for jollof sessions. Nobody was hostile. Nobody was ever mean. But I *felt* different and like I wasn't allowed to show that difference. I was the girl who took art classes and not econ; I preferred to walk everywhere and hadn't even tried to get my driver's licence; I kept my hair natural and not permed straight; I didn't go to church. They were small things, but added together, they painted me as *too different*.

'Me too!' I said, feeling refreshingly light. 'I literally ran away from my family in the Bronx. And in college, I only went to them when I was extremely homesick and needed comfort food.'

'For real?' She laughed. 'You used them! Yeah, mine are too judgemental. *Why is your hair red? Why don't you come to church? Why are you always wearing black? When are you getting married? We need grandchildren la.* It's exhausting, but I still love them.'

'We have a lot in common,' I said. 'With mine, if you weren't from a major ethnic group in Ghana or if you weren't Christian or related to someone who was important back home, then you didn't count. I feel small in Ghanaian circles. But I am curious: why *do* you always wear black?'

'Not you too.'

'Just wondering. I didn't know you always wore black until you said it.'

'To go with my hair. When I change my hair colour, I'll update my clothes.'

I marvelled that she could do a whole wardrobe change to go with her hair. Even if we were both outsiders, Mary Grace and I certainly had our differences, too. She wasn't an international student in the way I was an international student. International students like me, we toed the line. We didn't have money. We were inconspicuous. I observed her as she chomped down the rest of her pizza-flavoured pepper and pressed the pads of her fingers together.

'Heading back to BK?' she said after she'd swallowed. 'I can give you a ride.'

'Um, I didn't take the apartment.' I brought her up to speed. 'And now I'm sharing a bed with another grown woman.'

'That's hot,' said Mary Grace. 'But I take it you're looking for a place? I have one bedroom open in my apartment. It's small. Hold on a second, I'll be right back.'

She stepped out of the restaurant, and I watched people come to the counter to order their pizza. It seemed louder than before.

'Can I get two slices, mozzarella?'

'Pepperoni. Yeah, three pies.'

How do you know she hasn't run away and left you to pay?

She's not that kind of person.

Orders came and went, and Mary Grace was out for so long that I began to believe whoever the doubting voice was. Luckily, she came back in.

'Sorry about that,' she said. 'So, if you want the room, you can pay seven hundred dollars for it. Then we'll be roomies! And you can stay when you start grad school, if you'd like.'

It was a hundred dollars above my budget, but it was tempting. Could I survive on three hundred a month? The subway alone would eat about a third of that, phone bills, and then food . . .

Live a little!

Be cautious.

First make sure there are no cats.

'Can I come and see it?' That would be a prudent thing to do, in case it was just as bad as Mr Thomas's. Especially with what I'd seen of her car.

'Sure, let me know when.'

I went down the Delancey Street subway stairs and got decidedly confused trying to find the platform for the uptown F train, but not even that labyrinth could wipe off the smile I'd plastered on my face. Not only did I now have the keys to NYC's nightlife, but I also had a potential place to stay. One might even say I had a new friend in Mary Grace. The loneliness in my chest I'd been refusing to acknowledge since I arrived in New York crept out, thief-in-the-night style. Good riddance.

I opened Densua's creaky door and slipped into her studio. Her head popped up from her sheets.

'Sorry, sorry,' I said, slipping off my sandals. 'I didn't want to wake you up.'

'I just got in myself. How are you?'

'Good,' I said. 'You?'

There was silence, then she said, 'Zainab, my job is not a joke. I can't afford to put one foot wrong, so you can't just waltz in there as and when you please. It's not too much to ask of you to try to be responsible. You're not a child any more. I was in the middle of a really big meeting and they actually called me out because I had an emergency. I mean, come on, Zainab.'

She'd wrapped a silk scarf around her hair, which heightened her apple-shaped face and made her a spitting image of her mother. With all the words pouring out of her mouth, she really was her mother's twin. If anyone was good at blasting, it was Aunty Jane. She would always end her sermon with a Bible passage ('Girls, this room is a pigsty. First Corinthians 14, all things should be done decently and in order'). I was glad Densua didn't go as far as First Corinthians, but did she really have to make me feel so small? Anyone could get locked out of an apartment, couldn't they?

Yes, she's overreacting.

Well, she's entitled to how she feels.

'I'm sorry,' I said.

'After you left, I was thinking . . .' Densua started.

'Wow, you're *actually* allowed to do that at work?' I clamped my teeth on my tongue. It was too late to take back my words.

'Ha, funny. Good one. I was thinking that you've been like this since your parents split. Like a . . . zombie. You're just floating and letting life happen to you. When we were small, you knew where everything in your room was. You arranged your books from A to Z with little Post-it notes for people to borrow and return them. I remember the Zainab who wanted to be the world's most important doctor. Get your life together, especially if you want to survive in this city, or you won't last. You need to deal with what happened and move on. For real. Wake up, Zainab.'

I felt tears rising in my chest. It wasn't even about her calling me a mess. The raw nerve she'd struck had to do with my parents' divorce. I rushed into the bathroom and banged the door behind me. Her words split open the meaty wound and it felt like only yesterday I was the girl who'd been told her parents didn't love each other any more.

I sloughed off my clothes and decided right then that whatever Mary Grace's apartment looked like, I was taking it. Doing so went against all the advice I'd read about living on your own – paying more rent than you could afford – but I could always fall back on my unused credit card for purchases. Once school rolled around, I would pay it off. How dare Densua analyse me? She wasn't perfect either. Always trying to keep up with the Joneses or to look perfect. At least I was real and showed my true emotions.

'I'll move out by the end of the week,' I said when I came out of the bathroom.

'I'm barely here, Zainab,' she said. 'This is your apartment too. I just don't want work to be interrupted. These first two years are crucial. Your performance can decide whether you even reach management level or not.'

'Yes, so I don't want to bother you any more.'

'Where are you going?'

'Don't worry about it,' I said, sliding into the bed and leaving as much space between us as I could, which meant that one of my legs was almost dangling. But I would rather suffer.

'I can't deal with your only-child pettiness,' Densua huffed.

'I have half-siblings!' I muttered under my breath.

We didn't say a word to each other in the morning.

*

Mary Grace told me to use the L train, because the subway closer to her apartment wasn't working. When I got out of the train station, I was heralded with the sing-songy nursery rhyme of an ice cream truck, which was very quickly drowned out by scratchy merengue blasting from a speaker somewhere on the street. I walked by shops peddling records, musical instruments, interspersed with botanicas and a few restaurants. A green street sign proclaimed that this was Graham Avenue, also Avenue of Puerto Rico. It charmed me and chased away the bad mood I'd been festering in all day. Light poured through this road and Puerto Rican and Mexican flags stuck out under windowsills like insolent tongues.

I wondered what it was about places like Puerto Rico that tugged at my soul.

Because they are ours too.

As I was strolling by an old woman pushing a pram, I was startled to find in it a pug dressed in a baby's bonnet around its flat-faced head. I peered at the old woman and she didn't even bat an eye.

What a place to live in.

Only mad people live here.

Maybe I was mad too, with all this internal noise. I had always said I would come to the US, get a degree, work for some money and go back to Ghana, but New York was changing that dream and I could see myself living here forever. Maybe I truly was becoming of the mad ones.

As I walked to Mary Grace's, Densua's words kept repeating themselves. I'd had a childhood that was free from stress until the months leading up to the divorce. My parents didn't always have money, and it was only when I didn't get a present for my birthday that I could tell they'd fallen on hard times, but otherwise I spent some of the best moments of my life running around freely with my cousins. I was so blindly happy that I didn't even realise my parents hadn't been getting along for long before their cold war began. When Mma told me I would be moving out of the house with her, those words sounded like they'd been said in a foreign language. I'd thought going to Densua's and giving them room would help.

'We've decided to live apart,' she said. 'We both still love you very much. We're just not meant for each other.'

Densua was right in that my world shifted. I soon spent less time with my father, and my mother worked even harder than she already did. If I wasn't at school with Densua, I was at home reading poetry and sketching. Life became just Mma and me. And then I went off to boarding school.

Swimming in the past's sad waters still didn't stop me from basking in a moment of national pride when I walked past a large Food Bazaar adorned with flags from all over the world, including Ghana's red-gold-green. I knew right then I was going to live in this place.

After meeting with Mary Grace – I liked her roomy bohemian-looking apartment – I called Uncle Ali. She wanted one month's rent in advance.

You still haven't given him a gift.

A twinge of guilt passed through me, but I convinced myself of these facts: I was only twenty years old and change; I was his niece; he would understand if no gift came. And now guilt clawed even deeper into my skin because of what I was about to do.

'Zainabou,' he said. 'How's city living?'

'It's fine, Uncle. How are my dear aunty and cousins?'

'They're well. Your aunt told me what happened with the bathroom.'

I said nothing.

'If that's why you left, you shouldn't have. We could have talked through it.'

'It was always meant to be temporary, but I'm sorry if I hurt you.'

I couldn't continue boasting about the benefits of Densua's apartment when I was about to leave that too. And there was no way in hell I could tell him I'd called to borrow money for my rent deposit. He would definitely lure me back to the Bronx. I needed to think fast about an excuse.

'Uncle . . .'

'Yes?'

'Could I please borrow a hundred dollars?' I was still thinking about the excuse.

He hesitated. 'Sure, Zainabou.'

I held my breath, waiting for him to ask for an explanation. There was a heavy pause, but his question never came.

'How soon do you need it?'

'Before the weekend, please,' I said exhaling.

'Let's meet in the Manhattan Mall on Friday.'

I spent another two days in Densua's apartment, in which time I ordered out twice, which led to yet another chastisement for not even trying to cook. Even Densua, who had a strenuous job, found time to batch-cook, so what was my problem? Especially after I complained so much about not having money.

'I'm not grooming myself to be anyone's wife,' I retorted.

After that, she clammed up and our conversations skimmed the filmy surface of things until I moved out.

Chapter Ten

Old Flame

After scanning comic strips from the 1950s all morning, my eyes felt like sand had been thrown in them. I tried to get myself to think a bit like Densua, even though she had annoyed me with her 'grow up' speech. How could I become less of a zombie? How could I grow in this Altogether Media company over what was left of my three-month internship?

I couldn't focus. Today, the content of the comics was proving a distraction.

Big Augie was a comic about a man in the backwoods of the US. In the panels I'd looked at that day, his town was celebrating a day when women chased after men to pick their ideal partner. I loved it. Why was the world skewed the other way? If I as a woman wasn't being given the chance to choose, I could surely end up with trash. What if I not only channelled my ancestor Jamila's energy, but also acted like the women in *Big Augie*?

'You do know you can take a break,' said Sam, startling me. How long had he been there? I was relieved there was a scan on my screen and not Solitaire or my email, which I checked every five minutes. 'How is it going?'

His hair was hanging in a low bun. He was wearing a deep blue shirt tucked into khaki pants. His rolled sleeves showed a light sprinkling of hair on his arms. I wanted to press my fingers against them. Just because.

'It's going well,' I said, standing up and raising my own arms towards the ceiling, before I could stop myself.

'Yeah, don't forget to stop every now and then to stretch those muscles. I don't think our chairs are the most ergonomic. When you get back from lunch, let me know. I have a project I think you'll enjoy,' he said.

I almost hugged him.

Can we touch his hair?

She'll get into trouble.

Oh, let her concentrate on her work.

'I will do just that,' I said, surprised that I could come up with an answer that worked for both Sam and the voices in my head. He went back to his office and I took the elevator downstairs.

As I was crossing the street to go to my favourite pizza spot – I had plans to master the art of bringing my own food to work before the summer's end, but for now, cheap pizza it was – I saw a head I would recognise anywhere.

Kweku Ansah!

I hadn't seen him in close to eight years. He left our school because his father was posted to Malaysia for a job, and although we initially tried keeping in touch via letters – missives describing who had misbehaved in school, what we were reading, class trips – they trickled into one letter every three months, and then we just stopped.

'Kweku Nti Ansah!' I shouted, and waved. I couldn't believe it was him. My childhood boy bestie. He scrunched up his nose and peered at the mass of people on the sidewalk, probably wondering who would know his full name in New York City. His expression was familiar and sent little flutters dancing into my belly. I knew that face so well, even if it was now more handsome and stretched out. I pushed forward, stopped in front of him and waved in his face. It took him a few minutes, and then realisation smoothed the crinkles on his nose, widened the space between his cheekbones.

'Zainab? Zainab Sekyi. No way! Oh my God. All grown up! What a small world. I didn't know you were here.'

He was a hair taller than me. His skin was just like mine, a dark brown that reflected burnt sand undertones. He had a thin moustache and a tiny beard – both neatly trimmed.

His lips are juicier than the other one!

And he's African like us.

'Come here,' he said. He reached forward and engulfed me in a bergamot-scented hug. We held on for what felt like a good couple of minutes. The hug was warm and comforting and exciting, all in one. Kweku and I had spent a good part of our childhood doing homework together, taking long walks and watching cartoons. He *knew* me.

'So what *are* you doing here?' he asked when he pulled away.

'I work there.' I pointed to the important-looking edifice behind us, feeling immensely proud of myself.

'No way. Same here. I'm in an ad agency on the thirtieth floor.'

'That's where all the cool-looking people in the elevator must be going. What are the chances that we work in the same building? New York can feel strangely small.'

'Wow,' he said, placing his palm on my shoulder. My belly twisted in pleasure. 'How long has it been? Like Christmas 1999 or something. Was that the last time? Or maybe even earlier. Last time I went to Ghana, our trip was too short to see anyone but family. What are the chances of reuniting in this city?' He took his palm away.

Oh, but bring the hand back!

'It's been ages,' I said. I agreed with the voice – the hand could have stayed.

'I'm meeting my co-workers for lunch, and I'm kinda late, but let's have lunch or hang out soon. Please. What's your number? It's so good to see you.'

I rattled it off and waved as he walked away with a bounce in his step. A walk I knew so well.

Go back and take his number.

Let the man chase her.

They just met, no one is chasing anyone.

I ignored the chatter – I wouldn't let them bother me today. It had to mean something that I was working in the same building as one of my favourite people from growing up.

I often wondered what we would have become if he'd stayed. After junior secondary school, I went to boarding school. Would we have ended up in the same school like we'd planned? Would we have dated? Or would our friendship have broken down along the way? My heart was thumping as I ordered a slice of pizza.

I sprinkled on chilli flakes and thought of Mary Grace. How would her day be going? She waited tables in a restaurant in Brooklyn, even though I could tell she didn't need the money. There were small signs in our apartment that she was taken care of, but she didn't flaunt it. In any case, she had welcomed me there and I was already beginning to love my space.

Back at Altogether Media, I knocked on Sam's door and he stood up and offered me a chair. The bun had shifted higher up his head. It was probably my favourite of his bun looks.

Such a gentleman.

Our girl has choices.

I like the other boy better.

He rifled through the piles in his inbox, and I pictured myself getting up, walking over to him and resting my head on his chest. Was my wanting to lose my virginity making all the men in the world appear attractive?

'I know your dreams are to start drawing, from what I gather from your résumé,' he said. 'But how about a little writing work? Good illustrators who can write are rare!' His voice had lilted so high, I didn't know how it was going to come back down. He had to scratch his throat to regain his normal timbre. 'And you told me you were doing the visual essay MFA. Great programme, by the way, if I didn't say last time.'

'Thank you,' I said. As if I'd come up with the programme myself.

'So this project is a perfect chance to hone those writing skills. The writer of this piece, Aunt Abbie, is so old-school she mails everything in. Please type it up and look out for awkward sentences, typos, that kind of stuff.'

He handed me the sheet. It was an agony aunt column. I hadn't realised those were syndicated too. I wondered how much the columnist made. Could it be a good way to earn some side money? I let my eyes scan quickly through the letter and response. The question asked was how the writer was supposed to keep living with her smoker husband. They had both quit smoking the year before, and she was still going strong and staying away from cigarettes, while her husband had cracked. Now, she couldn't stand the smell of cigarettes any more.

'You're in this together' was Aunt Abbie's reply. 'You have to be as patient with him as you were with yourself.'

I don't know what I'd have responded.

Leave him, don't kill yourself?

Ay, these voices!

I typed it up, moved around a few punctuation marks, tightened some sentences and went back to Sam's office.

'That was fast,' he said, taking a look at it. He scrunched his chin and pouted. 'Impressive. Thank you.'

'You're welcome,' I said.

'And also! We have our monthly happy hour at the end of the week. You should come.'

Apart from Sam and Donna, I really hadn't interacted with most of the people who worked for Altogether Media, and I was curious about them, huddling all day long in their cubicles. I said I would.

I flung open the door to the apartment, saw Mary Grace's keys hanging on the hooks by the door.

'I'm in love with my boss and he invited me to happy hour!' I shouted theatrically. 'And I ran into the boy who used to be the love of my life but did nothing.'

'Whoa,' said Mary Grace from her room. I stood at her door, 'The boss situation . . . tricky.'

'Well, if I'm being honest, it wasn't just me he invited; it's happy hour for everyone.'

She was folding a very wrinkled T-shirt as if there were no

bones in her wrist, and I was filled with an urge to grab it out of her hands, give it a good shaking and do the folding for her. I resisted. The roots of her hair had curled up. Was her hair as naturally curly as mine?

'Then he was just doing his job. Tell me about this love of your life.'

'Seeing as we never did anything except sit in each other's homes to watch films and play games and do homework together, I don't know that he really was the love of my life. We spent a *lot* of time with each other, but our hormones must have been underdeveloped. Maybe it was a one-sided thing. I definitely liked him. If he had kissed me, I wouldn't have said no.'

'Did you ask him out?'

'What? No. But he said we should have lunch or hang.'

I thought of the comics I'd been scanning that day. Why hadn't I been bold? After all, Kweku wasn't some random guy on the street. But then if things went wrong and we ended up having the same New York circles, life could get unbearable. For one, we worked in the same building. It would be impossible to avoid him. It was good I'd been restrained.

'Also, what if he's seeing someone?' I said, continuing out loud the conversation I'd been having with myself. 'He *must* be seeing someone.'

'Well, silly, you won't know if you don't ask.'

'Oh, and then there's that Seth guy who's been texting me heys.'

'He sounds like a loser.' She stuffed her badly folded clothes onto the shelves of her closet. 'But keep him close. It's good to have options in New York.'

'You think?'

'Why hasn't he asked you anything up till now? Actually, you should ask *him* out. You have nothing to lose if he says no.'

It would be good practice.

No, he should do the work.

What did I think? I had no clue. I would listen to Mary Grace.

Chapter Eleven

Bushwick

At the close of the work day, Sam came to chaperone me, and others joined us.

'Some of you have met her,' said Sam, in a crumpled shirt with rolled-up sleeves. Ironing was clearly not his thing. 'Our new intern, Zainab.'

'Hi, everyone,' I said and studied the chipped yellow nail polish on my feet.

'Welcome, Zainab,' said the man I'd met on my first day, another dishevelled one.

'Nice to have some more ovaries around here,' said a woman in a Grateful Dead T-shirt and jeans. She laughed a body-shaking laugh and snorted. Her face turned beet red. Three other men joined us and we shuffled quietly to the elevator, down and out into the muggy evening air. It was a Thursday, but it felt like a Friday. People walked down Park Avenue, their jacket buttons undone, hair escaping from buns, stilettos traded for flip-flops.

We rounded the corner on one of the streets – I didn't notice which one – and walked into an Irish bar. On a huge screen, a match was playing and one of our team members stopped and stared at the TV as if he'd met an old friend.

'He's German,' explained Sam. 'So he watches all the World Cup games. Ghana is not doing badly, right?'

I nodded, even though I hadn't been watching the World Cup at all. I didn't have a TV – Mary Grace had one in her bedroom – but football wasn't really my thing. Although if Ghana qualified,

I would make sure to corral Densua and other Ghanaian friends in the city to watch the game.

'A round of beers?' Sam asked, pointing around the group. Here in the bar he finally seemed to have expanded and become our proper leader, very different from what he exuded in the office. Even as an intern, when he came to me with work it felt as if *I* were doing him a favour.

Everyone nodded. I supposed I couldn't ask for my usual Malibu-pineapple. This pub didn't seem like the place that would even stock my kind of drink. I would drink the beer.

Don't drink it.

She needs to loosen up, it's OK.

It came in a tall glass shaped like a dumb-bell. Thin in the middle, thick on the ends. I took one sip and it was bitter and frothy. Apart from sipping the dregs of my father's glass as a child, I'd never really drunk beer. I took a larger gulp and then another, until a third of the ghastly brew was gone.

I thought I would sidle up to the woman, female solidarity and all, but she had struck up a conversation with the bartender. Sam came to the rescue. My heart raced. There had to be rules about work romance at Altogether Media, but a girl could dream.

'So, grad school in the fall?'

'Yes,' I said, trying to ignore the cave-like feeling that was building in my belly. I was hungry. And nervous. And why was Sam always talking about grad school?

Be bold.

It's not proper home training. He's your boss.

'Where are you from?' I asked.

'Connecticut.'

'How come Donna isn't here?' I said, wondering about the only person with whom I'd had some affinity in the office.

'She thinks we're babies.' He paused, and when I said nothing, he said, 'I'm kidding. She lives in Yonkers, way above the Bronx, so she doesn't like lingering around in the city. What about you? Are you already in student housing at NYU?'

'SVA.'

'Right, sorry.'

'No. I just moved to Bushwick.' I swallowed another large gulp of my beer. It was oddly filling. At least the alcohol was good for one thing. It made me feel flirty. Did I look flirty? I'd lost track of our conversation.

Ask him where he lives.

'You?'

'Fort Greene.'

'It's really nice there.'

'It is. My girlfriend wanted to be near a park, and it's not too far from the city. It's great this time of year. There's even a book festival there you could check out.'

Girlfriend.

That punched me right in the solar plexus. It was probably for the best, having this new information. And was it written on my face somewhere that I liked books? Maybe that was why I hadn't met anyone yet. But didn't bookish types deserve love too?

'Thanks,' I said, belching loudly. 'I'm so sorry.'

'Want another?'

I shook my head as I downed the last drops in my glass. I felt my muscles loosen and I really liked the feeling. I'd drunk more alcohol in these first few weeks in New York than I'd ever had, and I was afraid I'd get used to it, or become an alcoholic like Uncle Ebo, my father's brother.

'So what are your hopes for the internship?' Sam asked.

I hadn't realised work was still ongoing, so his question threw me off. I wanted to learn the nuts and bolts of good graphic novels. No, I wanted to be able to come up with a project that I could simultaneously pitch to Altogether Media and also develop when grad school began.

'I want to learn as much as possible,' is what I eventually said out loud.

'Don't hesitate to let me know if you need anything from me.'

The rest of the happy hour went on in a joyful blur and I don't remember what I said to anyone, but I managed to get on the M home with no problems.

As the train crawled over the Williamsburg Bridge, surrounded by the dimming daylight, and onto the island that contained Brooklyn, the beer buzz cleared. This was my home now. My mind painted a picture of all the green that had once surrounded this area. I'd read somewhere that before it was Bushwick – Boswijck, the neighbourhood in the woods – the true owners of the land, the Canarsee, had called it Navack. Now, there weren't many trees left, and the neighbourhood had retained the name given it by the conquerors. In place of the red-brick behemoth of the Domino sugar factory, with its phallic tower, I could see a lush forest being felled to build houses for the Dutch, while a Native American family, the last survivors, peeked at what was left of their precious bushes before being pushed further inland. Ever since I was little, as long as I knew some small history of a place, I was able to see it in its previous incarnations, or I was able to place myself in a character who had lived in that time. It was almost as if I'd lived other lives. Or it was my super power? Did it have anything to do with the voices I was hearing?

My room in Mary Grace's apartment was small, and I slept on an airbed, which might have depressed someone else, but not me. I was as pleased as Punch. I'd gone to Fat Albert, a you-can-get-everything-here type of establishment tucked underneath the elevated JMZ train tracks just around the corner from our apartment, and bought myself a small fan. My room, with its surprisingly shiny parquet floor, now consisted of a not-so-comfortable bed, a fan, and my two suitcases. There wasn't space for a closet, but my plan was to get a clothing rack and some plastic drawers. All this would happen after my first pay cheque. I was living in my very own space!

On the second Saturday after I moved in, I cracked and texted Seth something more than the usual *I'm good* I would reply to his *hey*.

What are u up to?

Just chilling, came the response.

On my airbed, a cloud of my plastic-sheathed breath, I was also just chilling, feeling like I'd finally arrived somewhere, with a room of my own. Except for one very important part of my life I'd been avoiding: my drawing. OK, two important parts of my life: my work, and Densua.

First, I could take care of the drawing drought. Before moving into Mary Grace's, I'd had enough of an excuse because I didn't have a stable home. Now that I had my own space, the blank pages in my sketchbook needed filling. I'd tried a few times, but I had nothing to show for it, except for Sam's hair in its different states of bun. One of my soon-to-be professors at SVA, John Stephens, had emailed asking us to bring some ideas to our first day of class, and his email had grown spectral. I reached for the sketchbook I'd bought right before leaving Mount Holyoke. Then I saw my telephone and put down the sketchbook.

When are we hanging out? I texted Seth, emboldened. I waited five minutes. Ten minutes. Nothing. I walked out of my room.

Neither Mary Grace nor I knew how to cook, but we agreed that cooking had to flow through our veins, her being South East Asian, and me being West African. We had great cooking traditions and we were going to draw out our culinary ancestors kicking and screaming, even if domesticity was what we'd both been running away from our whole lives.

'I just asked the Seth guy to hang out, and he's literally left me hanging,' I said to Mary Grace, who was standing in our laboratory of a kitchenette, about to poke a piece of burnt toast with a fork. 'Please pull out the switch.'

'Oh yes,' she said, red hair now showing jet-black roots as she reached forward to yank out the wire of the toaster. 'How long has it been?'

'Now fifteen minutes. And we'd had a back-and-forth going. OK, three messages.'

She pushed the tines of the fork into her toast and led the

charred thing into her mouth. She beckoned me over and I showed her the messages, towering slightly over her. For some reason, I'd always thought of her as being the same height as me, if not taller.

'You know what we need to do?' she said. 'We should have a housewarming and have people bring their friends. If you want to invite this loser guy too . . . what's his name?'

'Seth.'

'Tell him to come, and invite all your guy friends and make him jealous. Like your childhood crush, even.'

I wouldn't do things that way.

Who would pay for all that?

But it would be nice to have some music and dancing.

It's true that a housewarming would involve spending money. Even if we told people to bring drinks, we would still have to serve them food. I couldn't have people come into my home and not feed them, never mind the fact that I couldn't cook myself.

'Let's do a housewarming when I have an actual bed,' I said.

'Yes, that way you can get laid properly. It'd be like the Cinderella ball, but with the roles reversed.'

I grinned. I didn't even want to begin to think of the mechanics of getting laid. It was what I desired, yes, but a good start would be finding someone to exchange saliva with, and then we'd work our way up to tangling legs.

I went back to my air mattress. My phone refused to buzz. This was a man I'd spent at most an hour with. Someone I hadn't even thought particularly interesting. But now the lack of a response from him grew into a force. It was powerful, converting Seth into larger-than-life proportions until he became the most important thing to me at that moment. Just hearing back from him was all I needed to calm my off-kilter heart. It was so quiet, even the voices in my head weren't saying anything. They seemed to emerge only when other people were around. When I was on my own, they fell silent. What was that about?

I reached for my sketchbook and a pencil and drew a straight line. Maybe I should draw our apartment building. It was a new building, around five years old. Why was Seth not responding? I picked up my phone and was tempted to fling it. This was madness. I came out of my pyjamas, threw on a pair of shorts and a T-shirt, stuffed ten dollars into my back pocket and walked out of my room, leaving my phone behind.

'I'm going to get some air,' I shouted to Mary Grace, now in her room. The living room reeked of char.

In the hot June morning, a train rattled by and the metallic singsong of an invisible ice cream truck became my soundtrack. I walked to the right, away from the shops that would tempt me with their cheap clothing: *Summer Ts for a dollar, dresses for 5.*

Water gushed down the street, and soon I passed by the offending fire hydrant. I winced, remembering days in boarding school when I'd had to carry a metal bucket to be able to have a decent bath. Densua's boyfriend Rodney carried her bucket for her, and would occasionally help me out, usually when he'd done something wrong and needed me to put in a good word for him.

Around the bend from the flooding street, I saw a block filled with graffiti and homed in on a colourful tag smack in the middle. I admired the strength of the lettering and the boldness of the colours the artist had used. Now that I thought about it, I didn't need to frequent expensive galleries to experience art. Art was everywhere . . . on the street in New York, and maybe I would chance on something to get me out of my drawing rut. Comic book artists had inspired many a graffiti writer, so it could go the other way, too.

Why wasn't I drawing? Mma's words, the voices, all the newness. I couldn't say what exactly it was.

I took a turn on Metropolitan Avenue, and in a little nondescript shop I discovered the most divine cream-filled cannoli. I bought myself three of them and stuffed my belly. I turned left on Manhattan and returned home.

My boy is DJing at Crime Scene tonight. Come thru.

The walking juju worked.

'Help,' I shouted, knocking on Mary Grace's door and thrusting the phone her way when she opened it. The cool blast pushing outside was welcome. Her bed was covered in a silk black sheet and her air conditioner was buzzing loudly. Clothes spread themselves on every free inch of space. Hadn't she just folded her laundry?

'Ignore it.'

'Why? I've been waiting for this message all day. Heck, all month!'

'OK, respond "I have plans, but we'll see."'

'I can't do that. I asked him when we were hanging. He'll know I have no other plans.'

'Who has more experience in New York?'

'You do,' I said, taking my phone back.

'This place will eat you alive if you don't play ball.'

'Will you please, please come with me?'

'I have plans, but we'll see.'

'What . . .' I shook my head. 'Oh, gotcha. You're showing me how it's done. What am I going to wear?'

'Something slutty.'

'I have nothing.'

'That's why we have Myrtle Avenue.'

'So now I don't have plans any more?'

'I see that you want to make your own mistakes, so I'm giving you the space for that. You might just land on that rare guy who doesn't play New York games.'

That would be nice.

We'll make sure it happens.

'Hold up. Didn't we both just get here? How come you know so much about New York?'

'While I was at Smith, I spent every single summer here. Trust me, I've seen it all. Text him "I have plans, but I'll pop by to say hi."'

'You're the best,' I said, grinning as I did exactly as Mary Grace had said.

She is wise after all.

Yes, we can keep her.

Chapter Twelve

Crime Scene

He definitely wasn't what my mind had clung to. His clothes seemed to hang on him too loosely. His T-shirt was oversized and his jeans baggy over his white sneakers. I wanted to apologise to Mary Grace for presenting her with such a shabby reality of my dreams.

'You look nice,' he said.

The slutty look I'd settled for was a halter-neck top that had cost me two bucks, with jeans. Mary Grace was in a black tube dress that showed off her legs and made her look less Victorian than I'd ever seen her. She struck up a conversation with a tall, striking man with dreadlocks, and my feelings of inadequacy shot sky high.

'Want a drink?' Seth asked.

'Sure. A beer, please.'

But that is not ladylike. This beer thing should stop.

A good calabash of beer every now and then never hurt anybody.

I was liking one of these voices. She was definitely not Grandma Fati, that was clear. Beer was as old as time. And it wasn't even like I'd asked for hard liquor. One or two nights in the apartment, Mary Grace had offered me a shot of bourbon she'd bought. I could only sip the stuff. The thoughts that ran through my mind were so conflicting. One minute it was good that I was being adventurous, the next was what if my mother saw me? Sometimes I couldn't even tell when the thoughts had come from me or from those strange beings in me. They felt like beings, people separate from me.

The DJ had a short attention span, but I couldn't bad-mouth him to his friend, Seth. He'd start one song and barely get through it, skipping over the juicy parts before switching. It got so bad that I decided to stop dancing.

'Sorry,' said Seth. 'It's almost like a DJ training school here. He'll get better.'

I drank my beer too fast and it unclenched my muscles. The volume of Seth's clothing stopped bothering me and I could focus on his baby face. It was smooth and pleasant to look at. His brows were perfectly shaped and thick, as if plucked, and his lips were plump. Before I knew it, he was closer and closer and then those lips touched mine and I liked the way they felt. Like cushions. Then his tongue was in my mouth and the warm fuzzies changed to a heat in my belly that melted down between my legs. I wrapped my arms around his neck and deeper and deeper the kiss went, until we were interrupted by his DJ friend. I was mortified. I had maybe kissed a couple of people on the dance floors of our Western Massachusetts college parties, but usually the shadows of those rooms had been my cover. No one had *ever* seen me kiss someone else. At least, not to my knowledge.

They all saw.

'Zainab,' Seth said, 'my bro, DJ Kelechi.'

'Ah, Kelechi, you're from Nigeria?' I said, not sure if it was worse that he was West African too.

'Yes, originally. You too?'

'No, I'm from Ghana.'

'Ah, ah, my small sister.'

I wanted Kelechi to go away, especially since he'd been such a poor DJ, so I could continue locking lips with Seth, but he was here to stay.

'Y'all hungry?'

They decided they wanted to go to a famous Belgian fry joint not too far from where we were. I went to find Mary Grace, who had plastered her backside on her tall man. It seemed so unlike her.

And so down the street the five of us went. Andre, the tall

man, knew Kelechi, but not Seth, so no one was really a fifth wheel, but I decided that Kelechi was.

'Are you gonna take him home?' Mary Grace whispered.

'I don't think so,' I said, the grease from the fries absorbing whatever alcohol was left in my body.

'Why not? I saw you two.'

'I thought you said I should tell him I had other plans, and I don't know if I like him like that.'

'Who cares?'

I hadn't confessed to my greenness in the sex department.

When the last of the fries had been swallowed, Seth looked at me expectantly and I stared at my feet. He was nice to kiss, but my first time had to be with someone I sort of liked, didn't it? I didn't know this man. Then again, I just wanted to have sex, so why was I dithering?

You're being too careful.

Better careful than sorry.

He's not all that.

'We're heading back to Bushwick,' Mary Grace said loudly, locking hands with Andre. How did she do that with ease?

'Mmm, yes, I'm coming, too,' I said, giving Seth a hasty hug and turning on my heel to join Mary Grace and Andre as they caught a cab. I didn't even leave room for Seth to insert himself into the equation.

I tried hard not to notice Mary Grace sitting on Andre and sucking off half of his face, and angled my body so I could look out the window. But I still caught their reflections in the glass. I should have sat in front. The taxi driver, head wrapped in a turban, said nothing. Oh, the things his eyes must have seen.

Luckily, it was a blip of a ride over the Williamsburg Bridge and under the train tracks. And indeed, it was a lucky thing, because the lovebirds forgot that *they* had decided to catch a taxi, and yet here I was paying for all nine dollars of the ride. In my head, it made up for the price of the drink Seth had bought for me.

Not long afterwards, not even the buzz of Mary Grace's air

conditioner could drown out the highs of her moans. I slid on my headphones and pressed play on my iPod, a gift I'd bought myself after my first summer at college, where I worked in the computer lab, teaching people Photoshop and Illustrator.

I had a good time tonight, I texted Seth.

Mary Grace would probably rip the phone out of my hands, reach into the cables and undo the message I'd just sent, but it was too late.

Me too, Seth responded a day later.

Chapter Thirteen

Mary Grace

I left work early, and couldn't wait to get home to lie on my airbed to think. My project for grad school was truly beginning to haunt me. I didn't know where to begin. After all, I had come to this city not for the *flânerie*, but to make something of myself as an illustrator. I had a slice of cannoli waiting for me that I'd been dreaming of, and opened the door and rushed to the kitchen, where I almost bumped into Mary Grace standing next to the stove wearing an apron I'd never seen, while Andre sat, bare-chested at the small table on which we ate our meals with a can of beer in hand.

I wanted the parquet floor to crack into two and bury me under its shiny lacquer. Why was I so embarrassed when I wasn't the one with a lover in such a domestic pose?

'Carry on,' I said, leaving the cannoli alone.

I didn't come out of my room again until I heard Mary Grace's signature loudness competing with the air conditioner. A small piece of chicken wing had been left on a plate, which I led straight to my mouth. It was surprisingly tasty, sweet, with savoury undertones of ginger and garlic. Mary Grace had outdone herself for someone who couldn't cook. It would be nice to have someone to *try* to cook for, I thought longingly.

I told her later that her chicken was delicious.

'I bought it,' she said. 'Just heated it up in the pan like it was my own.'

'So he's none the wiser? Poor guy.'

She shook her head, and I laughed so hard I almost wet my underwear.

'Let's learn to make one good dish,' I said.

'It's on,' she said. 'We are ancient people. We got this.'

The next day, we got off the J train at Canal Street and stepped out into the humid, fish-tinged air of Chinatown. Who was that first person who'd settled here from China? How different it would have been from their homeland then. And now, I wondered if these streets looked anything like the streets of Beijing. I'd only been here once, when Densua and other friends from secondary school had decided to go in search of authentic Chinese food. We wound round and round, finally settling for a restaurant proudly proclaiming an A grade on its facade. The ones with pending grades seemed the most suspect to us, mostly because the signs were tacked to businesses that looked well established. Pending seemed like a code word for not good. This time, Mary Grace led me along side streets, and I felt transported. Grandmothers slowly shuffled their wheeled shopping baskets along; merchants whipped by, offloading carts of familiar and strange fruits; the soft tinkle of bicycle bells competed with the Mandarin and Cantonese and the many dialects of Chinese on these streets, and the smells! Fried duck one minute, the stench of a not-so-fresh sea creature; the sweet warmth of freshly baked goods. We stopped in one of those bakeries and Mary Grace bought all sorts of squishy-looking confections that seemed to belong at a child's Play-Doh station rather than to be intended for consumption.

'Try this,' she said, splitting a green bun in two. A red paste oozed out.

I took it and bit into it, thinking it was probably full of food colouring. It was delightful. Sweet, but deep, with a tiny hint of bitterness in the bun that gave way to a rich full creaminess with the paste in the middle.

'What is this?'

'Mochi. On the outside, matcha, and on the inside, red bean paste.'

'Oh. My. God. Why have I never eaten anything like this?'

'Wait till you try the ice cream version.'

She bought a whole box of mochi and we walked out. We should have gone to Little Manila or to Woodside in Queens, to the real heart of the Philippines in New York, but Mary Grace didn't want to bump into her mother's sister, who lived there – the woman would hijack our day. Her shoulders hunched over and she greeted the woman sitting behind the counter in the Filipino food store. They exchanged long greetings in Tagalog. They spoke rapidly, a melodious song, with English words thrown in, and a few I recognised as Latinate.

It struck me how different Mary Grace looked from the other woman, whose skin was much lighter and whose hair was straighter. Even though we had grown closer, I didn't quite have the confidence to ask Mary Grace about how come her skin glowed almost as dark as mine, and how her hair, although straight, pushed out like mine in the days when I used to run perming cream through it.

'We praise God,' Mary Grace concluded. I had to do a double take. She was a chameleon.

With a name like Mary Grace, I knew she was Catholic by birth, but she hadn't set one foot at mass in the time I'd known her, and I had pegged her for an agnostic.

We picked up cans of coconut juice, rice vinegar, two kinds of soy sauce, lemongrass and various chilli peppers that she had grown up with, and the woman at the counter gave us each a bright yellow packet.

'For good flavour,' she said.

I studied the packing. Jolly Claro palm oil.

'We use palm oil, too!' I said excitedly.

'I knew we were one and the same,' said Mary Grace as we thanked the shopkeeper.

On the J train, as the light of day filtered into the car, I looked out and watched the high-rises of the Lower East Side abutting the East River, which we were soon crossing. My heart now belonged in Brooklyn. As a child, I'd listened in awe as a friend talked about visiting an aunt there. She had crossed the bridge into Manhattan and had said that was the New York City of the films. If only I had known that I would grow up to see things the other way round.

'The woman in the store knows my family,' Mary Grace said, apropos of nothing.

She's hiding something. She was too different in there.

People are different depending on who they talk to.

'That's why all your Hail Marys came out,' I said, ignoring the voices.

'That's the only way to get them off your back. Don't worry, when we go to the Bronx, we'll see how you behave.'

'Lucky for me, I'm a nobody in Ghana. I might be able to get away with bad behaviour.' Since our banter was smooth going, I decided to broach one of the many questions I had about Mary Grace. I wanted to know about her parents, about her hair, about why she wanted to write. I wanted to know how she was able to work as a waitress. How come she always seemed full of energy? But I'd start with a harmless question, one that wouldn't seem like I was prying too much, because it concerned me, too. Why did she intimidate me so much? 'How come you're able to work in a restaurant – as an international student?'

'So, swear you won't tell anybody this.' She glared at me, and I nodded so hard I must have pulled a muscle in my neck. There was no one to tell, anyway. 'My green card is arriving soon, so technically I'm not supposed to work. But if you just find the right people, you can get paid under the table for any job in this city.'

'Maybe I should get a bar or restaurant job like you,' I said.

'You won't last a day. You're too nice.'

Why did everyone think that? I'd only lived with Mary Grace for a few days and she'd already pegged me as *the nice girl*. I wanted to be less the nice girl and more like her, *the badass*. It was making me think of how I could supplement the stipend I was getting at the internship. I just had to find someone willing and able. That would be a badass move.

Back in the apartment, Mary Grace called her mother as I unpacked our bag of groceries.

'OK,' she said, hanging up, 'we're making my favourite dish, adobong manok sa buko. My mum says it'll be hard to ruin. But we need a whole chicken.'

'Do *you* know how to cut a whole chicken?' I asked. My privilege was undressing itself right before my eyes. I'd had help my whole life. Yes, my family was not wealthy, but I'd never had to descale a fish, defeather a bird or do any such drudgery. Even when we moved out of our nice house, my mum still employed a house help.

The girl paid for the shopping. You get the chicken.

Show you have good home training.

'OK,' I said out loud – I sounded like a toddler moaning, but Mary Grace didn't seem bothered by my tone. 'I'll get the chicken. You can start the prep.'

Good girl.

Down the street I went, and in a minute, I was in the giant Food Bazaar. I picked up a whole chicken, my eyes lingering on the pre-cut thighs, wondering why we couldn't use something that had already been prepared for us. Not far from the chicken, I saw what had to be a frozen rat. Sure, back home we had grass-cutter and the like, but to see a version of it here was like I'd put on my clothes inside out. A bit strange.

I walked to the counter and passed through the Asian aisle. All the food we'd bought in Chinatown, we could easily have picked up here. Mary Grace would probably be glad to know.

I returned to the apartment and she was sucking her finger. No way was *she* going to cut the chicken now. For a split second the thought crossed my mind that she'd hurt herself intentionally, but she spread a Band-Aid over the cut and proceeded to hack at the bird, mashing up some bits, splintering the bones in places I was sure should have been whole.

'I just saw a rat at the Food Bazaar,' I said.

'Why do you sound so shocked? This is New York. We live with them.'

'No, frozen.'

'Whoa. Next time, you have to show me.'

Mary Grace passed me the pieces of chicken and I cleaned them with lemon, like I'd seen my mother do. Then she took a back seat and delivered instructions. Soak the chicken in vinegar and soy sauce. Cut up the rest of the spring onions. Pour in the coconut juice. Add sugar.

I burnt the accompanying rice, and the sauce ended up very salty.

'How did we do?' I asked when we had both cleared our plates.

'Five out of ten. Next dish from Ghana. We'll do this until we get good. Deal?'

'Deal.'

Chapter Fourteen

World Cup

I stared at a blank page in my sketchbook, battling conflicting thoughts. One minute, my imposter syndrome was in fine form, dressed in a sharp suit, repeating words my mother had used in the past ('Zain, drawing is really a hobby'); the next, my brain had become my biggest cheerleader, screaming that I got into SVA in freaking New York City, I had to be talented, I was the best. Go Zainab! Go Zainab!

And yet neither of these two forces – neither the anxious one nor the confident one – could get the blank page filled. Nothing coloured the pristine white of the paper in front of me. I pressed the tip of my pencil to its hardness, deep. So deep that the pencil broke. I was left only with a smudge of black on white. I was a dry well in the desert, filled with sand.

I had seen Mary Grace's notebook lying on the sofa. Unlike its owner, it had a certain innocence about it, in its pink and green colours. But now that innocence had become a come-hitherness. Maybe it *was* just like its owner. On first blush, Mary Grace came off as innocent, with her big eyes, then she opened her mouth and she was like a crazy old lady who cursed a lot.

Don't do it.

I wouldn't, either.

Just one line. Maybe just one word from her work would inspire me. She was in her room and could come out any minute, so cat-like, I would make sure I wouldn't get caught.

I dragged my bed sheet and sketchbook with me, and made a

messy bundle on the sofa. I flipped through the notebook, pages and pages of surprisingly neat penmanship. I selected a page with a short poem:

> The day you released my fingers
> I felt bound & free
> Too early
> You let me go too early.

My phone buzzed and I almost jumped out of my skin. I left the notebook, took my property and went into my room, dropping the sketchbook on my bed and answering the phone. Uncle Ali wanted me to join him in the Bronx to watch the Ghana versus Brazil game in a Ghanaian restaurant. I actually considered it – even though I had sworn to stay away from the Bronx – but then my phone beeped. It was Kweku, texting me to join him in Fort Greene for the game. This wasn't a difficult decision to make.

'Uncle Ali,' I said, 'I'm so sorry I can't make it today, but I promise you I'll make it up to you. Pray for our boys!'

'All right, Zainabou.'

The blank page looked at me accusingly. Not only was I untalented and a sneak, I was disloyal.

Don't be so hard on yourself.

She should be. That was not good behaviour.

As I left the apartment, I paused for a split second as I saw Mary Grace back on the couch with a novel. I should invite her, especially after invading her privacy like that. Then again, she had a way of filling up the room and taking over situations. I wanted Kweku to myself. So I told her I was meeting Kweku without explaining more, and she gave me an enthusiastic thumbs-up and picked up her notebook – now returned to its innocence – as I shut the door behind me.

You are threatened by her.

Because she lives life as she chooses, as we all should.

And you shouldn't have opened her private book.

It hadn't even yielded any results, at least none that I could use in my illustrations. I couldn't crack Mary Grace, and maybe because of that I also couldn't completely be myself with her. I would have loved to talk to Densua to get her opinion on my budding friendship, but we hadn't spoken since I left her apartment – I couldn't tell if we were still friends. I brushed off these thoughts as I grabbed the G from Flushing Avenue.

I got off at Dekalb Avenue, and even though I'd been to Fort Greene a couple of times by now, I found myself searching all four corners of the crossroads at which I'd emerged to find a familiar point. Finally, I spied the Brooklyn Academy of Music, or BAM, with its iconic watchtower. It was my North Star in Fort Greene, and now I knew I had to leave it behind me to arrive at the park.

I went down a fabulous street lined on either side with brownstone buildings shaded mahogany, amber and deep chocolate. I was reminded of Mr Thomas, and wondered if he had managed to rent out his room. A mother sat on a stoop, watching as her toddlers wheeled about on their tricycles. Would life lead me down a road like this? Then I asked myself whether she had a partner and if they had a good relationship, or if one person took care of the children and the other thought himself the breadwinner, never mind that the two of them worked. Little resentments would build until they let their differences split their union and completely devastate their children. In any case, I was too young to think of children. First, I had to get laid. Second, come out of my summer internship with something incredible to show instead of just scans of *Big Augie*. Third, have a killer project to wow the likes of Professor John Stephens once school began.

At the end of the row of brownstones, I came upon the Fort Greene Park and strode alongside it until it ended. My heart raced as I saw the small crowd gathered around the front of Madiba, and I tried to pick Kweku out from the bodies that had come in their Ghana jerseys, kente head wraps and dashikis. What would he be wearing? Would something electric happen today? I got closer and realised that this was the spillover; the restaurant was chock-full of people. Kweku was not on the sidewalk, so I texted him and held my breath until he pushed his way out.

He wore a chambray shirt, jeans and a baseball cap. His dimpled smile made the crowd disappear, and when he grabbed my hand to pull me in through the bar-grocery-store area, I didn't want him to let go. But he did when we got through to the dining room, where a white screen rolling with ads hung above the heads of some of the diners. Behind the screen, various portraits of Nelson Mandela, after whom the restaurant was named.

Kweku introduced me to his friends, a motley crew. He had saved me a chair, and a girl with bouncy curls lifted her bag to let me sit. If this were a test of some sort, vetting me with his friends, I would have to play cool. The game started, and when the Ghana anthem began, Kweku and I and the large group of Ghanaians around us stood up and held our hands to our chests and belted out 'God Bless Our Homeland Ghana'. Within five minutes, Brazil's Ronaldo had scored a goal, puncturing our patriotic bubble. We were doomed. This was the first time we – Ghana – had gone into the round of sixteen, so all eyes were on us.

'If we lose to Brazil, I won't mind,' I whispered to Kweku.

Is that what you really feel, or is this playing cool?

'But the boys should try,' he said, forcing out his best Ghanaian accent. 'Want to eat something? Or drink something? Or both?'

I shook my head. I would go back home and eat, even if the thought of food was already making my belly gargle.

'OK, a beer,' I said. That shouldn't set me back too much.

If you don't stop drinking this beer, you will grow a pot belly.

I almost burst out laughing. *That* was funny.

The first half ended and not one goal from our boys. When the ads came on, the girl sitting next to me asked how Kweku and I knew each other.

'She's my oldest friend,' he replied.

'That's surely not true,' I said loudly, before I could stop myself. Beer wouldn't give me a big stomach, but it took control of my tongue. I was thinking of Densua and me – we went *way* back – and how we were currently not on speaking terms. Seeing what looked like horror flash in Kweku's eyes, I tried to explain. 'We met when we were nine or ten.'

'OK, fine,' he conceded. 'If she doesn't want me to be her oldest friend, we went to school together in Ghana.'

The conversation shifted back to analysing the game. People stood up and went to the bathroom. None of the women in the group seemed involved with Kweku, and whatever awkwardness I'd caused had vanished, because at some point his palm came to rest on my thigh. It just stayed there, warm and familiar and yet totally calling attention to itself. At first, I thought I liked it and I wanted it to press deeper, but it was funny how one small act could grow so noisy. It was as if just by placing his hand on my thigh, Kweku had marked me as his woman. And yet I wasn't. Stay away, that hand was warning any possible contenders out there.

Isn't that what you want?

What do *you want?*

When the game started again, the hand was extracted and sent to its other half in a clap. I was happy it was gone, and yet I missed it.

I tried to focus on the football, but couldn't. Instead, I was thinking of the what-next with Kweku. I forced myself to keep my eyes on the screen. I clapped hard, cheering the boys, hoping they would feel my vibes all the way in Germany. We barely held the ball in our possession, and lost the game. That was it. Africa was officially booted from the 2006 World Cup.

As people streamed out of Madiba, crestfallen, our waiter brought the check.

'We're splitting, right?' said a pasty fellow who had downed the most beers that afternoon. I had had one drink, but my protesting voice chose to hide, and I found myself nodding and grinning, even though paying for everyone else was the last thing I wanted to do. It came to fourteen dollars each, for one beer. I reached for my bag, annoyed that I hadn't at least ordered something to eat. My stomach's acids were definitely going to be eating all my internal walls now.

'I've got this,' Kweku said, pushing back my hand.

My protesting voice grew vociferous and high-pitched: 'Nooo! I can't let you.'

Let him pay.

'It's OK. Next time, you'll treat me.'

'Thank you,' I said, and looked down, sheepish. We walked out, and Kweku's friends hugged him and went their different ways.

'They were nice,' I said. Truth was, I found the pasty fellow rude, and the others were in their own worlds.

'My work colleagues,' he said. 'We started at the agency together. At first, there were ten or so of us, and now, we're six. High turnover. Anyway, what are your plans after this?'

'Have nothing planned. You?'

'Promised my mum I'd help her finally clean up the attic. Even though now I really just want to stay and catch up properly.'

Ah ba, then why did he talk about plans?

'Ei, Aunty Kim! How is she? Where do they live?'

'We live in New Jersey. I live with them.'

That was deflating. Why did he still live at home? Although if my mother lived in New York City, damn straight I'd still be at home too. I'd find another way to try to sow my wild oats. Maybe spend weekends at Densua's while she was working. My heart ached. Why did I keep thinking of Densua? She had opened a wound and had no right to do so. She should reach out first.

'Say hi to them,' I said. 'If they remember me, that is . . .'

'Of course they remember you.'

He stared at me and my heart raced. His eyes were slits, as if blinded by too much sunlight, but the sun was well on its way down. Under his eyes were the cutest bags, not from a lack of sleep; it was just the way he was moulded. All that made his way of beholding the world quite alluring. My gaze kept returning to his lips, and when he smiled, I was taken back to when we were little and how happy I was just to spend time with him. Roller-skating in his parents' driveway, playing Galaxian. Just the two of us. Why had we never kissed? At age ten, eleven, twelve, fine, too young. And now?

'Zainab Sekyi,' he said.

'Kweku Ansah,' I said, watching the blacks of his eyes. Was this going to be it?

'Let's for real hang out,' he said. I exhaled, disappointed. 'Like have a bite or do something. I wanna hear about everything you've been doing all these years.'

'I'd like that.'

'Let me go before Mrs Ansah begins to call the police thinking something has happened to her son.' He pressed his lips to the back of my hand.

Why not on her mouth?

He has good home training.

How long would I keep hearing Grandma Fati's voice? What would make it and the others go away?

I got home and Mary Grace wasn't there. I lay on my airbed, feeling the slight depression my body made. My back would be grateful for a real bed. It would soon be payday. But after rent and my MetroCard, I would be left only with grocery money. I closed my eyes and pictured Kweku's handsome face. He was cute when we were little, but now, he made my heart pound.

I slipped my fingers under my jean button and found the coils of my triangle. I couldn't relax. I took my computer and searched for Fleshbot. I had told myself long ago since that it was a blog, it wasn't really porn. I browsed through photos of people in undress and the insides of me began to swell with pleasure. I was feeling that familiar delicious build-up when a flash of black darted by. I would have missed it, but I was lying on my side, computer propped open, with a clear view of the skirting board, where the creature had made its mad dash.

Luckily, the door of the apartment swung open and I hopped off the bed, keeping my feet on their toes.

Mary Grace dumped a bag of groceries on the floor.

'I think I'm pregnant,' she said, before I could make *my* announcement.

No home training.

Is she sure?

'Are you sure? By whom?'

'Andre, who else?'

'Are you OK? Have you done a test?'

We walked over to the sofa, and I stared down at the floor, expecting the mouse to poke its little head out any minute. I would listen to Mary Grace first and then tell her about the creature.

'Not yet. But I'm *very* late for my period.'

'How late?'

'Three days.'

'Mary Grace!'

'What? I am a very regular woman. Even three days is enough to throw me off.'

'I thought you were on birth control.' I said this picturing the little pack of tablets she left by the bathroom sink.

'You know the pill is only ninety-one per cent effective. I'm the nine per cent. I'm sure of it.'

'Let's just say I'm glad *that* is one thing I've never had to worry about,' I said. 'You should take a test, just to make sure.'

She looked at me, at first maliciously; then, as if parsing through what I'd just revealed, she said, 'What exactly do you mean by you've never had to worry about *that*?'

'I've never had sex,' I mumbled.

'NO!' screamed Mary Grace. 'All this while, I'm vomiting out details about my sex life, and you don't have a single clue about any of it?'

'I mean, I've watched enough movies. I'm not that clueless.'

'Why? How?' she said. I looked behind me, avoiding her accusing look, but also to check that the mouse was not scurrying back into my room. I noticed her bag of groceries.

'Nothing in there needs to go in the fridge?'

'Oh crap!' She sprang up and extracted a tub of butter and a gallon of milk. 'So why haven't you had sex?'

'Before all of that,' I said, 'I think we have a mouse in the house. It was in my room and then went under the door, I think.'

'Aargh. I'll call an exterminator,' she said, pulling her red hair into a bun. She was wearing a long black dress with bell sleeves. Gothic! That was it! Her style was like a goth's, except she was more approachable.

'What if there's a whole mouse family hiding in the oven or something? I don't think I'll be able to sleep tonight.'

'Relax. This is New York. We have a guy who can fix these things. Don't worry. So now, tell me why haven't you had sex.'

'There's always been something stopping me. Like voices in my head or something.'

'We all have voices in our heads.'

'You do?' I said. 'Distinct voices?'

Mary Grace shot me a look that was a cross between suggesting I'd lost my mind, and suggesting that I was making a big deal about something normal. I couldn't tell which one she was going for.

'Stop trying to change the subject,' she said. 'You've come close?'

'Not really. I've kissed a couple of people, but whenever they've even tried to go any further, I've freaked out.'

In college, of the handful of people I kissed on various dance floors, only one made it back to my dorm room. The dance had taken place at the Betty Shabazz Center on campus. I had seen him around; he went to Amherst and would have been perfect to take back to Ghana. He was Panamanian and could dance and was studying economics.

We got to my room, which at that point was all mine – there were no room-mates to 'sexile' by way of a sock on the door or whatever signs college students have used over the generations. It was the perfect time to lose my virginity. I was a month or two shy of graduation; I knew I was going to New York for grad school; even though my grades from bio left much to be desired, straight A's in my art classes had helped raise my mediocre GPA, and I wouldn't fail college. Everything was set for me to finally cross that line.

He was in my room. Our kissing grew steamy. His hands roamed over my blouse, travelled down my barely there skirt and sped up, but just before they reached the divide between my legs, a voice in my head asked if his fingernails were clean, if he'd been tested, what his past relationships had been. Suddenly, a host of possible ex-partners, some of them questionable, flashed before me like a fashion show. The questions multiplied, raced, ballooned in my head and forced me off the bed.

'I told him I was saving myself for marriage,' I said to Mary Grace.

'Get outta here!' she said. 'That should have been your cherry-popping story. Now you have to wade in these dangerous New York waters. The Pioneer Valley was tame. I'm mad for you.'

She was so upset with me I thought she would suck her teeth like a proper Ghanaian girl. She didn't.

'Remember how the PVTA bus was an acronym for Pointing Virgins Towards Amherst?' I asked, apropos of her mentioning the Pioneer Valley.

'Yeah, you clearly missed that bus,' smirked Mary Grace.

I reflected on other moments and how, each time, something had intervened. Either my mind would spin out of control or the other person would suddenly find a reason to move away on the dance floor. Were those voices the same ones I was hearing now? Only now it was like they were through a megaphone. The big change was coming to New York. Maybe there was something in the air here.

I thought about Mary Grace's possible pregnancy. A part of me was convinced she was being a drama queen. I didn't know her that well yet, but she could sometimes be too much.

'So what will you do if you *are* pregnant?' I asked.

'This baby won't stop me. I'd get my MFA with my big belly. I'm sure I won't be the first. Nor the last.'

Chapter Fifteen

Breaking the Flower

Better to lose your virginity to a semi-random person, Mary Grace urged, than the love of your life, even though I didn't count Kweku as the love of my life. At least not yet. I was now getting to know him as an adult. And the more I thought about it, the more I agreed. It was like having a handful of candy and saving your favourite for last – the one you wanted to savour for a long time. In any case, since he still lived at home, he would have to come to *my* house to have sex, which would mean I would have to invite him, and I wasn't sure I wanted to have that discussion when I didn't even have a proper bed.

When I told Mary Grace I wanted my first time to at least be romantic, she said, 'At sixteen, it's romantic. At twenty-one, it starts becoming pathetic.'

So I listened to her, and not to the voice that screamed that I should not be chasing boys and that I was throwing away all the work my mother had done.

Which was how I found myself texting Seth to find out if we could do something, anything, that would lead to my deflowering.

Which was then how I found myself, on a Friday night, sitting on the red velveteen sofa of a man I'd met at an under-twenty-one rave spot, drinking a beer to calm my nerves. The incense-soaked room was stifling, and I kept choking.

'Can we open some windows?' I asked, getting up and tugging on my barely bum-covering dress, then sinking back down. My legs reminded me of an insect's. Twiggy and long. Why had I listened to Mary Grace? I felt naked.

He stood up and pushed open the doors to his bedroom and bathroom. There were no living room windows. This must have been what was considered tenement living back in the day. I could see a family huddled around a cast-iron furnace.

Seth sat down again, dragging me back to the present, and landed his hand on my thigh, the same one Kweku had chosen. Just Seth's touch was heavier. Maybe it was the more attractive of the two thighs. Soon, he was massaging it. I was at once thrilled and frightened.

Was this really the person I wanted to usher me into a brave new world? Or to be my guide to the underworld, if one was religious about these things? His lips touched mine. They were soft, and I tasted the vodka he'd been drinking and a lingering sweetness. He climbed over me and his hands tickled my sides and settled on my hips. His tongue was in my mouth and I welcomed it, licked it. We kissed deeply and then he reached under my dress and pulled off my underwear. That fast? He stood up, pulled his T-shirt over his head, sloughed off his jeans, and was left only in his boxer shorts, navy blue with orange Garfield motifs all over. Why had he chosen those boxers? This was serious to me, but it was coming off like a joke to him.

'Wait!' I said.

'Uh huh?'

'I . . . There's something you should know.'

He got off me and lowered his body next to mine, and I wondered what it was he thought I was about to say. Apart from venereal diseases and a lack of experience, there weren't a whole lot of options one could be presented with.

Don't tell him!

Honesty is the best policy.

Yes, his reaction will tell you everything you need to know.

'I've never done this before,' I exhaled, and it was as if my words squeezed the life-giving air out of him. He slunk back and scratched his head.

'Yeeeeah,' he said. 'I can't mess with that.'

'We could take our time.'

'Yeah . . . I don't know if *I* should be the person who does that.' His voice was suddenly soft and avuncular, and he turned to face me with a furrowed brow to match. 'Don't you want your first time to be special?'

His words unclenched my chest, which hitherto had been pumping a mile a minute, and I burst into tears.

'I'm so sorry,' I said, searching for my underwear on the floor, the lacy thing twisted into an unwearable knot.

'Don't go yet.' He went to the kitchen and tipped a gallon of water into a glass, which he brought to me. 'Damn, how did I miss the signs?'

'What do you mean? Nobody goes around wearing "I'm a virgin" on their head.'

'No, but you can tell when somebody's been banging. The hips bloom. It's in the voice . . . You *are* innocent. Wow, how did I not see that?'

Oh, he was annoying. Luckily it wasn't so late that I couldn't take the train. He lived in Prospect Heights, so it was two trains back to Bushwick.

'I'm going home. Thanks for the evening,' I said, pulling on the hem of my dress.

'Let me get you a cab.'

'I'm good.'

'At least let me walk you out.'

We went down all five of his storeys to a brightly lit street where diners sat al fresco outside restaurants. I held up my hand to wave, but he leant forward and wrapped his beefy arms around me. Just when I was starting to enjoy those arms. The rejection was beginning to sting. A man I'd met at an under-twenty-one club had rejected me. It didn't feel good.

'We should still hang,' he said.

Never.

I got home, and just before sleep washed over me, my phone buzzed. I was hoping Seth wasn't writing with more sage words. If I never saw him again, my life wouldn't miss a thing.

I'm coming in two weeks for a conference in Washington DC. I will spend a weekend with you then head down to Aunty Maimouna's. Let me know what you want me to bring you. I hope nothing dramatic happens in that city of yours when I arrive. Love you.

That flushed the sleep, melancholy and unsatiated horniness out of my system. My mother, texting late from Ghana. Thank God I was still a virgin, I breathed. She would have seen me from a mile away at JFK and sniffed the wantonness on me. At that point, I wanted to return to Prospect Heights to kiss Seth and thank him for saving me from a parental pogrom. I'd dodged a bullet!

Thank us.

Thank your ancestors.

The next day, when I was sure there was no Andre in Mary Grace's room, I knocked and poured into her room and onto her bed. I gave her a play-by-play of my evening.

'I wouldn't have said anything if I were you,' she said.

'He'd still have found out. His thing wouldn't have gone in.'

'Is he packing?'

'I didn't even see it! In any case, this project has to be put on hold, because is it OK if my mum stays here for a weekend?'

'You're not gonna let your mother sleep on an airbed!'

'She's cool.'

'Go buy a bed. I'll drive you to IKEA. And by the way, false alarm, I got my period. Whew! Imagine us clubbing away with my big belly. Ugh.'

'I'm happy for you,' I said.

'Thank you,' she said, then leant in and hugged me. The gesture, which made me envision Mary Grace as a toddler clinging to her mother, threw me off. The hug seemed to say that we were getting close as friends and could continue shedding off the layers we'd piled on to protect our respective hearts.

'I'm extra glad I don't have to share the apartment with a screaming creature,' I said, to lighten the mood after she released me. It was more that it meant I wouldn't have to move out. I went back to my room and straight to IKEA.com. My fear disappeared when I saw bed frames for forty dollars. I would buy the bed with my credit card and worry about it later.

Chapter Sixteen
IKEA

As Mary Grace drove through the Holland Tunnel, with its blinking lights, I couldn't help thinking of caterpillars and how this was not unlike slogging through the body of one. We pulled up at the parking lot of the giant IKEA in Elizabeth, New Jersey, though finding a parking spot took a good half-hour.

'Why is the whole of New York here?' groaned Mary Grace.

When we got into IKEA's hangar of a shop, she led the way through models of rooms decorated to make one salivate. A perfectly placed lamp casting an ambient glow on the clean design of a sofa; a fruit bowl with glistening fake fruit; a kitchen shining with wooden finishes. Maybe working for a company like IKEA would make sense to my mother as a career choice, instead of editorial illustrating. But story was everything for me. How was fake fruit telling me a story? It was pure advertising.

In one of the model bedrooms, Mary Grace plopped up and down on a bed.

'You need a solid bed to handle all the boning you're going to be doing.'

'Uh, you mean that I'll *not* be doing, especially while my mother is here.'

'She's here only a weekend.'

I decided on a full-sized pine bed, one that had been baptised Neiden, because I could slide my suitcases underneath it and finally not have to look at their outdated ugliness.

'And here we are,' said Mary Grace, who had procured two

baskets and stuck one under my nose. I'd come to buy a bed, and only to buy a bed, so I didn't know why I needed a shopping basket.

'We are upping our cooking game,' she said. 'Plus think of all the things your mother would be impressed to find in our kitchen. I know *my* mother would come and inspect everything in the house. I'm getting some stuff too.'

It made sense.

It does make sense.

I picked up a can opener (I don't know how we'd been getting by without one), a professional-looking knife, a wooden spoon set, a large multi-purpose pot (those small things we'd been using would annoy my mma), and a mortar and pestle (because I couldn't resist its design). When we arrived at the bed section, it dawned on me that the bed I'd seen online was only displaying the frame. I needed an assembly line of parts: the mattress, the slats that went underneath it, at least two sets of sheets, and a mattress protector.

At the till, I held my breath as the cashier rang up my purchases.

'That will be three hundred and fifty dollars,' she said perkily, as if she were saying 'Have a great day!'

I proffered my credit card, calculating that with payments of fifty dollars, I could pay off this damage in seven months.

We wheeled our spoils to the car, and as we unloaded the boxed bed frame with our slight bodies, Mary Grace said, 'I'm breaking up with Dre.'

I pushed a box in with my bum.

'Why?'

I don't know why she hadn't said anything on the ride over. What was it about packing boxes that made her think of her boyfriend? Did she even consider him her boyfriend? Was it that she thought this was a man's job? Or would she rather have had a man do it for her? I had to admit to myself that after four years in a women's college, it would have been nice to have some brawn to do the heavy lifting once in a while.

'Is it because of the pregnancy scare?'

'It's getting too . . . He's possessive. He came by the restaurant yesterday. He thinks I'm having an affair with Jay. Jay's cute, but no thanks. That's another immature person I don't need in my life.'

'I'm sorry, MG,' I said. 'Who needs men? We don't!'

'That's why I like you. You get me.'

Her words warmed me in a way I hadn't expected. They gave me the exact same rush the thought of a crush would.

'I need a man,' I said to myself later, as I was tightening the bed's screws. I was petrified about trying it out. I shook it and it seemed stable.

'MG!' I shouted. 'Come test this with me, please.'

My mother was twice Mary Grace's size, but I had no other choice.

Mary Grace threw herself on the mattress.

'Careful!' I warned. 'It's probably going to give in five, four, three . . .'

I eased myself onto the bed slowly and lay by her. She turned over and humped the mattress.

Ah, what is she doing? No home training.

'Not happening in this sacred space,' I said.

'You wait and see. Good job, you! Now I know who to call when I need a repair person. And FYI, the exterminator will come by before your mother arrives.'

Part Two
July

Chapter Seventeen

Mother

I held my breath until I saw the delicate white lace of the mayafi shrouding her face, the stride of her long limbs, that proudness with which she held up her head. I rushed into the warm cloud of my mother's embrace and felt grounded and calmed by it.

'My darling!' she said, planting kisses on my cheeks. 'But how have you lost so much weight?' she asked, pinching the flesh under my ribs. We were off to a shaky start.

'The New York grind, Mma,' I said. I had to remember not to take everything she said personally. She was a mother – it was her job to be critical of *everything.*

'What does that mean – the New York grind?'

'We walk everywhere. We run to catch the train. There are stairs everywhere. It's impossible to put on weight in this city.'

'Well, I'll do my best to fatten you in the short time I'm here with you,' she said, pinching my cheek.

That's right!

I pushed her three-suitcase-heaped trolley, marvelling at her need for so much luggage for a conference that would last a week. Her clothes – ensemble pieces – were on the heavy side, and for every outfit, there was a matching veil, shoes and handbag. It was excessive. Then she always travelled with one empty suitcase for all the things she would be hauling back home. She was one of those people who took home the most improbable things in their suitcase: curtains, gardening tools, knives, a toilet seat! As if she couldn't find these things in Ghana.

The quality is not the same.

We entered the AirTrain, then the A train, and switched for the J at Broadway Junction. I was glad my mother didn't fuss that I was making her take public transportation. She even seemed happy that the whole trip cost only a few dollars. Here was a woman who would happily pay for excess baggage, but not for a taxi. I was a bit like her, willing to spend only if we were gaining something tangible in the arrangement.

When we finally arrived at the apartment, I was relieved Mary Grace wasn't around – at least just for the time it would take Mma to settle in. My mother sloughed off her mayafi and scarf, and her long hair fell down her back. It was such a shame that the world didn't get to behold the thick wonder that was Mma's hair, but she was so fashionable with her veils that it didn't even matter.

'Your apartment is not bad,' she said, walking round, I was sure, to inspect the places where dirt took refuge. She opened the fridge. 'But you girls have to be cleaning your fridge. She drinks, your room-mate?'

I nodded. This was going to be hard to navigate. I'd have to send Mary Grace a message with some ground rules. I was excited to show my mother the world I was building, but I was also anxious. Would she approve? What if she told me I was doing life all wrong?

Mma said nothing about the fully stocked fridge. I'd bought the fruits I knew she missed when she was in Ghana: peaches, plums and grapes. I'd picked up three different types of cheese, and I'd even trekked to get cannoli, because of our shared love for pastries. And yet, not a single word of gratitude.

As Mma looked around, it was as if I was seeing our apartment for the first time. It was all Mary Grace, with its bohemian chicness. Different textures and fabric prints jostling for space. Prints of Parisian cafés on the wall. An empty pot, which we'd never filled with a plant because Mary Grace had killed its original occupant and didn't want that heartbreak again, because plants were living things too.

I opened the door to my room.

'You didn't tell me you'd bought a bed!' she said.

'Surprise!'

'I was expecting to sleep on an airbed. I even told Aunty Maimouna to book me a masseuse after my weekend with you.'

'Oh Mma!'

'It's truly a crossover point, buying a bed. It means you're on your way to growing up. Remember when I slept on a mattress on the floor?' she said. A vague memory was coming back, after the divorce. She made sure I had a bed, though. I nodded. 'I didn't mind it. Except for when I realised that we had a mouse in the house.'

'And remember when the monitor lizard got in?'

'Yes, that daft house girl . . . What was her name?'

'Agnes?'

'Yes, she could never get it into her head to close the door behind her.'

'We had a mouse here, too.'

'And?' She looked around as if it would suddenly resurface.

'We got an exterminator. Don't worry, we're mouse-free now.'

I pushed Mma's suitcases against my rainbow-colour-arranged clothing rack.

'They could have built a wardrobe, they too.'

'Yes,' I said, looking at the rack. In Mma's world, there was always a 'they' or 'these people' who had not pulled their weight. 'Do you want to rest, or you want to go for a walk?'

'A walk?' she snorted. 'These are things you do with your paapa, Zain. And it's too hot. No one would believe me at home if I told them New York is hotter than Accra. Let me show you the dress Sister made for you. I think you'll like this one.'

My mother had been patronising the same seamstress for years, and while everything Sister made for her fitted her like she was her mannequin, the same couldn't be said for the things she made for me. Mma unzipped the largest suitcase and a deep indigo smock cloth brightened up the whole room. Even if Sister's dress didn't look good on me, I would cut it up and convert it into something else – the fabric was truly beautiful. Thank goodness I could sew!

'Did you buy the fabric?'

'It was from Mma Fati's inheritance. You know how your grandma could hoard material. Well, I gave most of it away, except for the truly special pieces.'

It's from Bobo-Dioulasso.

That last piece of information gave me goose pimples. I'd had my hunches about the voices, but this was the first piece of concrete evidence that I was hearing Grandma Fati. Could I talk to Mma about it?

'It's from Bobo-Dioulasso,' I said.

'Yes,' said Mma, pausing and training her small eyes on me with their dark blue eyeliner. 'How did you know?

'Guesswork. I know she went there a lot. And smocks are usually from Burkina Faso or Tamale.'

'I should have kept more of the others for you, but when we moved, there was just too much stuff.'

'Did Mma Fati ever visit New York?' I asked, even though I was sure the answer was no.

'She travelled a lot in West Africa. And she was even an alhajiya. She went to Mecca at least once.'

Three times.

'Three times,' I said before I could hold my tongue. 'Maybe. The way she was super religious.'

'I think you're right. You have an incredible memory, Zain.'

If she'd never come to New York, why was I hearing her voice here?

Mma pulled the dress out of the suitcase, her bracelets clinking as she lifted it up.

'I'm glad you kept this one,' I said. 'I've never seen anything like it.'

It was a simple shift dress.

'I told her not to add embroidery. *Veerry* simple, I told her. I think she got it, no?'

I peeled off my T-shirt.

'Look at these bones,' Mma said, rubbing her palm over my ribcage. It tickled, and I wriggled away from her. 'Still so ticklish. Anyway, I should let you be. You've always been small. And I used to look just like you. When you have children, you'll get more meat on you.'

I pulled the dress over my head and Mma helped me zip it up. It fitted perfectly.

'For the first time, Sister didn't fail me,' I said, hugging Mma. 'Thank you.'

'I've told you, with Sister, you have to keep going back and making sure she doesn't get too creative. You never have time to do that work, so *your* laziness is to blame for Sister's failed designs. That's exactly what I did with this dress.'

'She thinks she's a designer,' I said, remembering all the clothing disasters Sister had made for me in the name of fashion. 'And it's as if she gets inventive only for me.'

Mma laughed and shrugged. I needed to talk to her about the voices.

Say you're asking for a friend.

Was this voice actually helping me out?

'Mma,' I squeaked. 'I'm asking for a friend. Do you think people are capable of hearing their dead relatives' voices?'

'It's sort of what shamans and juju men back home claim to do,' she said. 'And as you know, in Islam we have our djinns, so anything is possible. Actually, your great-great-grandmother, Jamila, was quite gifted. Sometimes we felt as if she could read minds. But that's not what you're asking. Which friend is this? I hope it's not Densua. Working so hard can give a person a breakdown. Ah, this thing you brought up, you and your father must be in sync . . .'

She went back to the suitcase and wordlessly dug out packs of plantain chips and three tubs of shea butter. I greedily grabbed and ripped open a bag of chips and crunched into their sweet and salty goodness. Her answer didn't satisfy me. In one go, she had said yes, it's possible, but only if you're suffering a breakdown.

'Paapa sent you this,' my mother said, handing me a picture frame.

'Aww,' I said. It was a framed photocopy of the cover of *Captain Africa*, a 1970s comic by one of Ghana's famed comic book artists, Andy Akman. 'Return of the Dead: Is it possible for a dead man buried years ago to come back to life?' read its caption. Was the universe playing a trick on me? It was so apt. My dead people hadn't come back in their physical bodies, like Lazarus, but as voices in my head. Who were the others? I opened the book and there was a note from Paapa: 'Search your bookstores to see if you can find an actual copy. It'll inspire you. Love, P.'

It was comforting that at least one of my parents supported my current choice of work. Mma and Paapa saw each other at least once a week, which I knew his wife didn't appreciate too much. Even though I'd wanted them to stay together, I loved that my parents had worked their way into a good post-marriage relationship. And in some ways, it was my mother's fault that they didn't work out, so she had to be nice to him. She married a Christian man and then couldn't handle that he drank whisky every night, or that there was no way he was going to stop believing that Jesus died for his sins. But maybe there was more – in my short life, I already knew that parents only revealed the tiny tips of things. One time, when I was maybe ten or so, we were dancing to a song from the seventies and I caught her dabbing her eyes and wiping at her cheeks. She did it so fast that I would have missed it. I was sure in her chest was buried the story of a lost love. One day I would find the courage to ask her about her past.

'Save some of the chips for Aunty Maimouna, please. She wanted me to bring her palm oil and smoked fish, but I had to stop her in her tracks,' my mother said. 'What would she say if the palm oil spilt on my clothes? Eish, but it's hot here.'

I laughed as I went to switch on the fancy-looking fan, which fitted snugly in the space under the sliding windows. It even came with a remote control, and made me feel like I had the next best thing to an air conditioner.

'This evening, I'm taking you to a concert,' I announced.

She started to protest.

'It's Angélique Kidjo . . .'

'Ah, you should have told me yesterday! I would have packed some jeans. All I brought are my maame-maame conference clothes. Oh, Angélique Kidjo is fabulous.'

'But you *are* somebody's mother, so no one will judge you.'

'Then let me rest a bit.' She reached out and planted a big kiss on the V between my eyebrows. 'I've missed you papa, Zain.'

'Me too, Mma.'

My body felt warm and full. That kiss was enough. I took my laptop, closed the door of my bedroom and sat in the living room. I had to text Mary Grace immediately. I didn't want anything upsetting the happy peace between Mma and me.

FYI: I don't drink & pls no boy talk, I typed. Don't forget concert tnite.

Don't worry. I gotchu. Mine think I'm Mother Teresa ;), she replied.

My bedroom door swung open, startling me.

'Invite Uncle Ali, too,' my mother said, sticking her head through the doorway. 'You know he loves his music.'

I did as requested and went to use the bathroom. By the time I came out, the apartment's odour had changed to the aroma of our home in Accra: the redolence of caramelising onions, the heat of blended ginger and garlic and the meaty promise of a can of freshly opened corned beef. My mother was at our stove, hair in a bun, changed into a T-shirt and sweatpants.

'But Mma, is this how you rest?'

'I changed my mind. I want to make sure lunch is ready before my nap,' she said. 'You girls should always wipe down your stove after cooking. The leftover crust on this cooker is unhealthy. Project Fatten Zainab begins now.'

She ran the wheels of the can opener along the mouth of a can of tomato sauce and poured its contents into the newly bought IKEA pot. Then she opened the freezer, extracting a pack of mixed vegetables.

'You don't have Maggi?'

'I've heard it's not good, so I've stopped using it.'

'Hmm,' she said, reaching above the stove for spices. 'If you follow these people, you'll just stop eating. Next time I'm coming, I'll bring you local spices, then.'

I had picked up curry, black pepper and adobo, sure that with those three, I'd be covered. Apparently not.

'But local spices – dawadawa and things – would give your clothes a smell,' I said, laughing.

'Fine, if you don't want them, it's OK,' she said.

'But why is dawadawa so stinky, for a vegetarian condiment?'

'It's because it's fermented. But it's very nutritious.'

'Mary Grace and I are learning how to cook.'

'Alhamdulillah!' Mma said. 'Words I never thought I'd hear coming out of your mouth.'

She didn't like cooking as a girl, either.

That was good information for me, but I didn't repeat the words out loud.

My mother hunted through a bowl of rice that certainly bore no stones or weevils, since she'd already washed it three times. She rubbed the now pristine grains between her palms, and they squeaked *squish-squish* squeaky clean.

'So how are you liking your internship?' she asked as she wiped down the tomato sauce splatter on the stove. 'Have you upgraded from scanning?'

'My brain is seriously going to flatten out like the scanner. And no one talks in that office. It's as if there's an invisible strict librarian ready to pounce on the person who dares make any noise.'

Mma laughed. 'You and your sense of humour and imagination. But at least it's paying, and maybe they'll offer you a full-time job when you're done. But maybe you want to move out of New York to somewhere more wholesome, like Virginia?'

I hadn't thought that far, but it would be gratifying if Altogether Media gave me an offer. Although I couldn't imagine scanning comics for the rest of my life. At least I had grad school after the internship and didn't have to worry too much about having a job lined up. And Virginia? Why would I ever want to live there?

Mma napped for all of five minutes and came to join me on our couch, where she proceeded to regale me with gossip from her office and from home. Even though she was quiet, my mother was so good at mimicking people that without even trying, she made me laugh. When she imitated her boss, she transformed into a gregarious woman with her eyes constantly popping out and a deep belly laugh. In another life, she would have been an actress.

The lock of the apartment door clicked, and in walked Mary Grace.

'Mmm, I have perfect timing!' she said. 'It smells so delicious in here. Welcome to New York, Aunty Jamila. I hope you travelled well.'

So she has good training after all.

'Mary Grace,' said my mother. 'Thank you, my trip went well. It's finally nice to meet you. But you're also so thin. Is this what New York does to you people?'

Since our dining table was made for two, we dished out our plates of jollof rice and settled on the sofa. When Mary Grace and I both went for seconds, my mother smiled.

Later that day, my mother decided the best outfit for the evening was a striking indigo boubou.

'It's roomy,' she said. 'And our Senegalese ancestors dance so gracefully in these things.'

She was convinced her father's family had come from Senegal and said it explained the deep black undertones of our skin. I looked at this skin in the bathroom mirror as I undid my twists and dabbed on lip gloss. Maybe with my new super power I could tell her whether she was right or wrong.

'So, voices,' I whispered, 'do we have Senegalese roots?'

They ignored me, yet again. Why was this a one-way relationship?

Mary Grace offered to drive us. Once we arrived, finding parking took so long that we had to trek what felt like ten blocks. I was sure Mma wasn't too pleased with all that walking, but she said nothing. She finally expressed her disappointment about something when she learnt Angélique Kidjo wasn't singing her own songs, but Brenda Fassie's songs instead.

'These people, too,' she said. 'They could have warned us.'

Uncle Ali rang and I went to the entrance of Celebrate Brooklyn to meet him. He hugged me tightly. At our last rendezvous at the Manhattan Mall, he'd had a meeting to get to, so he'd handed me the money I'd asked for and rushed back up to the Bronx.

'I brought you this.' He gave me a wad of a newspaper. 'Our new paper for Ghanaians in the Bronx.'

'Congratulations, Uncle. You actually made it happen,' I said. I did not think it possible for Ghanaians to be so fast and efficient.

'By the grace of Allah.'

I led the way to my mother and Mary Grace. Mma dashed to hug Uncle Ali and they held their embrace for a long time. The last time they must have seen each other was when Uncle Ali visited Ghana about two years before. They talked and talked, and I wondered how they could get a conversation going with all the music and chatter around us.

'Jamilatou, let me treat you and the girls to dinner,' said Uncle Ali.

There he goes again.

He should save his money.

But he did give our girl cash. It's better for him to spend it on his family.

As we were leaving, I felt a tap on my shoulder, and when I turned around, I met Kweku's wide smile. Since the World Cup, neither of us had made a single move. My heart did a little skip, or maybe a big jump, so I surely liked him. And yet something in me was holding off, simply biding its time. Maybe the voices. What was *his* hold-up?

'Kweku!' I said, my voice twenty times higher than its usual register. He was with some of the group from Madiba. 'Mma, remember Kweku Ansah? From Achimota Primary?'

'Ah, your little husband?'

I could have died. Mary Grace smirked. Uncle Ali put on a grave face. He was trying to look so serious that it came off as comical.

'These two would be on the phone for hours talking about goodness knows what. Ei, you've become a man. How are your parents? Kim and Dominic?'

'Fine, Aunty.'

'This one didn't even mention that you were around. She keeps secrets.'

'She sure does,' said Mary Grace, who hadn't yet met Kweku.

'OK, we're heading off to a bar close to here if you want to come,' said Kweku, too loudly. I don't know if it was meant for just me, or Mma and Uncle Ali too, but he should have known better, unless he'd lost his Ghanaian ways.

Maybe he doesn't have good home training after all.

'We're going to dinner,' I cut in. 'Mma is jet-lagged.'

Bar and Zainab could not exist in the same sentence. At least not yet. I was still, in my mother's eyes, innocent. One day I'd work up the courage to tell her I'd lost my faith and all that it came with. But not today.

'Next time, then. It's good to see you, Aunty Jamila,' said Kweku, waving. 'Uncle . . .'

'Why don't you two go out?' said Mma, and I wanted to burrow a hole and hide in it. 'He's a foreign Ghanaian, but still Ghanaian. I know he's your taste.'

'He has nice teeth,' said Mary Grace.

'Dentition *is* important,' said my mother.

Why were Mary Grace and Mma getting along so well?

'Until she has procured her doctorate, Zainab is not going to be marrying anyone,' said Uncle Ali, laughing. Then he opened his mouth again. 'But if he wants to persist, his parents should get their pockets ready and come and see me, as the abusua panyin.'

'You people, he's like my brother!'

Was that why I was hesitating? Did he feel the same way? My own words sounded false to me.

'Mary Grace and I don't believe you,' said Mma.

Uncle Ali knew a restaurant he used to frequent in the days his taxi circuit sent him to Brooklyn. Now that he worked as a city clerk in the Bronx, he hadn't found the time to go back to this place of his youth. He had also driven over, so we had to walk to Mary Grace's car, drive to Uncle Ali's, where Mma joined him, and then tail him to Flatbush. That way, we could all drive straight home after the meal.

In the food joint – it could hardly be called a restaurant – there was barely any place to sit, but Uncle Ali secured a chair for my mother, while Mary Grace and I stood around a small table. I ordered the chicken roti, my mother and uncle the beef one, and Mary Grace went for the vegetarian version.

'Do you not eat meat?' my mother asked, with a tone that suggested something might be wrong with Mary Grace. She'd forgotten that Mary Grace had polished off the corned beef jollof at lunchtime.

'Oh, I love meat, Aunty,' she said. 'I just overdid it today. First at the restaurant, and then your delicious cooking.'

My mother side-eyed her, then took a bite of her roti and chewed slowly. I wolfed mine down, while everyone else was taking their time to savour theirs, which gave me free hands to peruse Uncle Ali's newspaper. The headline was 'Ghana Bronxhene Declares Parade a Success!'. Another was 'CPP Branch Holds General Meeting'. I groaned internally – royalty and politics, was that all that interested Ghanaians? Then I folded the paper and waited for the others to finish their food.

When I was ready to go back to Ghana, down down down the

line, would I fit in again? I hoped there would be space for art and film and culture. Uncle Ali should change the model and not just make it about events in the Ghanaian community. It could become a well-rounded paper; contain fully researched articles, features on people doing earth-shattering things. Maybe I should write for him for pay. But about what? I could barely get my illustrations going. Now was not the time to add in more stress.

'Where are you from?' Uncle Ali asked Mary Grace.

'The Philippines,' she said.

'And your parents are?' he continued. I wanted to pinch him to stop with the interrogation, but Mary Grace was good-natured and didn't seem bothered.

'My father is an engineer and my mother is the house manager.'

'I like that,' said my mother, dabbing at her cheeks with a red paper napkin. 'Keeping a home really should be a paid job.'

'Yes,' said Mary Grace emphatically.

On the ride back home, I looked out at the row of houses of Park Slope and dreamt. Would I stay here or go back to Ghana? This would be a nice place for grown-up me to live. Wherever I lived, grown-up me would not be a house manager. I would have a whole roster of published comics, and two children. A boy and a girl.

We don't make boys in our family.

And it's too soon to be thinking about children.

Wasn't Uncle Ali a boy? The voices obviously didn't know everything.

Let's hang next weekend, I texted Kweku. Maybe grown-up me would end up with grown-up him, when we both sorted out our feelings.

A warm bubble formed in my belly. At least I was setting things in motion, even though my own feelings were like clothes tumble-drying. What did I want? What direction would or should my life take?

You're being hard on yourself.

Back at the apartment, my mother sat on the bed I'd bought just for her use, and sighed.

'Zainab,' she said. The B became a heavy thud at the end of my name, and I knew I'd done something wrong. My belly churned. Life was annoying. No good moment ever seemed to last long. What had I unwittingly said or done that evening? Was it about Kweku? 'Uncle Ali told me you borrowed money from him.'

The traitor.

I warned you.

'You can't imagine how embarrassing it was for me,' continued my mother. 'Next time you need money, call me or your father. Uncle Ali has enough troubles as it is. It doesn't look like it, but life is much harder for people who live abroad than for those of us at home. He's constantly having to send money back home to be able to retire there one day. Please don't add to his wahala. I paid him back, right away, but I don't want this to happen again, understood?'

I nodded. I felt like I'd shrunk in size and was back to being five. How did Uncle Ali go from offering to pay for our dinner to letting on that I'd borrowed money from him? It didn't seem coherent. I shouldn't have let them ride together in Uncle Ali's car.

You can't control everything.

'What did you use it for?' Mma asked. 'He said you were very mysterious and didn't say what it was for.'

'For my rent deposit. I was going to pay him back with this month's pay cheque. And I didn't want him to know that I was borrowing money for housing and doing everything I could not to stay with him.'

'Next time, you call me. Did you ever get him that gift I asked you to?'

I shook my head.

'Ay, Allah,' said Mma. 'Zain, you can't just take take take from people. You have to learn to give back, too.'

I nodded.

My mother spent the next day cooking and sent me to buy a stack of Tupperware, which she filled with groundnut soup, chicken light soup, corned beef stew, and a tomato base I could use to make bean stew or spinach stew.

'That way, you people will stop losing weight. It's not nice to look so waif-like. And that way, you're not too homesick either. Don't you get homesick?'

I shook my head. 'You can find everything in New York,' I said.

'I remember when I went to Brighton in my twenties,' said Mma. 'Just nine months away from home and I swore I'd never live outside Ghana again.'

She had kept her word.

The day, a beautiful cloudless one, went by, and we stayed inside the whole time. The *flâneuse* in me itched. I would have liked to walk down Graham Avenue with her, but she would probably complain about the loud music, why people had to stick their heads out of windows, and that woman with the dog dressed as a baby – if we saw her – would surely give my mother a heart attack. So indoors it was.

My phone rang. And after I looked at the caller ID, I almost didn't pick it up.

'Zainab, I can't believe you didn't tell me your mum was coming to town,' said Densua. 'You, if you're angry with me, it's OK. But can I speak to her?'

I wanted to find out how she knew my mum was here when we hadn't spoken since I moved out, but Accra was a small place.

'It's Densua,' I said, thrusting the phone towards Mma.

'Oh, wonderful. Hi, darling,' Mma said. 'I would have loved to see you, but I hear your job keeps you busy papa. Ehnnn, I'm off to DC tomorrow.'

I wanted to hear what Densua was saying on the other end. All my mother was responding was 'Yes . . . Yes . . . Ehnnn . . . That so? . . . Hmmm.'

'OK, let me pass you back to her,' she concluded.

'Zainab,' said Densua. 'I miss you and I'm sorry if I upset you and pushed you out of the apartment. Let's meet up during the week, OK?'

'OK,' I said, and she hung up.

'Poor thing even sounds like she's lost her voice,' said Mma. 'She should really take it easy. I ran into her mother at Sister's, when I was picking up your dress. Does she have time for anything else?'

'Barely,' I said. 'I think life only gets better after they get into senior positions.'

'Well, take care of her, OK? You're sisters.'

She's not my sister, I almost said. The forgiving with Densua would be easier when we were face to face.

I sent Mma to Port Authority early the next morning, and before she left, I asked her about my namesake. For some reason, I'd dreamt about her the night before, a dream that was now fuzzy.

'Mma, why did you name me after a person who had bad luck in life?'

'You don't know that Zeina had bad luck,' said my mother.

'OK, but her death was mysterious?'

'She died young, in her sleep. I think it could have been a blood clot.'

'The story changes all the time. Uncle Ali told me sickle cell. But why name me after her?'

'The name chose you. Trust me, Paapa and I had picked out all sorts of names. You might have ended up with a nice Fante name like Araba, but Zainab was the name that you wanted.'

She hugged me, and when I saw her climb up the steps of the Greyhound bus, I exhaled. I could go back to being myself, or to the me I wanted to become.

Free as a bird.

Chapter Eighteen
Surprise

I knew we had a rooftop, but I'd never ventured up there. It was the Tuesday after my mother left, 4 July. I spent the day, a scorcher, watching *Sex and the City* with Mary Grace. We binged on so many episodes that my eyes hurt.

I needed air. Graham Avenue would be full of everyone and their mother rocking red, white and blue, and I didn't really want to deal with crowds in the heat. That was when the rooftop became interesting. So I went up the staircase and pushed at the door, which gave easily. I hoisted myself up, and what a world! I could see all the jagged outlines of downtown Manhattan: to the south, the curves of the Williamsburg, Manhattan and Brooklyn bridges; then, shifting my gaze along Manhattan Island's east coast, the Empire State Building and the Queensboro Bridge. As I walked towards the edge of the building, I caught sight of people sitting on lounge chairs behind me: a black man with two white men. In shorts and T-shirts, they looked like they were in their late twenties.

'Hey,' I said, waving at them. 'Happy Fourth of July.'

'Happy Fourth,' they shouted back.

The sun was setting and had painted an orange and purple skyscape to go with its descent. A slight breeze was chasing away the heat of the day.

'It's beautiful,' said a voice, suddenly next to me. I started, and remarked, relieved, that there was netting all around the rooftop. It would be hard to fall from here. Why was I so jittery about falling?

It's the fear that you want to do it.

Heights are *scary.*

'Here,' he said, offering me a bottle of beer. I didn't know whether to take it or decline his offer.

Live a little.

'Sure, thank you,' I said. 'I'm Zainab.'

'Alex.' He could have been southern European or South American. I couldn't tell. His eyes were a piercing green. He was about my height and his hair was cropped short. 'Join us, if you'd like.'

'Thank you,' I said, doing something I'd never done before. Sharing a drink with random people. The message *don't talk to strangers* was one I'd truly imbibed. Until now. Maybe watching *Sex and the City* the whole day was to blame. It was such a Samantha move.

Alex was visiting his friends Kyle and Simon, who lived in our building.

'You're Mary Grace's room-mate,' said Simon, whose hair had been carefully gelled back. 'Now that you know us, tell her to reduce our rent,' he continued. 'We've lived here forever.'

This was news to me. Why was Mary Grace connected to *their* rent?

'I'm sorry, why would Mary Grace reduce your rent?'

'Oh no, I shouldn't have said anything,' said Simon.

'The maker of gaffes,' said Kyle. He and Alex laughed at Simon's expense. 'This is Mary Grace's building,' he explained.

No wonder she said 'we' about everything apartment-related. It was a comforting and chilling thought. At least I should be able to keep my rent stable. But what if we fell out? And why was she charging me so much? If we were now friends, couldn't she reduce *my* rent?

'I was joking, about the rent thing,' Simon said. 'But she's great. I would love to own real estate at twenty-something.'

Alex took a swig out of his bottle and asked me where I was from. Kyle and Simon faded away. He told me he was half Puerto Rican, half Moroccan. Hot, I thought. He was a physical therapist in New Jersey and he and Kyle had attended college together. It had become a tradition for him to spend holidays with Kyle and his boyfriend. We talked about our families. His father brought the Puerto Rican heritage and his mother was from Tangiers. I felt kinship with him, even though his mother was Jewish. We were from the same continent! Puerto Rico, too, was an extension of Africa, I told him. We talked about food, and he said he loved to cook.

'I love food, but I'm not good at making it,' I said. 'I want to learn to cook all the dishes my mum made when I was growing up. But the easy way. And I want to cook things I like to eat, not because someone expects me to.'

I'd said too much. Or at least I thought I had, because he was quiet.

'I have a book I think you'd like,' he said, finally.

Why is he saying all the right things?

I don't trust him.

A splash of red, white and blue brightened the Manhattan skyline, and loud awe-filled applause echoed across the five boroughs. The four of us stood and watched the ancient magic of pyrotechnics. Blue, yellow, green astral confetti exploded and lit up the firmament. We stood speechless and marvelled at the impossible stories being woven by light, sound and smoke.

Alex stood next to me and our bodies touched. His skin grazed mine and I leant in just so. Was he feeling the same thing? When the stars twinkled brightly above us, and after the fireworks had fizzled out, Kyle and Simon said they were going downstairs to scrounge around for dinner. Alex gave me another beer.

'Your friends are nice,' I said.

'Yeah, they're like an old married couple. There's a big case in court now, and as soon as same-sex marriage is legal, they'll be first in line to get married.'

He told me about his childhood, here in the US, and how both sides of his family were big and into celebrations. I told him my father's family was enormous, but for some reason my mother,

her mother, her mother's mother, they'd all had just one child each.

Maybe you'll break the chain.

These things are just the way they are. She'll have one too.

She needs to study hard before having children.

I swept the thought of having children out of my mind and instead leant into the excitement zapping through my bone marrow. Alex had something about him that my body seemed to like. We were sitting across from each other, and somehow we had shifted closer and closer, and before I could even trace how it happened, we were kissing. He pressed his chest into mine and we inhaled each other's breath. It was as exhilarating as it was scary.

When we came up for air, he said, 'Can we go to yours?'

I hesitated, then said, 'OK.' Only because he was friends with the gay men in the building, one of whom was black. In my warped brain, it meant he would be harmless, non-prejudiced, a good person.

I opened the door quietly and was glad to find the living room empty. We snuck into my room and I locked the door and turned on the highest setting of the fan. He peeled off his clothes faster than I thought possible, and suddenly here I was staring at my first real-life male member. All my art classes had featured only women. Even as the flesh between my legs warmed, my heart raced in fear. Titillation and fear, sitting on a tree.

Was this going to be it? Should I say something? Was the thing that always intervened going to interfere?

'I need a drink!' I said. Not a promising start. The two beers had already faded away. I needed to relax. 'Want something?'

He shook his head.

I ran to the fridge and took one of Mary Grace's Coronas.

Make sure you replace it.

I twisted the top off and took a large swig, then went back to the room where my potential-lover-to-be now lay on my IKEA bed, expectant. I took another gulp of beer, then another. Now my head felt good and woolly. I was nicely lubricated. I slipped off my short shorts, suddenly realising that they were probably to blame for Alex's boldness. I'd seduced him with my mma's legs. Then I pulled off my sleeveless T and went to join him on the bed. I took one more sip of beer, and my bra came off, my underwear. Just when his thing was about to do its thing, I froze. Should I tell him?

'It's my first time,' I spat out.

He didn't shoot up and bolt out.

'You're sure you still want to do this?' he asked.

I shook my head. Then I nodded.

'Yes,' I said. 'Yes. Yes. Um, do you have a . . .?'

'A condom?' He shook his head.

I wasn't sure if that was a good sign or a bad one. If he had one, then he was on the constant search for adventure. If he didn't have one, then he didn't play it safe. In any case, I had many. As a student adviser in college, I had organised a safe sex event one evening and had been donated a whole pack of condoms by the health centre. I rummaged through my underwear drawer and brought out a handful of them.

'Whoa, just one,' said Alex, picking one and tearing off its plastic with his teeth.

We kissed and I lay mummy-like as he climbed on top of me. He took his time, and when he finally entered the threshold of me, the triangle between my legs, I felt myself fill up. A line was crossed. And just like that, my girlhood was over. I was now, I thought, a truly free woman. Just like Mary Grace.

Inside, I felt a celebration, as if all my cells were clapping, and I laughed, even though my thighs now seared from pain. I wanted this. But that, I suddenly realised, was only the beginning, because now he was grinding slowly into me, staring intensely into my eyes, and I wanted to simultaneously laugh and cry. I was being killed and reborn, with a stranger for a midwife. It also felt normal. I'd always expected my first time to be some huge event, and yet here we were. He pushed in harder and I yelped, and he pulled out.

'I'm sorry,' he said. 'It was too much, no?'

'No, don't be sorry,' I said. 'Let's go slowly.'

I woke up the next day with soreness between my legs and another person lying next to me. It took a minute to replay what had gone down. I needed this time to curl into my cocoon or to go for a long walk to revisit the images from the night before, even if they involved said person. I put on my pyjamas, then shifted around, but he didn't stir, so I picked up a book and dropped it loudly. That did it.

'Hey,' said Alex, his eyelids pushing apart. Even without the beer-Photoshopping, I still found him cute, and I was thankful. I'd at least lost my virginity to an attractive stranger. But whoa! I had lost my virginity. Celebrations. The horror. All the roller-coaster feelings. I was no longer a girl. There was no going back. Like, this was signed, sealed, delivered. Well, not sealed, because the seal was broken. I was a child no more.

The skin above his eyes creased. Was I making faces?

'Good morning. How are you feeling?' he said.

'Fine. But, um, I have to get to work,' I whispered. I'd learnt that people often mirrored your tone. If you shouted, they shouted back. I needed us to be as quiet as possible.

'Right,' he said, also whispering. 'I had a great time yesterday.'

'Thank you. Me too.'

He stood up and pulled on his boxers – grown-up boxers. I hadn't given up my precious pearl to a man who wore Garfield underwear. Then on went his T-shirt and Bermuda shorts. All these details I'd missed the night before.

And he's well hung.

Give him something to drink.

I *should* at least give him something to drink. Even when Mma was fighting with someone, she offered them water. Like the time her landlord had refused to cut the grass in the compound for weeks, and she'd left stern messages with his wife asking him to come and see her. When he finally showed up, she gave him a cold glass of water, before blasting him and telling him there could be snakes and scorpions breeding in there. So now, a man who had unlocked something for me? But what if Mary Grace were there? I didn't want my night sliced and diced by her. Not yet, at least. He would be offered water another day.

Shame.

I stepped out of the room, and when I was sure Mary Grace was still in her room, I gingerly herded Alex out of the apartment.

'Can I have your number?' he said, his smile bright. He didn't seem offended that I was shooing him off.

'Um, yes,' I said, rattling it off.

He nuzzled my cheek and hugged me.

'I'll call you,' he said, before heading down the stairs.

One door closed, another swung open.

'Was someone here?' Mary Grace asked. Our walls were thin, and apart from dropping the book, I'd made sure I was discreet. Had she heard anything?

'No,' I said. If Mary Grace could keep secrets about owning the apartment, I could have my own, too. For now . . .

Liar.

'I could have sworn I heard you talking to someone,' she said.

'Radio,' I said, trying to head into my room to prepare for the day. 'I had the radio on.'

That boy was nice. You have to see him again.

Now that what you've done can't be undone, what are you going to do?

The voices were even louder now, and insistent. Like they finally wanted me to engage with them.

Mary Grace headed for the fridge. 'That meat sauce your mother made is banging. I'll have some for breakfast.'

I barely heard her. I had had sex! A part of me wanted to freak out, but where would that get me?

On the subway, I played back images of the night before. I thought of Alex kissing me on the rooftop, and my nipples hardened. I looked down, grateful for the extra-thick padding on my bra. I remembered his nose pressing against my neck and I squeezed my legs closer together while I looked about.

The car was so packed I could only see the face of the Asian woman to my left and the Hasidic Jewish woman to my right, with her perfect wig. If only they could see into my head. As I looped the video of the night of my deflowerment in my mind, I decided Alex seemed cool. I felt both relief and sadness. I would never be that girl I had been again, but that girl was also too guarded, too scared. I was on the brink of a new life and it thrilled me to the inside of my bones.

Sam handed me a letter to type and proofread, and it was as if it had been written about me. In the letter, Embarrassed in Westchester asked of Dear Aunt Abbie what she should do about her daughter, who had started dating. She was happy her daughter was discovering life, but wanted to have a talk with her about safe sex and didn't know where to begin. Aunt Abbie's response was for Embarrassed in Westchester to take her daughter out for a fun mother–daughter outing and to simply begin by asking, 'How are you?' That would probably not be Mma's approach. Mma would be Tight-Lipped in Accra. Not just tight-lipped; she would willingly don a scold's bridle so she wouldn't have to have the talk with me.

And I would give the girl a good tongue-lashing.

No, it's good she learns now. She'll know how to take care of herself later.

I hushed up the voices, edited the piece and went into Sam's office.

'Here you go,' I said.

'Awesome, Zainab. You rock!' said Sam, hair down this time.

Now that I'd had sex, he seemed to have lost a bit of the shine that once glowed around him. Alex was shinier. It was good. I hadn't liked feeling so attracted to Sam. It was distracting. Now, I could be a professional and maybe be confident enough to ask for work that went beyond scanning and proofreading Aunt Abbie's letters.

The next day, Mary Grace handed me a package. I slid a knife under its seal, and when I popped open the box's flaps, there was a thick hardcover book covered in laterite brown.

'*The Africa Cookbook*,' read Mary Grace, who I hadn't realised had been lurking. She could be quite nosy, that one. Could it be? I opened the cover and a note stuck out. I read it and gasped.

'What? What?' said Mary Grace.

I grinned, feeling warm all over and so giddy that I couldn't help it, I couldn't keep it a secret any longer.

'So,' I said, lowering my voice, 'I finally had sex. Two days ago. He sent me this.'

'I KNEW IT!' screamed Mary Grace. 'I was sure I heard a man's voice. Wait, wait, wait. You did *it*. You're now a sexual being. How are you feeling?'

'I don't know. I'm still processing.'

'Was it good? C'mon, tell me more.'

'I don't know.'

'Did it hurt?'

'A little. Yes.'

'Hmm, your first time was very memorable . . .' she said, side-eyeing me.

'At least it's done,' I said.

I got up and pulled open the door of the freezer and took out a bowl of frozen chicken stew that Mma had made. I put on the kettle. I was so hungry I had to melt the stew as fast as possible.

You should have taken it out before you left for work this morning.

'So do you want to do him again or do you want to see other people?'

'I haven't thought that far. Eish, Mary Grace, must you put it so crudely?'

She had a glazed look in her eyes – as if she'd gone to another dimension.

'Mine was at sixteen. My first boyfriend in high school. Very vanilla, when I think about it. But we were truly in love. I couldn't stop touching him.'

'And you told me not to do it with someone I liked,' I said.

'Different situations.'

'Anyway, I can't imagine having had sex in boarding school.

Where would we have gone? And in any case, boys didn't like me.'

The kettle hissed.

'We did it in my house, when my parents were travelling.'

I wondered if it was him she wrote about in her diary.

If Mary Grace had enough money to own a building in New York, I was sure she lived in a mansion back in the Philippines. There would be more than enough rooms to hide and get up to naughtiness. In my mother's two-bedroom bungalow, even masturbating had to be a well-orchestrated activity. I thought of asking Mary Grace about being my landlord, but I let it go. It was a topic that could be charged, and I didn't want my high brought down. I had had sex.

'If you had a good time, you *should* see him again.'

'He took my number. I don't have his.'

'He must like you, if he sent you a gift. Or he's trying to tell you he wants you to cook for him. Like he's looking for a wife.'

'He knows I can't cook. And he doesn't seem like the traditional kind. But this is sweet, no?'

'Well, since he seems to enjoy food, we should go on a double date,' said Mary Grace, casually.

'Who's your new guy?' I asked.

'*She* is a chef, actually.'

'Oooh,' I said. I hadn't realised Mary Grace dated both men and women. But I wasn't surprised. During my four years of attending a women's college, I'd had crushes on girls, but hadn't dared do anything about what seemed to be a result of my environment.

Yes, but you'd be surprised.

'And how long have you been dating?' I asked. Just when I thought we were on the same playing field, she brought in a hat trick out of nowhere. She was good.

'Right after I broke up with Dre. I went to this place called Employees Only. It's mostly for industry people. And this girl . . . she sparkled. Dre was such a drag. Nothing was ever good enough for him. I already have you as the sensible person in my life. Now, I need effervescence.'

I liked Mary Grace's vocabulary. I especially warmed at being part of her life, even though I didn't like being equated to being a drag. Maybe I was overthinking what she was saying. I touched the book on my lap. What did it mean that Alex had sent me a gift? Was I going to be seeing a lot of him? The thought made me smile.

I couldn't text him my thanks. And just as I thought of him, my phone buzzed to life. Not Alex. Kweku. Asking what my plans were for the weekend.

Poor Kweku. I hadn't thought of him in a while.

I didn't respond. It wasn't good to mix flavours, was it?

Chapter Nineteen

Investment Banking

Densua invited me to a work social. I sighed in relief. Our cold war had gone on long enough. It also gave me something to text back to Kweku.

Going for drinks on Friday, but Saturday's free. What r you up to?

Party at MoMA on Sat. Come!

There would be no sleep for me that weekend. But something was itchy in my brain. Every time I checked my phone, there was not a single word from Alex. Why hadn't I taken down *his* number? Was he trying to make me like him? Because it was working. His lack of contact made me live and relive the magical evening we'd shared, the fact that he'd sent me a gift, and how beautiful every part of his body was. All these took on wilder proportions, and as usual, my brain filled in more colourful details as the days wore on.

That body of his WAS beautiful.

I'm telling you I don't trust him.

I can't believe our girl isn't a girl any more.

There were clearly three different voices. When I first arrived in New York, they sort of muddled together. Now, it was like three separate people lived in my head. Had I lost my mind the minute I arrived in the city? Maybe Densua – who knew me so well – could help. I honestly didn't feel any different from the girl who had left South Hadley, or even Accra years before. But what if Densua discovered I'd had sex and grew disgusted with me; what if I never heard from Alex again; what if things became weird with Kweku? What if Densua confirmed that I was truly lost in my head?

These thoughts plagued me as Sam handed me an Aunt Abbie letter. I went through it with my usual lightning speed, but after I returned it to him, I had a niggling feeling that I should take it back and double check. But it was done. I went back to scanning comics into the infernal database.

When, finally, the day was over, I rushed back to Brooklyn to prepare for my night with the most stuck-up people on the planet, according to Mary Grace. You couldn't pay her to date an investment banker.

The J train was held up on the rails for a long time, so when I arrived at the Gansevoort Hotel, Densua was already there, talking to two people, hair waving down her back, in a curve-hugging trouser suit. A lone swimmer did laps in the lit pool in the middle of the bar. This was one of the places that had been on my NYC radar for a long time. But now that I was here, it seemed cheap, with its purple fluorescence. In front of us, the Empire State Building was still sparkling red, white and blue for Independence Day. It suddenly hit me that I'd chosen quite the day to lose my virginity. It was a sparkly day.

'So sorry,' I said, and we stood there awkwardly. I hoped my apology would be an umbrella apology not just for my lateness, but also for the way I'd left her apartment and our friendship – in total limbo.

'My colleagues, Nayantara and Wambui,' she said, introducing them to me. With a lot of diplomacy, she freed herself from their conversation and soon had me to herself. 'Brooklyn girl!' she exclaimed, twiddling her ear lobe.

She didn't appear upset with me. If anything, she seemed a bit nervous. Ever since primary school, she'd had this nervous tic of singing her words and tugging on her ear when she was keeping secrets. I knew what I wasn't telling her, but what was *she* hiding from me?

I smiled, also needing to appear as normal as I could. Could people truly sniff out the experienced from the inexperienced? Had my hips bloomed? Wasn't that what that idiot Garfield-boxer-wearing Seth had told me? And how would Densua react to my news anyway? Did it even matter what she thought about my being deflowered? Even if she thought I was the scum of the earth for having premarital sex, would it hurt me? Surely not.

We sat at the bar and a heavy silence filled the space between us. This wasn't our first fight – we'd fought plenty of times – but it was the longest we'd gone without speaking.

'Has your mum left?' Densua asked, chipping at the ice between us.

'Yes,' I said.

'And you like your new place?'

'Yes.'

She's definitely the adult.

I almost said 'Leave me alone' to the voices but caught myself just in time.

'I said some things,' Densua said.

'Which I'd have liked for you to keep to yourself,' I said.

'Zainab, they were facts, as harsh as they were.'

'They hurt my feelings.'

'Everything hurts your feelings. If the sun doesn't come out, you feel hurt.'

'Did you call me out here to continue insulting me?'

'That wasn't an insult. OK, OK, I'm sorry. I just reacted the way I did because I thought you could have been more thoughtful.'

Her tone was nicer, but she was still not saying things I wanted to hear.

You also weren't the best behaved.

'Fine, I'm sorry if I was thoughtless.'

'That really doesn't sound like an apology,' Densua said, reaching for her hair and pulling it through her fist. 'OK, how about I go first? I'm sorry for the things I said. I was harsh.'

'And I apologise for disrupting your work.'

'Much better.'

'And I'm sorry I left the way I did,' I said, and stretched out my arms. She shuffled into them, and we hugged and it felt like home. 'Let's never fight this way again.'

'I think we said that our last fight. It's life; we'll fight again one day,' said Densua.

'Well, I don't plan to start the next one.'

'Yeah, since you always start them.'

'I don't. The last one was all you.'

'When you asked for my boom box right before I left for college? I'd already sold it. You overreacted.'

'I did not. You knew how much I loved it. You should have anticipated. Anyway, water under the bridge . . . I'm so happy we're back to us.'

'Me too. What can I get you?'

'A beer.'

She snapped her head back, as if I'd asked for a whisky.

'Ei, Brooklyn is changing you papa. A specific kind?'

'A Corona, please.'

She ordered it from the bartender, along with a glass of white wine for herself. The rooftop filled up with suited types, and it didn't seem to matter how different I felt from them. Everything was better now as Densua and I clung to each other, dancing to the DJ's selection of insipid pop songs. I don't know if it was Mary Grace's influence, or just having had a bit of time to design my own taste in music, but maybe Densua was right that I was changing. I would rather listen to classic highlife music from home, or an independent band, or music from the seventies. All the same, when the DJ played Rihanna's 'SOS', I realised there was still a place in my heart for great pop songs. Densua forgot she was surrounded by her colleagues, future competition and professional grown folk, and dragged me to the dance floor. We shook our bodies wildly. And when the DJ was back to his less interesting tracks, we went to sit at the bar again.

'How's work going?' I asked.

'Same old. I don't sleep. Are you enjoying your internship?'

'So-so. I like reading the agony aunt letters.'

'They're from real people?'

'Yes, I think so. By the time they get to my desk, they've already gone to the agony aunt. I just edit the final letter and response.'

'I should get her address. Dear Aunt Agony, how do I cleave myself into multiple people? Work Densua is exhausted. Life Densua would like to get some attention, too. Fun Densua, where's she hiding? Have you seen her? Tell her to come back from vacation. I miss her.'

'Aww,' I said, relieved I had my friend back. I loved Densua's funny bursts. 'I also have an agony aunt problem.'

'Oh yeah? Tell me. You know I love konkonsa.'

'You do love gossip!' I said, and laughed.

'I don't get enough juicy info at work. I'll do my best to give you good advice.'

'So I heard that my new room-mate apparently owns the building we live in.'

'Ei, saaa? The girl must be Mama Cash then.'

'Mmm-hmm. But it's strange, she still waits tables in a restaurant. Anyway, do you think it's right for her to be charging me rent, if we're friends? I mean, she should have told me, no? Or cut my rent in half or something.'

'You know I would never charge you rent, if it were me,' said Densua. 'I think it's a cultural thing. I see the differences when we go out with work friends. When it's other West Africans, we take care of each other. It's not the same with—'

She suddenly stiffened. Some tall man came and put his hand on the small of her back. Her body leant into his. His hair was shaved close to his scalp and he wore a crisp white shirt with jeans. He seemed very clean. He smelt like expensive cologne. He was maybe in his thirties.

'Um, Zainab, this is Edward,' she said.

'Finally! Hello, Zainab,' Edward said, stretching his hand towards mine. 'I've heard so much about you.'

I hadn't heard a thing about him. Granted, it was probably my fault for not reaching out to her for the last couple of weeks. But she had also been ignoring me. Fine, she was the one who asked me to come out, so she was the bigger person in this situation, but this was major. Why hadn't she just called me?

You didn't call her either to tell her about Alex.

She and Edward started whispering to each other, and I took my Corona and inched closer to the bar, suddenly feeling more kinship with the bartender than with Densua. I nursed my beer and watched as her colleagues debated with each other; as spectators kept their eyes glued to the large television screen flashing brawn and football; as lovers whispered into each other's ears, palms lingering on shoulders, backs or backsides; as some patrons simply drank, and as three brave souls splashed in the pool.

I was about to roll up my jeans and dip my feet in the water when Densua grabbed my arm and led me to the bathroom.

'So what do you think?' she asked.

I wanted to be rude.

Be nice.

You didn't even talk to him. No training.

'He seems cool,' I said, watching Densua apply a layer of deep brown lipstick.

'He's at Credit Suisse. On his way to becoming a VP.' She smacked her lips together.

'How wonderful.'

'Nigerian-Ghanaian. Went to HBS. Checks all the boxes. Maybe we'll do this marriage thing and I can become a kept wife.'

Good for you.

But you've worked so hard to be independent, I wanted to say. I swallowed all of my thoughts – mine and the intrusive voices'.

We went back out and I sat at the bar and drank another beer by myself. Then I went to Densua and Edward.

'Densua,' I said, 'I'm feeling a bit tired. You don't mind if I head out?'

'Call me when you get home.'

I hugged her and nodded at Edward, who mouthed his goodbye.

It wasn't that late when I left the hotel, so I strode out onto 14th Street, where the last stragglers were exiting closing shops. The two beers had given me a nice buzz, and sitting on a train seemed like an especially sad end to what had been a rather deflating evening. If there was such a thing as a runner's high, there had to be the equivalent for walkers like me. There was nothing like a walk to get the good feelings going. This weird evening warranted a long walk.

Ahead of me, travellers melded with revellers, and office workers made a dash for their weekends. I lingered at Union Square, where break dancers and bucket drummers had pulled a crowd to them. I made a right on Broadway, the thoroughfare once known as the King's Highway, which went all the way up to New England, my old life. I strode past Forbidden Planet, where I'd spent many late afternoons fantasising about the day I would have a comic book of my own. I liked walking down this way because this part of Manhattan was like one giant campus: Blockbuster, bookstores, NYU student discount signs all over the place, college-aged types huddling together. I went down to Houston Street, which I was rudely taught to pronounce correctly one day I had to meet Densua in SoHo.

'Not Huuuston,' an old lady had groused. 'House-ton.'

I admired the graffiti competing with peeling advertisements near the Bowery, and it brought to mind Keith Haring and his iconic shaking people, and how the New York City of his time must have been so different from mine. When I realised there were fewer people around, I found myself constantly peering over my shoulder, especially in the treed area as I approached the Lower East Side. Maybe it wasn't so different. But I calmed down. This New York *was* tame, Uncle Ali had told me one evening, as Miles Davis poured out of his computer speakers. I don't know why the whole moment had stayed in my brain, but I could remember it clearly. 'Before Rudy,' he said, referring to one mayor of New

York who had supposedly cleaned things up, 'you wouldn't catch me walking down the street.'

I could have taken a train home at any point, but I was driven by an impulse to just keep going. The heat of the last couple of days had lifted, and it was the perfect summer evening – warm with a hint of a breeze. I went down Ludlow Street, where party people had lined up in front of Pianos and the various places Mary Grace and I had found ourselves on one Thursday night too many. At Essex and Delancey came my last chance to get on a train, but it was too beautiful an evening. The moon was now clear in the sky, above the brown silhouettes of the housing projects, wisps of cloud around her waxing half. So I continued on Delancey, the lights of the Williamsburg Bridge calling.

Bicycles shot past me, cars and trucks rattled by, and I began my incline up the bridge. By summer's end, I wanted to have crossed as many of the bridges in New York City as I could. They were such feats of engineering genius and design. My father had wanted me to do structural engineering – his own dream job (he'd ended up teaching physics instead) – but I was too much of a storyteller to live his dreams. When he next visited, we would walk on this bridge and as many as he would allow me to show him. I missed him and wanted to talk to him about things I couldn't broach with my mother, like how he lost his faith and found it again. Maybe he'd have an explanation for the voices, and everything would make sense. He'd told me he was agnostic in his university days – and maybe even when he'd met my mother, which she'd probably chosen to interpret as someone she could convert to her religion. Mma saw the world along very specific lines, like everything had to be pristinely clean, and life's big changes happened because Allah willed them so, and these beliefs weren't to be crossed or coloured out of. Maybe because she and I had spent too much time together, we knew how to annoy each other – me with my mess, she with her rules. And because of that, Paapa had fewer faults in my eyes.

Why don't you call him, then?

He was too busy with his new family to listen to my troubles. Or what if he said something that destroyed the image I kept of him? I loved the way he was a dreamer and left room for doubt. He was the one who taught me to love walks and to notice the things everyone seemed to be ignoring. He introduced me to the word *flâneur.* He loved French literature and movies. 'Let's go, *ma petite flâneuse*,' he called out every time we left the house for a walk. I felt a twinge of sadness – was it only Paapa who truly understood me? And yet I couldn't even call him. Maybe there was hope with Alex. If we worked out, I hoped we would have a good relationship, that he wouldn't annoy me, judge me, belittle me or keep things from me.

As I approached the middle of the bridge, my thoughts shifted to people who had ended their lives by throwing their bodies into waters like this. They had to have been pushed by very powerful forces – physical or spiritual. That evening I was feeling sad because I couldn't understand my relationships. Why did it feel like Densua and Mary Grace kept things from me? But even that sadness couldn't push me that far. I looked behind me to make sure no person with designs on shoving me was close by, even if a large cage had been set up to prevent any falls.

The fear is ancestral.

I stopped to look at downtown Brooklyn and pictured people travelling by ferry boat to cross over from Manhattan before this bridge existed. I could see the men smoking their cigars, separated from the women. What would it look like in another hundred years?

When I landed on Brooklyn soil, such a rush of accomplishment spread over me that my sadness was replaced with pure joy. *This* was the walker's high. I was descending the ramp when a body bumped into me. I tripped, and before I realised what was going on, the person had snatched my bag. I wanted to shout, but my voice got stuck in my throat. So much for Rudy, the mayor who had cleaned things up!

'Hey! My bag!' Finally my voice was squeaking out.

Let it go.

But how could I? It contained my keys; my wallet, with my credit card and ten dollars in it; my phone; a small make-up kit; my notebook filled with sketches of Sam's hair; my passport! My beloved passport.

'Hey!' I said again, a small croak of a sound, but it was too late. The person had disappeared into the blurry grey of the New York night.

My passport. At this point, it wasn't even about New York City nightlife. My passport contained my I-94 card, my student visa. It was going to be a bureaucratic nightmare to replace. I'd have to call the international students' office at SVA to find out about my visa and all the rest. The only things I had left on me were my MetroCard and debit card, in a small cardholder I'd thankfully slid into my jeans pocket.

It was only three stops to home. I would feel safer on the train. I climbed up the metallic stairs to the platform, feeling leaden with each step I took. In the train, I tried to contain the feelings, but I started heaving. I couldn't control it – I burst into giant sobs. When I calmed down, I looked about and not a soul glanced up. What a place this was. No one asked me if I was OK. No one offered me a tissue. I had nothing to wipe off my snot, except for the back of my hand. I did just that.

At least he just took your bag and didn't hurt you.

I ran from the subway steps to the house. Mary Grace wasn't at home when I buzzed. I panicked. I couldn't stay out here. What if it happened again? This time, I had nothing to bargain with except for my body.

Breathe. You know people inside.

Kyle and Simon. It was strange sharing walls with complete strangers. In college, because I was a student adviser, I knew every single person in my dorm.

You're getting distracted. Try and get inside.

Only problem was, I didn't know which apartment they lived in. So I found myself trying every button in the building, until Simon answered.

'Hi, it's Zainab. Mary Grace's room-mate. Um, we met on the rooftop, with your friend Alex. I got mugged.'

There was a long, uncomfortable silence and I imagined them arguing with each other on whether to believe my story.

'Simon's coming to get you,' finally announced the scratchy buzzer.

As I told them what had happened, the tears started again. They offered me a cup of chamomile tea, and it was only after that that I could look around. Their apartment was a dream space! Simon and Kyle had good taste. It was colourful, but not saccharine, with clean lines and relics of their travels arranged like they were in an art gallery. I found myself looking over and over again at a red coral they'd displayed above a black and white photo of an okapi.

I asked for a Post-it note and stuck it to our door. MG! I'm down in 2A. Crazy story. Don't have keys. Z

By the time Mary Grace came to get me, it was well past midnight. Kyle and Simon had graciously fed me and given me a space on their couch, and we'd all diplomatically avoided the subject of Alex.

'I'm so sorry, Z. See, I told you investment bankers were bad luck,' said Mary Grace. 'Call the bank tomorrow to cancel your credit card. I have an old flip phone you can keep. You just need to get a SIM card for it.'

'Thanks, MG,' I said, hugging her. It made no sense to me how she could be so generous and yet could be charging me so much rent.

Just ask her.

Right now, that was the least of my worries.

Home, I texted Densua – hers the only number in New York I had memorised: Borrowed room-mate's phone.

It hit me that I didn't even want to call her to tell her about my traumatic evening. What was happening to our friendship?

Chapter Twenty

Work Drama

The Monday after my mugging, carrying a woven Mexican bag I'd borrowed from Mary Grace, I made my way up to the thirtieth floor, to the bright white offices of Kweku's ad agency, and asked for him. He showed up at the reception in a blue shirt, jeans and a baseball cap, a big smile brightening his face.

'I'm so sorry,' I said. 'I got mugged and couldn't call you.'

Truth is, if I'd really wanted to find him, I could have searched for him on TheFacebook, but I told myself a long story of how I didn't want to go on there and find out that he had a whole other life, like a girlfriend, so it was better to stay in denial and to avoid him altogether. And there was Alex, too.

'Whoa. Are you OK?' His brow had furrowed, and his dimples had deepened. 'There were so many people at the event, I was hoping you'd come but somehow hadn't gotten round to saying hi.'

'Ah, Kweku, how would I have come and not said hello?'

'Shyness?' He smiled and shrugged, his eyes closing. 'Do you have time to see my office?' I nodded, and he led the way around the reception. 'But you're sure you're fine? That was a proper New York baptism. I've lived here for so long and that hasn't happened to me. Touch wood.' He knocked on the wall in the corridor we wound through.

'It happened so fast. Apart from my notebook and passport, the rest can be replaced. The passport is the one bugging me papa. Please give me your number again.'

'Mum knows someone at the embassy,' Kweku volunteered, as he flipped open my phone, pressed in his number and passed it back. 'He gets us our visas to Ghana and arranges for everything Ghana-related. I'll ask her for his info, or rather, let me ask Mum and tell you how we can help. So, this is me.'

His desk, a white semicircle, was neat. Next to his desktop were folders and figurines. He hadn't outgrown his love of superheroes. The next desk was covered with signed baseball gloves, framed photos of players I didn't know, at least five caps, a shrine to the game.

'Your neighbour loves baseball,' I said.

'Nope, he loves the Yankees. I think he goes up to the Bronx, like, every weekend. It's all he talks about. I try to tell him about the World Cup, and somehow we end up on Derek Jeter.'

'If I had a work neighbour I could even just see, I would endure whatever they wanted to talk to me about,' I said.

'No, you don't want Dave next to you,' Kweku whispered. 'I think he manages to insert baseball in some shape or form into every single one of his campaigns.'

'That's funny. How was the MoMA? I really wanted to come.'

Not true.

Let's give them some space.

'Also,' I said, more to explain to the voice in my head, 'because I haven't been yet, and as an art student that's a travesty.'

'It was good. My band played.'

'You're in a band?'

'I dabble,' he said, and grinned. 'Guitar. But work got so busy I'm putting it on pause for a while. It was my goodbye show with them. For now, I think.'

That was attractive. What else did I not know about Kweku?

Shallow.

Musicians are sensitive souls.

It's true. Talk to him.

'Can I ask you something?' I said. 'So, I was feeling sad, decided to walk home, and then got mugged. My girlfriends are keeping a lot from me . . . hence my sadness. Is that normal?'

'The sadness?'

'That they don't tell me things.'

Kweku sat on his desk and clasped his fingers on his knee.

'We have different relationships, boys and girls. Boys, we don't talk. Like, if I had to talk to someone, it would probably be to you, not one of the guys. So I don't know what to say. Is it big things they're keeping from you? Tell me more.'

'One of them might be really loaded and she hasn't said a thing about that.'

He laughed. 'Sorry, but I'm not sure how she would tell you that. Like, "Hey, Zainab, I'm rich"?'

'OK, fine. But the other one, who's my bestie, didn't even tell me she was dating someone new.'

'Ouch,' said Kweku. 'Maybe it's too soon, and she's not sure about the person yet. I'm sure soon she'll be telling you all these details you don't even want to hear. Give her time.'

'Okaaay,' I sighed. 'Anyway, I have to go back down – not that anyone will notice I'm gone – but I wanted to let you know that I didn't flake on you.'

'I appreciate that,' he said, walking me to the elevator. He leant in for a tight hug. Warm, happy sparkles lit up my belly. But Alex. He kept showing up. I hadn't hugged him yet, had I? For now, Kweku was winning in the hug department.

Whatever good buzz had been building dissipated when I got to my desk.

See me – a note from Sam. Two words. No salutation. No explanation. Two words that meant something was off. Had I come in too late?

I took a deep breath and knocked on his open door. He motioned for me to come in.

'Good morning,' I said, sitting down.

'Morning. Zainab. What happened? We sent out an Aunt Abbie column this morning riddled with mistakes. A couple of papers spotted it and called me. Others published it as is and have been receiving calls and emails from their readers all morning. One would have been forgivable. But three or more? This is a shit show. Pardon my French.'

I hadn't realised I was the last stop on the train before the documents went out. It was a lot of responsibility to be placing on the tiny shoulders of an intern, wasn't it? He should have read it himself before sending it out. I felt the tears building: my chest heaving, liquid pooling in my eyes. I liked feedback, but I wanted it to be good and congratulatory. I didn't like making mistakes like this.

'I got mugged,' I croaked, and the dam broke, tears ran down my cheeks. He didn't need to know that the sequence of events had nothing to do with each other.

Shame.

There was certainly one voice that liked shaming me, or, more like, making me feel ashamed. There was a difference. It knew how to get to me. I now felt like scum for having lied.

'Why didn't you say something?' he said, rummaging through his drawer and pulling out a crumpled plastic pack of Kleenex. He extended it to me.

'I'm so sorry, Sam. This won't happen again.'

'It's my fault. Your previous work was so good, I thought I didn't need to keep double-checking.'

He stood up and came to pat my back. In a movie, this was the point where he would get up to close the door and draw the blinds, and as he was comforting me, we'd passionately make out. But instead his palm had somehow managed to encourage me out of the seat and I was being led back to my cubicle.

That's a good man.

Later that evening, I came to the sobering thought that I'd done this to myself. Having sex was bringing me bad luck. The mugging, the heightened voices, then this work fiasco. But sex was a thing that couldn't be undone. Perhaps there was an ancestral curse I'd broken? 'Ancestral' *was,* after all, one of the words that had seeped into my head. There were all sorts of pacts that our grandmothers made. Maybe one of my female forebears had promised that all her daughters had to remain virginal until married. Or betrothed – the word they would have used in those times. And no one had bothered to tell me. Probably because they assumed that as the good Muslim girl I had been, a choice I'd made when I was thirteen, mind you, I was in no danger of having sex. They hadn't counted on my flipping the whole damn script. I almost cackled as I thought of donning gloves to fight my ghostly grandmother and whoever the other voices were – grand-aunties? My grandmother and her sagging breasts with her hands in boxing gloves versus svelte me with perky breasts tucked into a Wonder Woman suit.

Well, if they had made a pact and wanted to use it to scare me, they were wrong. They just hadn't met me. I would fight them with everything I had.

Meet us then.

Get paper.

Well, that was a first. They had never responded to any of my direct questions. Maybe joking with them was what I needed to do more often.

Stop joking. Let us come through.

So I set my pen on paper. Ever since I arrived in New York, I hadn't drawn anything of value. I was highly sceptical about what was going to ensue.

Chapter Twenty-One

The Grandmothers

They asked me to get my colours. I reached instinctively for my set of brown pastels.

Take your time, they said.

Zeina was the one whose details emerged first. My namesake, but mostly called by her nickname. Her skin was red laterite, red like Rafiki's mud on Simba the lion cub, red like the Dogon Hills in Mali. She with her sharp, biting tongue said she was the only solace I needed. Acerbic Zeina, a great-grandmother I never met. I drew her with short hair, a finger pointing at me. She was slender and exuded a beauty that made you want to stop and study every etch of her face. Hers was the deepest of the voices, definitely the one who had been saying all those *shames*.

Jamila, my oldest ancestor, appeared next, the sweetest. The voice that encouraged me the most. Hers was skin like milk toast, like the sands of the Sahara, like ochre. She was a short woman, wearing grey cornrows. Her eyes were small and piercing, like my mother's. She asked me to sketch a pipe in her mouth. The most distant ancestor. She was delicate, like a fossil, to be treated with utmost respect. So Jamila of frail bones, woman after whom my mother was named, was to be handled with care. I drew her with the biggest grin on her face.

Then appeared Fati, the one whose skin I had inherited. Dark, so dark we shone. Me and Fati. The one who tempered the saccharine of Jamila and the acid of Zeina. Fati had thick hair braided down her back, a ring lying delicately in a braid on her forehead.

She was where my mother's confidence came from. I drew her with a hand clasped on her hip in an indigo boubou. The one who had kept me zipped up until Alex. It was her voice that had appeared the most familiar to me. I even sketched a scar on her cheek, because it was a detail I knew. She was the tallest of the three. Maybe the one I looked like the most.

So you've met us, they chanted.

Dear Zainab, don't forget to put my mayafi on, said Fati.

So I drew a sheer veil over her thick hair.

'You're not real,' I said loudly, my words echoing off the walls in my room. Mary Grace, who had been pottering around her own room, stopped. If she'd heard me, she let it go.

Holy cow, I thought, wiping my face over and over, as if doing so would bring me back to something real or believable. I closed my eyes and opened them and the drawings were still there. The voices were real. They belonged to people connected to me. And now I had visuals to go with them. This was too much.

I considered the drawings. It was funny that my ancestors had grown taller and darker over the generations. They had also become more conservative.

I didn't know whether to laugh or cry. So I had somehow willed my ancestors alive and they were speaking to me right here in New York City, through my drawings? It was nice to have some solid explanation as to what the voices were, if I could call any of this solid. But what the hell?

'Why are you now coming out?' I whispered. 'Can you even hear me? How do we communicate? Why didn't you tell me someone was going to rob me?'

We've always been there, said Jamila. *And we can call others, too, if you want. There are a whole lot of us.*

'No,' I said loudly. 'You're enough.'

We're those strange thoughts you have out of nowhere, said Zeina.

And we've always lived in the lessons your mother passed on to you, which she got from me, which I got from Zeina, and on, said Fati.

You never walk alone.

'Why now?' I whispered.

You came to the right city, said Jamila. *Estuary towns have power.*

You have the power with your pencil, said Zeina.

And sad as I am to see you leave your girlhood behind, you are ready, said Mma Fati.

My head hurt. I knew a little bit about shamans and mallams and marabouts. Had I become a shaman, able to commune with these old ladies? This was nuts. I called Uncle Ali. Where to begin?

'Zainabou,' he said. 'How are you?'

'Fine, Uncle.' I was about to launch.

Ask him how the family is doing first, ah! said Zeina.

'How are Aunty Emefa and my cousins?'

'Well. Dzifa has started her summer camp a few blocks from the house. She seems to like it. Ibrahim categorically refused to go to camp. I tried to convince him, but your generation knows what it wants.'

How to broach the topic?

'They're much younger than me,' I said. 'I think my generation still listens to parents. Uncle, um, was there anyone in our family with gifts?'

'What kind of gifts?'

'Like, um, spiritual gifts. Hearing spirits, seeing the future, talking to ancestors?' I didn't even know if I was making any sense.

'One of your mother's uncles was a mallam or a marabout, you know, a religious leader in the community. And people consulted him when they wanted to commune with those who had left us, or when they wanted to take a more sure-footed path towards the future. But he was a very distant relation. Why?'

'It's a project I'm thinking about,' I said.

'Mallam Sile. His name was Mallam Sile. I don't know if he's still alive. Scared all of us children in the village. Your grandmother Fati would threaten to send us to him if we didn't behave.'

And it worked, said Fati. *But he's not blood.*

So he wasn't a direct relative.

'Thanks, Uncle,' I said.

'My pleasure.'

That hadn't brought me any resolution.

Thank you for these shrines, said Jamila.

So my drawings were shrines to my ancestors? What a concept! Shrines were usually places where blessings would be received. But from what I remembered of the films I watched growing up, not all juju in shrines was productive. Or like that man in Kweku's office, shrines were a sign of obsession, or madness even . . . Did this power mean good things for my future, or was it a bad omen?

I looked at the drawings again before I went to bed, a bit in awe, a lot frightened.

Chapter Twenty-Two

Two Dates

My phone rang, startling me awake. A few days had gone by since that weekend from hell, in which I got mugged and it was confirmed that I could hear my dead grandmothers' voices. Having drawn them, I now knew when each grandmother was speaking, but I still couldn't believe any of what I was experiencing was real.

The call was from Densua.

'What's your address?' she said. 'I'm coming to Brooklyn. I've finally found a church that has evening meetings. So I'll come say hello, then head to church.'

She knew how to heed my advice after all. I gave her the address.

'Hmm, are Bushwick and downtown Brooklyn close?' she asked.

'You can take the bus from ours downtown.'

'It's OK, I'll take a cab. I don't want to get lost in this place.'

When Densua buzzed at the door, Mary Grace was back home, much to my annoyance. I'd hoped to get Densua's undivided opinion on how to deal with the topic of rent and to tell her about the voices I was hearing.

'That's my friend Densua coming up,' I said. 'Is that OK?'

'Of course,' said Mary Grace, in a tattered T-shirt and blue biker shorts. 'You live here too. You really shouldn't have to ask, Z, you can be so proper sometimes.'

I let Densua up, unsure if we would all get along. One person was churchgoing; the other was anything goes.

And you? asked Zeina, with her deep voice. I could even picture her as she spoke.

'I'm figuring me out,' I whispered to myself as I unlocked the door.

Densua breezed in, wearing a grey trouser suit, her hair in a long weave with bangs. I don't know where she found the time to do her hair.

'I like the new do,' I said.

'Oh my word, Brooklyn is far papa,' said Densua, then she held her mouth when she realised I wasn't alone. 'Oh, hello.'

'Hi there,' said Mary Grace. 'You must be the wealthy banker. I'm Mary Grace.'

'I don't know about wealthy. Densua.'

Mary Grace had no right to call anyone wealthy.

Maybe you don't know the full story, said Jamila.

'Welcome to our casa,' said Mary Grace. She was darker-skinned than Densua. 'I hope you're both hungry. I brought home a shit-load of dumplings. I must be PMS-ing.'

I watched Densua hesitate. She studied the sofa, covered with a furry blanket – the same one on which I'd sat on the drive to New York – then she placed her bag gingerly down and sat right by it.

'Sure,' she finally said, and I sighed, relieved. 'Let me wash my hands first.'

'The bathroom is that way,' I said. 'Or use the kitchen sink.'

'I need to pee, too,' she said, heading for our bathroom.

I got three plates and set them on the table by the sofa, then went for my Nepali scarf and placed it on the floor. Densua came back out.

'One thing you have out here is space,' she said, settling down by her bag. 'So what do you do, Mary Grace?'

'I'm an artist, like your friend here, but the less tortured kind. But ladies, how clichéd are we? We're following the same old roads taken by all those other newcomers to New York. It's either make money in a bank or struggle as an artist. We could have been more original, no? Chopsticks?'

Densua and I shook our heads. Mary Grace handed us forks.

'Question for both of you,' I said, finding my voice at last. 'If you hadn't come to New York, where would you have gone instead?' I bit into a dumpling. The juice from the minced meat flowed down my chin and I rushed to get a napkin.

'For sure, Paris,' said Mary Grace. She twiddled her chop-sticks, grabbed a dumpling and dipped it in a coffee-brown pool of soy sauce. 'After New York, it will be Paris for me.'

'I can see that. Densua?'

'I don't know. Even New York I came to only because of my job. I don't know. Probably back home in Ghana. And you?'

'It's up to you,' I sang and raised my arms in a wide V, 'New York, New Yorrrk!'

'Boo!' hollered Mary Grace. 'You're cheating.'

'I love it here, you guys,' I said. 'This is the only place where I've felt like I can be myself.'

'It's good for you artists,' said Densua. 'Me? I could be any-where in the world, and it wouldn't matter. Work doesn't let me do anything. No church, no museums . . .'

'I'm too cheap to do museums,' I said.

'Use your student ID,' said Mary Grace. 'It's not free, but it reduces the price, sometimes by half.'

'I'm glad I didn't lose my student ID in the mugging. But I'm too cheap,' I repeated. 'If it's not free, it's a no for me.'

They laughed.

'I believe the MoMA and Brooklyn Museum have free nights every month,' said Densua.

'Mmm, ladies, I have the perfect white wine to go with these dumplings,' said Mary Grace. 'Sorry for cutting you off. Just remembered.'

You've been drinking too much alcohol since you arrived here, said Mma Fati.

'No thank you,' said Densua. 'Another time. I can't show up my first time at church reeking of alcohol.'

'All my priests reeked of alcohol,' said Mary Grace, and

shuddered as she reached for glasses in the cabinet above the kitchen sink and grabbed the bottle of wine. One day, I would be able to buy a whole bottle of wine for myself, just like Mary Grace. 'There was one who taught us history in Catholic school. He would take sips of whisky all day and in class he would talk and talk and talk about politics. By the time class was over, we'd learnt nothing. I'm surprised it didn't kill my interest in politics. Maybe he knew what he was doing after all.'

'That's like . . .' I started.

'. . . Mrs Enum!' Densua concluded. We looked at each other and smiled. 'Jinx!' we would have said if Mary Grace weren't here. 'The woman was an alcoholic. It was rare to see women drink in Ghana then. But she managed to make geography interesting.'

'So what kind of church is it you're attending?' asked Mary Grace.

'It's non-denominational,' said Densua. 'It seems laid-back, like the kind of church you can wear jeans to.'

'But I don't understand why you've decided to come all the way to Brooklyn for church,' I said. 'I'm assuming you have to go back to work tonight. Wouldn't one closer to the office be better?'

'Not today, thankfully,' said Densua. 'I've listened to their albums and sermons for years, not realising they congregate right here in New York – well, here in Brooklyn. Seeing as I'm not able to go to church often, I want to make it count when I do go, you know?'

'You're dedicated,' said Mary Grace, popping the wine cork. 'The last time I went to mass was my cousin's wedding. Like four years ago.'

'Thank you,' I said, as she set a stemless glass on the floor next to me. 'How's Edward? Edward is Densua's new boo.'

'Fine,' said Densua. 'We both work so much. We need to find a way to spend more time together.'

'And you've been together how long?' asked Mary Grace. I

wanted to know, too, but hadn't felt brave enough to ask; also maybe because I didn't really want to hear the truth.

'Mmm, officially it's been three weeks or so.'

She's hiding something, said Zeina.

When you're in love, you get precise about dates and things like that, said Mma Fati.

Mma Fati's words were so surprising, I almost repeated them.

Densua pressed her silver wristwatch between her fingers and looked at it.

'If I don't go now, I'll be late. I can catch a taxi from downstairs?'

'Yeah, a gypsy cab,' said Mary Grace.

'Now I know where you live, let's please do this again soon!' said Densua, grabbing her bag. 'Mary Grace, thank you for the dumplings, and a pleasure to finally meet you.'

'Likewise, and any time.'

'I'll walk you down,' I said.

We crossed the Food Bazaar's parking lot, under the flags flapping in the wind, and stopped under the JMZ tracks.

'She seems down-to-earth,' said Densua. 'Not stuck up for someone who is Mama Cash.'

'You can't even tell she comes from money, right?'

'Ah, miracles! A yellow cab,' said Densua, flagging it down. 'We'll catch up soon?'

'Thank you for the surprise visit,' I said, hugging her.

At least one thing in my life was righting itself.

Densua is always the one fixing things, said Zeina again.

Let her be, said Jamila.

The doorbell rang, and I answered it before I realised that I hadn't been expecting anybody. I hadn't even asked 'Who is it?' This was how people got murdered in New York – by just opening the door to strangers.

Outside the apartment stood Kyle in a crumpled T-shirt and shorts. He wasn't as meticulous as his partner, but I was relieved it was a dishevelled Kyle and not a serial killer. But what if Kyle was a serial killer?

Stop, said Zeina.

'Someone wants to speak to you,' he said, spreading a wide grin from brown cheek to cheek.

I took the phone from him, and when the other person spoke, my heart began a sprint. For the first time, I was hearing Alex's voice on the phone. His voice was even-pitched, not deep, not high. After a whole week and more of not hearing from him, here he was, or here his voice was, whispering into my ear. It had to be working, the grandmothers' powers. First Densua visited me, now Alex had called me?

'I heard you got mugged,' he was saying, but I was so excited I could barely focus on his words. All I heard was '. . . graffiti. I'll pick you up on Saturday, then.'

Wo yo, said Jamila. Her favourite expression of surprise, shock and everything in between.

'I do have a phone now, you know,' I said, giving him my new number.

I wanted to hug Kyle as I handed him back his phone. Finally, after what had felt like abandonment, a date. My first real date!

My phone buzzed. Was he already texting me sweet nothings? It was Kweku, with more good news. His mother's man in the embassy was happy to help me get a new passport. I had to send a copy of my birth certificate and passport photos as soon as I could.

The grandmothers were surely blessing me.

When the date finally arrived, we were in the middle of the most stifling heat I'd ever experienced. I felt like the air had transformed into a being and draped its heavy woolly mass around me. I got into Alex's air-conditioned car, surrounded by an entourage of Kyle, Simon and Mary Grace. All they were missing was confetti to throw on us.

'They are ridiculous,' I said, settling in the passenger seat, relieved it was cool. His car smelt woody and fresh, like aftershave.

'Our very own cheerleaders. What about this heat, eh?'

I had enough cheerleaders already with my grandmothers bouncing around in my head. I didn't need any more.

'It's hot,' I said.

We drove down Flushing Avenue to the deserted patch that separated our neighbourhood from Bedford–Stuyvesant, home to the Notorious BIG and to Mr Thomas. When Alex turned right onto Mr Thomas's street, I hoped I wouldn't see the poor old man. I still felt a hint of guilt for flaking on him. At Atlantic Street, we left Fort Greene's browns and greens behind and came upon an expanse of shopping and a construction site that was said to be a Jay-Z project in the works.

In the sky, a lone hawk or falcon swooped and coasted, free and brave. Alex and I chatted about music, mostly hip hop. He slotted in one of his old-school CDs, and of course, I didn't know a single song.

'Because you're a baby,' he said.

'How old are *you*?' There were all these biographical details we hadn't bothered about when we hooked up. I thought he was in his late twenties.

'Thirty-two,' he said. I liked his profile. His skin was sun-baked, and his hair cropped neatly. And he had lips!

'Wow,' escaped from my own. It really wasn't a big deal, was it? My father was fifteen years older than my mother. But at thirty-two, think of all the experience Alex had had.

And all the women, said Fati.

'You?'

'Twenty-one.'

Not true, said Zeina.

I was just shy of it.

'The world is opening up for you.'

At twenty-one, I'd already had three children, Jamila boasted. *Even though only Zeina survived.*

For now, this was the 411 on the old ladies: Jamila was on my side. Zeina was not – or she was the one who got to me the most. Fati was still sore I had lost my virginity.

We got to Prospect Heights, and I thought of lowering my body, in case Seth the Garfield-boxer-wearer was out there on those streets, but why should I shrink myself? No. Seth should see me with my new guy.

Everything isn't about you, admonished Zeina. *How could you think that at this very minute Seth would be waiting around just for you? And this isn't even his street.*

Then another thought floated up – this one mine. I was like a dog, leaving pee traces all over New York City. And I had just arrived. I snorted.

Alex turned to regard me.

'What's so funny?'

I didn't know what to say. Help, grannies?

Tell him it's funny how it took you getting mugged to have him invite you out, said Zeina.

I found myself repeating every single one of her words, cringing all the while, but I really didn't have the gift of repartee.

'Shame on me, eh? I really wanted to call you,' said Alex, 'but I don't know what folks did over Fourth of July. I had so many clients come in for therapy. And then I tried calling you at the weekend, but you didn't answer.'

Liar, said Zeina.

Well, we'll never know, will we? said Fati.

Yes, he's here now, so let it go, agreed Jamila.

Maybe it was rather Zeina who was on my side. They were so bothersome, these grandmothers.

'When Kyle told me you'd been mugged, I understood why my call didn't go through.'

At the Brooklyn Museum, which was nice and cool, Alex paid for my ticket even though I made a show of reaching into my bag. I considered telling him we'd get a reduced rate with my student ID, but I thought of the photo on it, taken when I was sixteen, and then I pre-empted what Fati would say – *let the man pay* – and eventually said and did nothing.

We started out in the huge atrium, where I saw a banner

advertising 'Magic in Ancient Egypt' and my heart raced in excitement. The exhibition wouldn't start till October, though.

'We should come back for this,' I said. October was a whole three months into the future. Why was I so loose-lipped? I tried to save the situation with a lame explanation. 'I'm obsessed with ancient Egypt. See, it is to Africans what Greece is to Europeans.'

'Word?' he said. 'The museum has a good permanent collection on Egypt. I used to come here all the time.' He and Kyle had gone to college in Brooklyn and lived walking distance from here. 'It allowed me to reset myself.'

It would be nice to get married here was the thought that slipped innocently into my mind, and this time, I clamped my tongue to prevent myself from spitting it out, like I had earlier. That was my own thought, not an ancestral one. Years of watching *Sex and the City* told me that nothing scared a single male New Yorker more than the thought of marriage, so I was glad I'd acted faster than my tongue. The three-month slip was bad enough. For now, feasible goals were: not driving Alex away; surviving the summer and not dying of starvation; arriving at grad school in one piece with a bomb thesis project idea; and, icing on the cake, lots and lots of sex with this beautiful human being.

I don't like hearing this, said Fati.

Leave her alone, said Jamila. *Good goals.*

We took an elevator up and ended up on the fifth floor. His hand reached for mine and we walked to the gallery entrance marked 'Graffiti', above a canvas tagged in splashes of red, green and black. This was pure happiness: holding hands with the man you liked, going to look at art, and not just any art, but street art. It *felt* right. Alex was lean and handsome in his white shirt and jeans. In my jeans and black wrap blouse, I was sure we looked good together.

Inside, we stopped before a canvas of a sunset. Below the bold orange and yellow sky, a black silhouette of cityscape, and beneath that, a tag that read 'Sunday' in greens, blues and whites. It was signed 'Bear'.

'*Sunday Afternoon*, 1984, Kwame Monroe,' I read. 'Ooh, maybe he's from Ghana. Kwame means "born on a Saturday".'

'Dope,' said Alex. 'What's my Ghanaian name?'

'I'd say . . . you're a Kofi,' I said. Fridays were sexy.

'Alex Kofi Sanchez,' he said. 'I like it.'

'If I were truly bold,' I said, 'I would leave a mark somewhere in New York. Not as audacious as this one – I mean, this is breathtaking – and not as wild as those guys who tag the subway, but something to show that I too was here.'

'I dare you to do it,' said Alex. 'You *are* bold.'

He looked deep into my eyes, and then planted a big long kiss on my lips. Every cell in my body vibrated in bliss. I liked it so much that I made him keep doing it. I was too giddy to focus on any of the art, and there were beautiful canvases of graffiti. I was just head over heels, or like they said back home in Ghana, my heart had slid into my stomach.

After the exhibition, we went to The Islands. A hole in the wall just around the corner from the Brooklyn Museum, it welcomed us with the aroma of stewing meats and grilling chicken. They had loud fans blasting everywhere, which for some reason made me feel transported to an island, or to a boat next to an island. The skin under my arms itched wildly when Alex asked me if I would like a drink.

That used to happen to me, too, said Zeina. *The itching.*

I didn't have my passport, and any ID I had would reveal that I was very much underage. I didn't want anything to ruin what was going splendidly so far.

'Pineapple,' I said.

Our food came, and when he picked up his piece of browned oxtail with his fingers and ate it, I fell deeper in love. This was a man I could take home to meet Mma and Paapa. He sucked the bone clean and set it on the plate as if it were the most normal thing. In college, I had watched as girls left fat pieces of chicken still dangling on perfectly chewable bones. This man was a keeper.

So I dawdled in the passenger seat when we got back to my apartment, then said, 'Do you want to come up for tea?'

His brows shot up, but he didn't ridicule me. *Tea?* his eyebrows said. *What are we, British?* 'I'd love to . . . but I can't today. Rain check?'

I pouted, and he kissed me. Even though the heavy weight of disappointment was slogging down my belly, I still convinced myself that this must be what love felt like: sometimes a little frustrating.

Back in my room, roasting all by myself and upset that Alex wasn't in my bed sweating in my sheets, I caught sight of the newspaper Uncle Ali had given me at the Angélique Kidjo concert. I thumbed through it and got a brainwave. A really good brainwave. The kind of thought that made me want to jump up and down and exclaim, 'I'm a genius!'

Uncle Ali *had* asked me about content once. I could now give it to him. I would write my own advice column – yes, I was twenty and didn't know anything about anything, but I could hear three wise women who had lived rich lives. I wasn't sure if Uncle Ali and his cohorts could pay me, but nothing ventured, nothing gained, right?

She's planning on using us, said Zeina.

Isn't that what we exist for? said Jamila. *Ancestors have lived. We know. Use away, Zainab.*

What happens if she's asked a very modern question? asked Fati.

'We'll cross that bridge when we get there,' I said loudly, reaching for the phone. 'And that's why I have you, Mma Fati! You're the most modern.'

Don't forget to ask your mother first. Remember when you borrowed money last time, warned Zeina.

Mma gave me her blessing, telling me it was a brilliant idea to write for my uncle, and told me to stay cool, because she'd heard New York was in the middle of a heatwave. She probably got updates in her email on all things New York to keep track of me. I called Uncle Ali and he asked me to send him a writing sample. I got straight to work. Editing letters at Altogether Media had shown me what was going on in the minds of middle-class American women. I could guess the preoccupations of Ghanaian mothers in the Bronx. Talking to Uncle Ali alone gave me fodder.

I would write about a woman whose teenage son was talking back to her and threatening to call social services every time she tried to discipline him.

Fati's advice was to give him a few slaps – if he ended up calling social whatwhat, who would suffer in the end? She was clearly not going to be the one I listened to.

Zeina suggested sending him back home to Ghana.

Jamila said teenage years were like toddler years, but more complicated. She said the mother had to understand that her son needed to find his own way, but whenever he talked rudely to her, she should move away and not give in to his bad behaviour. I lapped up her every word.

I needed a name. Jamila. Zeina. Fati. JaZeFa. Aunty Jazefa. I especially liked that it sounded like Jezebel.

Is that a good thing? asked Fati. *She was not a good woman, was she?*

A woman after my heart, then, chuckled Jamila.

Chapter Twenty-Three

Basil and Lemon

It was the last week in July, temperatures had cooled a bit and school was drawing nearer. My goal before the end of the summer was to will the universe to get Alex to make me his girlfriend. It didn't seem complicated.

Is Alex what you truly want? asked Zeina.

Kweku texted to go for drinks after work, and I had to consult my relationship guru – the one carrying breath in her lungs, Mary Grace. What did three dead old ladies know about the modern rules of engagement? Where did Kweku fit in?

As long as u & Alex aren't official, ur not doing anything wrong. Its just drinks.

Maybe you don't want Kweku, which is why you're confused, said Zeina. *Don't waste the man's time.*

I went with Mary Grace's advice.

Kweku and I met in the lobby of our shared work building, and just as we were exiting, my phone buzzed.

I wanna be like u when I grow up. Playa playa ;)

We walked down Park Avenue, against the rush of people heading for Grand Central Station. We passed by Turkish rug stores and one eatery after another.

'Good news,' he said. 'Mum's guy in the Ghanaian embassy is a miracle-worker; the passport is ready. We're always doing things last minute, and he always gets us out of binds like a magician.'

'Hallelujah!' I said. It would be good to have my passport back. I'd missed going out dancing. 'Thank you.'

'But . . . it takes a couple of days to ship. Mum has paid for it to be expedited.'

'Aww, Aunty Kim. That's so kind of her. I have to call to thank her!'

'Which way do you want to go?' he asked.

'You know this city better than I do.'

He closed one eye and squinted out of the other, puckering his lips. If I were bold, I would lean over and kiss them, because they were beautiful. But of course, I wasn't bold. And Alex's face flashed before Kweku's. Was that an ancestral trick, too?

'OK, we'll try this,' he said, herding me west, and then down Madison Avenue. 'I hope you'll like it.'

Soon, we were strolling through Madison Square Park, where a curved white sculpture hugged the hem of a lawn.

'Good choice,' I said. 'This is probably one of my favourite places in the city.' I pointed to a sculpture that was a wall bending in waves. 'The artist, Sol LeWitt, calls them structures, and isn't that exactly what this is?'

'But of course . . . you like art,' Kweku said, as if he were answering a question he'd previously asked himself. 'We should check out the Whitney one of these days, if you haven't been?'

'If it's not free, I haven't been. If my student ID works for the Whitney, I'm game. I did go to the Brooklyn Museum over the weekend.'

Why aren't you saying who you went with? joked Zeina.

'Yup, when I was studying in France, that's where I saw how powerful a student ID could be. Here, they don't have the same kind of power. Museums were free there. Here, I think it's just reduced, right?'

'You were in France? Where haven't you been, Kweku? You're like my room-mate. She knows all these places.'

'Just a semester abroad. You know how the parents are. Pops really wanted me to end up at the UN, or some international organisation, so languages were big for him. And now *I*,' he stretched it out, 'have something to make him proud. All the late nights . . . also why you haven't been hearing much from me, is because I just officially won my first account. It's not my own account – maybe in a few years – but I'm the project manager on it.'

'Congratulations,' I said, extending my hand for a high-five. I honestly hadn't noticed that he hadn't been in touch much. It was Alex's absences that had screamed at me. Poor Kweku.

For this you could give him a hug, said Jamila fairy-grandmother. So I wrapped the stretched-out hand around his back and pulled him in. He held on for a few seconds and then squeezed me before letting go.

'So what's the account?'

'A cigarette company.'

'Oh.'

'Don't sound so disappointed. It's like the dipo ceremony in advertising.'

I laughed and snorted. 'The dipo ceremony? I just pictured you with your breasts on display and chalk circles on your body as you danced your rite of passage. That's funny, Kweku. I love how you haven't forgotten about such things from home. Dipo!'

'I have shapely breasts too,' he said, palming his chest. 'No, truth is, after this, I can be more selective about who I work for.'

'Well, if you need any illustrators . . .' I raised my hand.

'Noted! By the way, how are your complicated friendships going?'

We were walking into a small restaurant off 18th Street. Outside, it was painted blue and green, its bottom half decorated with pots of herbs poking out of a planter. Inside, patrons sat at the bar or in clusters on cane chairs and tables.

He remembered, said Jamila, and I thought she would say 'aww', but it wasn't part of her vocabulary.

Fati and Zeina didn't seem to care for either Kweku or Alex, for different reasons. Jamila I got the sense was Team Any Man for Zainab.

'This place is adorable,' I said.

'I thought you'd like it. There was another place I was considering, but it's farther west. I did good?'

I nodded. 'And yes, my friendships. One of them is sort of OK. The other, I still haven't been able to bring up. The money one.'

The barista said we'd have to wait about twenty minutes for a table, so we were seated at the bar. I couldn't even order the tequila cocktail – this place's speciality, according to Kweku, so I went for a Sweet Sunrise – orange, fizz and grenadine. He went round in circles studying the menu, and eventually settled on the tequila cocktail.

'Time has a wonderful way of working,' he said. 'Let it do its thing. Like, I can't tell you how glad I was to run into you.' He smiled brightly. 'After I left Ghana, I lost touch with old friends like you. You see anybody from APS?'

'Remember Densua? We ended up attending boarding school and then college together. She's also in the city, working with J. P. Morgan.'

I almost added that she was one of my complicated friends, but I could already imagine Mma Fati saying 'He doesn't need to know.'

Yes, he doesn't, she confirmed.

'Densua . . .' His irises danced to the tops of his eyes and backwards, as if searching through a cabinet in his brain. 'Ah, your twin! It was annoying how she was always first in class.'

'That's why she was Mr Amankwah's favourite.'

'I don't think she liked me, or maybe it was because I took you away from her. She wrote down my name a lot for punishment.'

'Maybe because you *were* always talking.'

'It wasn't me! Eli was the chatterbox.'

'Eli Okudjeto! Wow, I haven't heard that name in a minute! Do you know where he is?'

'We're friends on TheFacebook. I think he's out in California, working with Apple. He got out of college and landed this sweet gig. Or maybe he didn't even graduate. I can't remember.'

'Wow. He's made it. People like Densua and Eli are already so successful. And you, of course, are doing so well, too. I feel like a loser.'

'Patience, my blue friend,' said Kweku. 'Our time will come.'

'Huh?' I said.

'*Star Wars*, Zainab.'

'You're still the same. I have to confess that I never read any of those sci-fi books you'd get me on my birthday.'

Kweku sighed and clutched his chest. Our waitress appeared and seated us next to the vitrine with the herb pots.

'Don't you just love this city?' I said. 'I feel like I was born to live here.'

'Thank you,' Kweku said to the waitress. 'Zainab Sekyi takes New York City. Tell me all about it. You feel this way because?'

'I'm finally at home in my skin here. Even when bad things happen, I'm able to shake them off. I'm not constantly pretending to be someone else to please anybody else. I'm finally learning to fly.'

'Yup, New York has a way of doing that to you.'

'Do you think you'll stay here forever?'

'I don't know . . . It makes sense now: I don't have a family, I work in advertising. Maybe ask me again in five years. Maybe I'll want a big house and space, who knows? I technically don't even live here yet.'

The waitress came back to take our order.

'You'd like some wine? We could buy a bottle?'

A whole bottle of wine? Who's paying for that? said Zeina.

The grandmothers were meddlesome.

And wine plus the other alcohol, it's too much, said Fati. *He's drinking too much. All these people in this town drink too much.*

'My passport is my ID,' I said in hushed tones.

'She had her passport stolen,' Kweku said to the waitress. 'But she's the same age as me; we were classmates.'

'I'm so sorry, with no ID, I can't serve her alcohol,' said the waitress. I didn't like that she was talking over me, and then I noticed that she had a tattoo of an ankh on her wrist.

'Nice tattoo,' I said, before I could even control my tongue.

'Thanks,' she said. She paused, then went back to the kitchen.

I looked at Kweku, and on his lips he wore an amused pout. Whatever he wanted to say stayed shut behind it.

'Let it out!' I said. It was as if we were finally shedding our stiff outer layers and could get back to our original ease with each other.

'Nothing,' he said, and cocked his head to the side. 'I see you were trying to soften her up. Nice try.'

'I swear I wasn't. I just liked her tattoo.'

She came back and hadn't changed her mind on my getting alcohol, so I decided to go straight for the entrée.

'The bass in basil reduction, please.'

Kweku took an eternity to decide, and finally ordered the entrecôte.

This one can't make up his mind, said Zeina.

'Have you been here in New York since college?'

'Yup. Luckily Pops got transferred here not long after that, too.'

'I'm already worried about grad school, but at least I'm more mature than I was at sixteen. I hope I'll be able to focus in school!'

'When you're at Columbia, you don't forget you're in school. Yup, we were in New York, but when you had papers and finals and you were a resident adviser, nothing would lure you to the downtown scene. Unless you'd decided you could afford to fail college, or you were a trust-fund baby.'

'I was an adviser, too. Why are we such overachievers?'

'It's the Ghanaian-ness in us. But Nigerians, too,' said Kweku. 'They were even more gung-ho than I was about getting A's.'

'It has to be a West African thing,' I conceded, as our steaming plates were set before us. 'Truth is, I was the ugly duckling. Far from overachieving.' I took a bite of the fish. The sauce was tangy and perfumed with the freshest basil. I led another forkful to my mouth.

'I find that hard to believe,' said Kweku.

'This is so good,' I said. With each bite, the acid and the

freshness of the sauce awoke every sensory nerve in my mouth, and I knew I'd have to try and make it at home, even if I was still just an embryo of a cook. 'How's your meat?' I didn't want to butcher the word entrecôte.

'Delicious. So how do you like working at Altogether Media? It seems . . . quiet. Or serious. Or both.'

He didn't ask you about your food, said Zeina.

Well, he's still asking about her, snapped Jamila. *Let them be.*

'It is. I don't know if I'm growing there. And I messed up royally on a very simple assignment.'

'Zainab, it happens to all of us. You see, you're *still* Miss Perfection.'

'Hey! I let go of that a long time ago. Secondary school was tough, mehn. You were probably breezing through wherever you were.'

'I was in Malaysia. I got my ass whopped in everything but English. But tell me more about work.'

I talked about Sam and how unbosslike he was with his ponytails, about scanning, about editing Aunt Abbie's columns, then excitedly told him I wanted to do the same thing – for Ghanaians in the Bronx, of course, leaving out the part about using ancestral knowledge to help me.

'That's a great idea,' he said.

'What do you believe?' I blurted out, testing the waters. Kweku was someone I could talk to. The blocks that were there with Alex – because I couldn't just ask Alex such a question – weren't there with Kweku. I still needed to talk to *somebody* about the grannies. Densua was always busy. Mary Grace I wasn't sure about. Uncle Ali would call my mother and the two of them would have me locked up.

'Like what my faith is? I go to church with the folks on Sunday, so I suppose I'm Presbyterian on paper, but I'm still searching for meaning, you know?'

'I hear you. But what if our African ways of being are what we *truly* were meant to believe? Like our traditional religions?'

'Honestly, we don't package our religions well. One of my aunts comes to visit and she brings these DVDs from back home and from Nigeria. The way it's all raffia and cowries and just hocus-pocus, well, it doesn't attract me. It's honestly scary. And kind of violent. Or straight-up ridiculous.'

That's not at all what our religions are about, said Zeina.

'You know who packages well?' Kweku went on. I shook my head. 'Brazil. You see the way they present their religion and you think, wow, this looks really cool.'

'My goodness, Kweku, you're in the right job. Packaged religion . . .'

He shrugged. 'How did we even end up on this topic?' he asked.

'Let's just say I'm also questioning a lot. I feel like there are things that our senses are too underdeveloped to catch, and that the people in our traditional religions might know a lot more than we do . . . and that some people might have gifts.'

'Yup. You might be on to something. Like with all our science we can't explain dreams. My mother and I share the same dreams sometimes.'

I nodded; there was hope yet.

This is the man, Jamila said, clapping. *There is plenty of hope.*

'What was the dream you shared?'

'It's happened a few times. Like we'd both dream of eating cake, or the same person appears in our dreams.'

'And you don't want to know what it could mean for both of you?'

'My mum says we're in sync, but I don't know. It could be pure coincidence.'

I wasn't convinced yet that Kweku was ready to hear my story. Instead, we talked about travel and reminisced about our prepubescent selves and ordered dessert. I didn't see where the time went. He walked me to the subway to catch the F train on 6th Avenue and enveloped me in the tightest hug. Nothing more. And I found myself relieved. What would I have done if he'd leant in for a kiss? Kweku was confusing. Alex was confusing. My situation was confusing.

Confusion notwithstanding, I got back home feeling full and warm, and opened the door to find Mary Grace and a pretty woman with ringlets of hair haloing her face in the kitchen.

'Zainab! Come and meet Aliya. Aliya, Zainab is the best roomie in the world. And I truly mean that. She's a calming force in my life. And she knows how to put things together. She's the man in this home.'

'So that's why you keep me around,' I said, laughing. 'Hi, Aliya.'

'Nice to meet you, Zainab. We were just about to eat. Join us?'

'I would love to,' I said, 'especially since I've been told you are an amazing cook, but I'm stuffed. Had the most delicious fish I've ever eaten.'

'She was on a date,' said Mary Grace, holding a wooden spoon and inspecting whatever was stewing on the stove. She had this annoying and rather unhealthy habit of sticking the cooking spoon into her mouth.

'Not a date. I just met up with my childhood friend.'

'And?' they both said.

'It was nice. Good conversation.'

'And?'

'We hugged at the end.'

'Hmm,' said Mary Grace, spoon now in her mouth. Maybe Aliya would knock the bad habit out of her. 'Maybe he has a girlfriend?'

'Or maybe he's not interested,' I ventured.

Or maybe you're *not interested.*

'Or maybe because you know each other, he just wants to do you right.' This was from Aliya. 'You're not just some girl he picked off the streets, so he's taking his time. Some people need to plot and put every piece in place before making a move. But what do *you* want?'

'I don't know,' I said, throwing myself on the couch. I only then noticed they had spread a scarf on the ground and had laid a whole table, with forks and knives in the right places, and candles and wine glasses. A fancy indoor picnic, obviously inspired by the time Densua had visited. I felt a twinge of pride that I'd been able to have some effect on Mary Grace. 'You guys, this is too cute.'

'Since we both work in restaurants, we thought we should switch it up and stay in for a change,' said Aliya.

'Well, it works. Let me leave you to it.'

That evening, as I drowned out Mary Grace's loud cries of pleasure with music from my headphones, I realised I hadn't heard from Alex all week.

Chapter Twenty-Four

Where Did That Come From?

It seemed like I was the one doing all the texting. And Alex's responses were of the *busy day, call you later* flavour, which left me with quite a bitter aftertaste in my mouth. So when we finally managed to have a date, I wanted sweetness. I wore the dress Mma had asked Sister to make for me.

I love that fabric, said Fati. *I bought it thinking it was the most stunning pattern I'd ever seen. I'm glad you get to wear it. You look beautiful.*

That was such a nice thing for her to say to me. Her words sprayed bubbles of happiness around me and I felt sparkly. I wanted to surprise Alex with just how good I looked, so I declined his invitation to pick me up. Also, meeting in a place seemed more romantic than driving in together like we were some old married couple.

All my trains arrived on time. I took the M to the F, got down and walked up Essex Street and across the Lower East Side. It was a beautiful warm evening, but I arrived at the Angelika Cinema annoyingly early, even after taking my time to stroll there. Alex showed up in a linen shirt, jeans and a two-day beard. His hair was longer than usual and was curly, and my legs warmed when I thought of what we'd do after dinner. He'd given me a small taste of what it was to be with someone, and now I was ready for more.

'Hey,' he said, and kissed my cheek. 'You look nice.'

She wore it just for you, said Zeina.

We went inside the theatre, and at first, we sat stiffly. Then I was bold, reaching for his hand and resting it on my thigh. I squeezed in closer to snuggle up to him. This having a boyfriend business could grow on me. I could barely focus on the movie. I just wanted us to go back to my apartment. I was even ready to go to New Jersey, and to do the walk of shame to work the next day. I was ready for sex to be good.

'Are you hungry?' he asked as we walked out of the cinema.

'Yes please!'

'There's a wine place not too far away. They have tapas.'

We walked down Allen Street, and wound down a few streets until we stopped in front of a vinoteca. It was sparkly new, with straight lines and perfectly rectangular bar stools.

The place you went to with your friend was nicer, said Fati, and the other two old ladies agreed. What did three dried-up hags from another century know about wine bars? I shooed them from my mind, of course, with plans to apologise later. I needed them for my advice column – if Uncle Ali ever got back to me with feedback.

We sat at the bar, because it was the only place available to sit. Alex ordered olives, razor-sharp slices of cheese and ham. I was sure to be hungry after this, but I could always fix myself an after-shag sandwich.

The old ladies threatened to comment.

'Shh,' I whispered under my breath.

Alex was mostly quiet, so I forced myself to fill the silence.

'Scarlett Johansson is a woman I'd do,' I said. 'She's gorgeous and was so believable.'

'Many women say that.'

Our conversation reached a lull after we'd cleared our plates.

'I have something to tell you,' he said, downing the dregs in his wine glass. His teeth were magnified by the curved bowl. His tone was too serious. He inhaled dramatically, then just launched. 'I think you're beautiful and I like you a lot, but I got out of a relationship not too long ago and I still need time. I really like you, but I don't want to disappoint you, and we're going fast,' he exhaled, but wasn't done, 'and I think we need to take a break.'

His words crashed into each other. Large verbal blocks making fender-benders. An unwelcome run-on sentence I didn't want to hear. The wine shop's straight lines grew wobbly. I wasn't going to cry. I didn't want to cry.

The old ladies screamed, *Don't cry!*

And yet an errant tear escaped from my eye and trickled down my cheek. I should have seen this coming. Why did the grandmas not help me dodge *this* bullet?

When he offered to drop me off or even ride the subway home with me, I said I was good. I let him kiss me on the lips as we parted ways at Essex and Delancey; I bawled all the way home, falling on my bed in a cloud of pity. The grandmothers huddled close and wrapped their stringy arms around me.

'Why did you let this happen?' I whispered. 'I built you a shrine, it wasn't enough? You didn't like it. Was I supposed to add more to it?'

No one can control life, said Zeina. *No matter how many altars you build.*

It was a chilling and strangely comforting thought. What purpose, then, did the grandmothers serve?

We're simply your guides, said Fati. *But you choose what you want to do with what life throws at you.*

Then it hit me: my life would make a great graphic novel. *Zainab and Her Grandmother's Ghosts Take New York. Zainab Finds Her Ancestors in New York. Zainab and Her Ancestors Take New York.* This was not just about my grad school project. This could be big. Like a whole book big. I opened my sketchbook and set my charcoal to paper, sketching a few ideas. I stepped back. On the sheet, I'd drawn a girl with long legs, surrounded by her ancestors, the New York cityscape in the background. Bam! I had my grad school project right there. Then I remembered I'd just been dumped, and the sadness seeped back into my chest like deep blue ink pouring down the side of a table.

Mary Grace walked in with a bowl of something vinegary, which I was sure I wouldn't want to eat.

'My mother's recipe. It was *her* mother's recipe. One of those things that goes way back. I think I actually nailed it.'

It smelt vile. I shook my head.

'Tell me when you want it. Yoooo . . . what are these?' she said, pointing to the sketches on my bed. 'Girl, you can draw!'

'Heartbreak seems to have inspired me,' I said, holding up the sketchbook. How else could I explain it? I couldn't tell her the truth, could I? I told her it was imagined. 'What do you think? A graphic novel about these three and me as we navigate New York City's mind-and-heart labyrinth.'

'Mind-and-heart fuckery, you mean. I didn't know you had such talent, Zainab. These drawings are so good!' she squealed. 'Amazing concept. Pitch it to that guy you're in love with at your office. Wow, I can tell that's you, and you haven't even drawn your face. You're good.'

'I don't know if I'm his favourite after that editing fiasco.'

'It's more reason to do it. If you get famous, he can say he discovered you. No, *when*, because it's going to happen. When you get famous, that Alex fool will regret dumping you.'

'But why does my heart hurt the way it does?' I said, shutting the sketchbook on my bed and leaning my back against the headboard.

'Time heals. But if you can't wait for time to do its thing, there's another solution,' she said, scratching her scalp with both hands. Her roots were curly and black.

'I'll do anything. Tell me.'

'Hop in bed with someone else.'

'Surely *that* doesn't work. It will only leave me confused. And with whom?'

'The Garfield guy?'

'Eww. No thank you. Kweku?'

'Something tells me you don't want him to be your rebound guy. I mean, you guys are being all high school about each other. But no, don't make him your rebound.'

She's right, said Fati.

'Why not?'

'Because it'll set the tone for the rest of your relationship. And you're already in love with him and you just don't want to wake up to it. Why, only you know.'

'No, I loved Alex,' I said. 'He sent me a book. He took me to see a freaking exhibition on graffiti. Like he knows me. If that wasn't love, what is? Waaah!'

'You didn't just say waaah . . . That book was probably something he picked off the sidewalk. Listen, this weekend, you, me and Aliya, we're going out. You can tell Densua, too. I'm taking you to a dyke bar.'

'Yes, because men suck. But no, I need to stay in my hole. I really liked him, MG. My whole body was happy when he was near me. And he was so hot.'

'Is that *why* you liked him? It's called L-U-S-T. What does that spell?'

'He made me feel good.'

'It's coz he popped your cherry. It hurts, but this too shall pass.'

My initial thinking was perhaps wrong. No, I didn't want to be free. I longed to be entangled limb over limb with Alex's body. My thighs on top of his, his legs entwined with mine. Stuck to each other forever. Alex and Zainab forever. It even went together. A to Z. A plus Z. We were beginning and end.

The next day, I kept ruminating on the topic of liberty as I stood in the M train, as I inhaled someone's unfragrant armpit on the F and as I walked across 34th Street and down to work.

I had tried to dress nicely, because Fati insisted on it. She said I needed my outside to give my insides a boost and some courage, that I didn't want to be that person who showed up to work with bloodshot eyes, eyeliner running, hair in all shapes of dishevelled, clothes mismatched. No, the grandmothers said to hold my head up high. I had to be a professional.

Maybe show Sam your work now, said Zeina.

'I can't,' I whispered. I would choke and start crying, and anyway, it wasn't ready. So I sat at my desk and looked at my drawings, and any time I heard someone approach, I popped open the scanner and pretended to work.

Chapter Twenty-Five

Lesbian Bar

As I was entering the laundry room downstairs (thank you, Mary Grace, for installing laundry in the building; I still hadn't found the courage to bring up the rent topic), I bumped into Simon carrying a wicker basket full of perfectly folded clothing. I never folded my clothes in the laundry room. I dumped the whole dried load into my plastic basket and then left the clothes to sit crinkled, and only when I felt motivated did I fold those clothes. Once I got started, I *was* very good at folding. Although lately, not much had been motivating me. And now here was Simon. A person two degrees removed from that person who had unmotivated me.

'Hi, Zainab,' he said, pausing and setting down his basket.

'Oh hey, Simon,' I said, trying to sound chipper and unbothered.

'How are you?' he sang.

'I'm good. You?'

'Good. I heard about you and Alex. Sorry it didn't work out. For what it's worth, Kyle says he really liked you.'

Oh really? I wanted to say, but I bit my tongue. I shrugged. 'It happens.'

'It's just . . . That Vanessa witch came back, and she *really* has a hold on him. I don't get it. If it makes you feel better, Kyle and I really preferred you. You're much cooler, and that skin pops.'

My grandmothers clapped.

That's MY skin, Fati hollered.

It didn't change a thing. I was still heartbroken and I'd been lied to, because clearly he was back with his ex. Ours wasn't a *break*, it was a break-up. I felt sick.

Simon went up and I followed him with my basket.

'Weren't you going to do your laundry, honey?'

'I forgot something upstairs,' I lied.

'I learnt a trick,' Simon said, 'to dance when everything around you seems to be falling apart. It'll fall apart anyway, but when you look back on it, the fact that you danced your butt off will always put a smile on your face.'

'Thank you, Simon,' I said.

Back upstairs, I dropped my basket of unwashed clothes on the bedroom floor, flung myself on the bed, and wept like I'd lost a family member.

When Mary Grace showed up later that day, I told her I wanted to go to the lesbian bar after all. I couldn't invite Densua, because she needed advance notice for these kinds of things.

Fati said, *That's not our culture.*

Jamila said, *You should have seen these two girls I knew. No man would marry them because they kept running back to each other, until one was forced to break their connection. Love is love.*

The acerbic Zeina said nothing.

When we climbed out of the subway station, Mary Grace and I were welcomed with the sounds of a plastic ball pounding the pavement, basketball shoes skidding back and forth, and guttural *ughs*.

'Give me the testosterone in this place on a spoon,' said Mary Grace, 'and I'll lap it all up!'

'Says the person who's taking me to a lesbian bar.'

'Hey, you're the one who needs the healing. I could stand here and watch these men all day. Besides, I'm an equal opportunity kind of person. Look at that muscle. Mmm!'

'You're insane,' I said, and laughed.

We cut across West 4th Street with its rainbow display of Pride flags, and shop after shop selling the most complicated paraphernalia I'd ever seen in my life. How did people even use some of those contraptions? One looked like a rabbit with very long erect ears. I could only guess.

As we crossed 7th Avenue, I saw a woman sitting in front of a curtained door. 'PSYCHIC', her sign read. Did my grandmothers accord me psychic abilities?

'Have you been to a psychic before?' I asked Mary Grace.

'I go all the time.'

'And you call yourself a Catholic. Tsk tsk tsk.'

'Hey, just like you, I am a colonised person. We have our old ways . . . It sounds to me like this is another virgin situation for you. I don't know if this one is any good, but it doesn't hurt. Wanna try?'

'What about Aliya?'

'She arrives late to everything. Don't worry, we have time.'

She grabbed my hand and we approached the woman, who wore a black lace blouse, thick black eyeliner, and hair as red as Mary Grace's but curlier. She was like a Caucasian version of Mary Grace, really. She smiled and asked us who wanted to go first.

'Just her,' Mary Grace said, twiddling her fingers at me to go in. 'And only do tarot cards.'

My skin pocked. My eyelids twitched. My underarms itched like crazy. I thought of all those times at school when one thing or another was labelled as demonic – books we were reading, films, even the clothing we wore. It was hard enough deciding to be Muslim in a country that had more Christians in it, but at least I was tolerated. Anything out of the Christian–Muslim binary was suspect. Never mind that most people combined said Christianity and Islam with their traditional beliefs the same way some people mixed fish and beef and chicken in one soup (an abomination!). Now, the words demonic and occult were flashing wildly in and out of my head. Sweat stuck my dress between my thighs and I peeled the fabric off my skin. You'll end up in hell for this.

Calm down, said Jamila. *She's using an ancient technique.*

You can always ignore what she tells you, said Zeina.

And we're here for you, said Fati. *Whatever she says, we'll help you carry.*

The psychic sat down, separated from me by a table shrouded in red velvet. I was disappointed she didn't have a crystal ball, like the old man in *The Wizard of Oz*. The room was dark and incense-filled. She took her deck of tarot cards and shuffled them, thumping them on the table, as she began to look at me intensely. My heart raced. The incense tickled my nostrils and I sneezed.

'Pick a card,' she said, finally.

I stretched out my hand and did so. I passed it to her and she laid it down on the table and pushed it to me. There were two women in the foreground, one blonde, the other red-haired. The blonde knelt before the red-haired one, and behind them an old lady in yellow, holding a candle. Underneath the candle was inscribed 'Eight of pentacles'.

'So?' I said, before I could stop myself from speaking.

'What interpretation would you like? Love, career, spirituality?'

'Love and spirituality, I guess.'

'Each reading is separate.'

Her eyes told me that what she wasn't saying was that I'd need to pay more money to get the complete reading. I wanted to know that I'd chosen a good career path, but that wasn't bothering me a whole lot. I was going to grad school, interning at *the* place for comics, and now I had a project idea that I was sure would make a mark . . . Heartbreak, I knew everyone and their mother suffered at one point or another, so even though I really would have liked to know if Alex would come back into my life, it wasn't the most pressing issue either. It was the grandmothers. *That* was confusing. Since arriving in New York, I hadn't gone a day without hearing their commentary.

'OK, spirituality, then,' I said.

'Rose Red, the mother priestess, is sending her knowledge on to Snow White, just as the crone in the background holds the light. Your female forebears are showing you the way. You are learning and you are working hard towards what you want. You're getting stronger in your spiritual gifts. You are young, but your soul is ageless. Everything you need, you already have.'

The skin prickled on my arms.

This is just right for you, said Jamila.

'Is it normal that I can hear, um, these female forebears?' I asked, for the first time.

'You can really hear them?' the woman asked, and her head snapped back ever so slightly. When I nodded, she arranged her face and said, 'If you came here today, it means you're in tune. When you're in tune, they speak to you.'

This was the thing about New Age spirituality that annoyed me. The part where it was all so woo-woo and you couldn't put your finger on it and it seemed like they just made it up on the fly. What did it mean that I was 'in tune'? Bloody hell!

'What does it mean that I'm in tune?'

'You could have moved to any place in the world, but you chose to come here. The fact that you chose a new path instead of staying on the old shows you're in tune.'

When she said nothing more, I got up and was about to walk away when the woman coughed. I turned to regard her and she rubbed her thumb against her middle and forefingers.

'Oh!' I said. 'Sorry. How much?'

'Ten dollars, please.'

I groaned inside as I searched in my purse. I guessed I would be having one drink tonight instead of two. What did all that mean? Was it switching from science to illustrating? If I were a scientist, would the old ladies not have chosen me? One of them had mentioned my pencil.

You modern people like to explain everything, said Jamila.

Isn't it comforting enough knowing you're fine? asked Zeina.

No, I'm not fine, I wanted to say as I left the witch's lair. Mary Grace was puffing on a cigarette outside.

'New habit?' Mary Grace and her hat tricks.

'Only when I'm bored and waiting outside. So how did it go?'

'I don't know if I learnt anything new, except for the fact that maybe I'm on the right track?'

'That should count for something, no?' Mary Grace said, dropping the cigarette butt on the pavement and crushing it underfoot. I shrugged.

We arrived at the end of a short line of women showing their IDs to the bouncer, and my armpits twitched for the second time that evening. Even though I'd found a hack for entry into New York's nightlife, I was always scared I would land on that one bouncer who happened to be from Ghana, who happened to remember that we wrote our dates differently. But this one nodded and let Mary Grace and me in. Me with my brand-new passport. In it, I looked just the way I wanted to look in my passport pictures: happy, shiny, with a big halo of an afro around my face.

I'd never been to a lesbian bar before, and yet I felt right at home. It was as if I'd been transported back to college. Before us were girls who looked just like Mary Grace and me. Others were butch, in shirts and buzz cuts. Some were very girlie girls. Some wore skin as dark as mine, others were brown, others were very pale. There was every kind of girl in this place. Aliya came in not long afterwards, and she and Mary Grace both took my hands as Nelly Furtado's 'Promiscuous' dragged everyone onto the dance floor. Mary Grace and Aliya soon grew cosy and I was left by myself. I was a hair, *just a hair*, self-conscious, but I would dance my sadness away, like Simon had advised.

I liked the way my body fitted with Alex's body. I liked his eyes. The way he looked at me. I was so grateful that he hadn't been afraid to take away my virginity.

It hurts more when you go deeper than this, said Zeina. *You will heal.*

I closed my eyes to stop myself from crying, and when I opened them, a girl with the biggest orange curls was dancing across from me. I tried not to laugh as she drunkenly twirled her hands in the air. We kept our distance from each other, but her being there prevented me from slipping into sadness.

More and more girls filled up the small space of the bar, and I couldn't see Mary Grace and Aliya any more. Before I knew it, Curly Sue had wrapped her arms around my waist and wanted to slow-dance with me. I didn't fight her off, but danced stiffly.

'Ouch,' I shouted, feeling a hot sting on my arm.

'Sorry,' said a gangly, boyish-looking woman holding a cigarette. Not one bit of remorse was present in that apology.

'Go away, Len,' said my dance partner, then she turned to me. 'Ignore her.'

This Len person had burnt me with the cigarette intentionally.

'OK,' I said, extricating myself from what must have been a lovers' squabble. That was just my luck. Even in a lesbian bar, I attracted a person who was not available. I'd have to ask the grandmothers why that kept happening. If I was on the right track, that was not very comforting. I finally found Mary Grace and Aliya and told them what had gone down.

'Whoa!' said Aliya.

'Do you want me to go talk to her?'

'This person was skinny, but I'm sure she would knock you out, MG.'

'Fine,' she said, and the two of them drew me into their circle of two.

I let my sadness climb out of my chest and cloak out its rough woolliness over my whole body. I cried quietly, and Aliya and Mary Grace held me tight, in the way only girls know how to take care of each other.

Part Three
August

Chapter Twenty-Six

Housewarming

The winds of change seemed to be blowing through. Or that was what I felt every time August rolled around. For as long as I could remember, August was always a bookmark to the end of freedom and the beginning of something new – usually school and a lack of freedom. So not only was I feeling that ever present tick-tock of time, but I also realised that my days as a fresh arrival to New York were about to end. That wide-eyed wonder with which I'd once regarded this city would never come back. I was truly a virgin no more. Would the grandmothers leave me once I found my way around this city?

She wants to get rid of us, Mma Fati said.

I convinced them and myself that I would be lonely without them. I didn't want them to go anywhere. But if I really sorted through my thoughts, it was because for now their being there stopped me from wallowing. Even though I couldn't stop thinking about that person I'd given three whole weeks of my life and who had just twisted and wrung my heart, the grandmothers stuck their gnarly imaginary fingers under my chin and told me to keep going.

Densua texted me.

Edward & I having a housewarming. Please come! Bring Mary Grace & cool ppl.

I couldn't envision her having a housewarming in her studio, especially since she'd already lived there for a year, and when she sent me a follow-up message with her address, it made sense.

Tribeca! She had hit the jackpot. If she hadn't told me she was moving out of her apartment, maybe we still weren't quite where we needed to be. Maybe this time she would have enough time for me to tell her about the grandmothers. And if I confided this to her, maybe she would feel like she could also start telling me things again.

I had to take wine and appropriate housewarming gifts over, so the next day, I hauled myself up to Trader Joe's on 14th Street, where, even in the morning, a line snaked its way through every single aisle. What would please the person who had it all – a job that paid handsomely, a perfect boyfriend and now, presumably, an envy-inducing apartment? Also, it wasn't a gift for Densua alone. It was for Edward, too. Trader Joe's hand soap? A frozen dessert? Honey?

In the end, I went for two bottles of wine, moisturising balm, hand soap and lavender salt scrub, all for under twenty dollars. I felt very pleased with myself, thanking heavens that Trader Joe's existed for people like me with bourgie tendencies and no money. All I had to do was find some way to present these nicely. I made my way back home and went to prepare. There was no one to impress, I told myself, but still . . . Maybe I would meet someone nice at Densua's.

Or you could tell your friend to come, said Jamila.

I'd told Mary Grace about the housewarming and she said she was down, and now, with the prodding from the grannies, I invited Kweku.

I flung the phone on the bed and went about sweeping, mopping, scrubbing, scouring and dusting every bit of space, except for Mary Grace's room.

You do this every week, said Zeina. *You're the only one constantly cleaning. Your problem is you don't stand back and watch your patterns.*

Don't start trouble, she has to prepare for her afternoon, admonished Jamila.

But your toes, Fati said. *At least look nice. Get some polish on those toes.*

I went over to Myrtle Avenue. The first nail salon was brimming, so I walked on and found another one, where I was able to have my toenails cut, trimmed, cleaned and pampered, all for under ten bucks. Exactly $9.99. Did I want to have my eyebrows threaded, the lady asked, while I was at it?

'They too bushy,' she said.

'Sure,' I said, never having done a thing to my brows my entire life.

She set my head back in her salon chair and powdered my brows, then took a spool of thread, roped it around her finger, pushed a piece into her mouth and hovered above me.

Reminds me of when I got the scar on my cheek, said Mma Fati.

If I were still alive, I would never have let them do that to you, said Zeina.

I didn't have time to figure out what they were going on about, because it suddenly felt as if the woman had run a dull knife along my brow.

'Ouch,' I said.

She didn't even flinch. She just repeated the motion over and over. And when at one point I touched my brow, she slapped my hand away.

'You on your period?' she asked.

Had I stained her chair?

'Yes,' I said.

'That's why it hurts. Next time, don't come when Aunt Flo's here.'

When she was done, I could have cried. I had endured all that physical and verbal abuse to end up resembling a surprised clown.

It's very fashionable, said Jamila.

I should remember to thin out her eyebrows in my sketches – which I added to every time I learnt something new about the grandmothers.

I forked out another ten dollars for the torture, then pushed my headscarf down over my brows and walked across and into Fat Albert's to search for wrapping paper.

Back home, regret built in my chest like rising water in a

clogged toilet bowl. Could I uninvite Kweku because I looked like an ancient surprised clown? Mary Grace was at work and would come directly to Densua's, so there was no way I could get a read on how bad my face situation was. Should I tell him I suddenly wasn't feeling well?

If he sees you at your worst and isn't fazed, you know he's a good one, snapped Zeina.

I took a long nap, showered, shaved my legs and tried to fill in my brows with brown lip liner. I put on the same dress I'd been dumped in, refusing to make it my bad-luck charm. My mother had had the dress made for me with love. The material came from Bobo-Dioulasso, goddammit! I slipped my feet into open-toed sandals, appreciative that at least my toes were cute. I combed out my afro, puckered my lips and walked out.

I thought I would arrive at Densua's early to help her set up, but other people were already milling about the apartment when I walked in. I gave her the Trader Joe's gift pack, glad it was concealed in silver wrapping paper. The people in the apartment wore silky summer dresses and linen suits, the stuff of J. Crew catalogues, at undiscounted retail prices. There was the dress I'd been coveting in the window display in Anthropologie, now draped over a girl's pale, waif-like body. Their gifts certainly wouldn't have come from Trader Joe's.

I went into the kitchen area, separated from the living room by a large industrial-looking island, and gave Densua a big hug. She was wrapped in a red dress that traced the double U's of her backside, and I was sure every male eye would be trained on her. My friend was a bombshell.

'You look scrumptious,' I told her, handing her the gift.

'Thanks. You look lovely, too. I like your dress.'

'Finally, a Sister creation done right.'

'Wonders!' said Densua, and laughed. 'Remember those giant sleeves she put on our APS graduation kabas?'

'Don't remind me. At least you had a plan B. I was forced to wear that horrible outfit.'

'You over-plucked your brows?'

'No. I had them threaded for the first time, and disaster.'

'You're brave papa. By the way, where are your people?'

'On their way. Who are all *these* people?'

'Edward's friends.'

Densua worked so hard, she really didn't have time for a social life. I was her only friend, and I should do better. Even though we weren't the kind of friends that went around gushing every single detail of our lives – she was private, I was private – we could change things. If she was the one who'd brought us back together, I should make us get closer, like I should be the glue between us.

'What's it like living with your man?' I asked.

'Chale, it's a learning experience.'

'When did you guys really meet?'

'In March, I think. He's such a kind person.'

So they'd been seeing each other even when I'd stayed at her place. She hadn't shared one word. How had I been so blind to the signs? I couldn't be *that* clueless. No, Densua, was super stealthy. I would not be like her, I decided right then. There was private and there was unhealthy. We had to be more open in our friendship.

'Why didn't you tell me? March, April, May, June. I met him in July, no? That's a looong time.'

'I wanted to make sure it was legit.'

'How come you never tell me anything?'

'You're exaggerating. I tell you a lot. Although, to be honest, I don't feel like you always want to hear about these kinds of things. Remember when I started dating Rodney in secondary school? You didn't care one bit about him.'

'Rodney and I were buddies, and I listened to you talk all the time about him.'

'In any case, you were only into things that concerned you. No one else mattered. There was one time – and this really pained me – I still remember it like it was yesterday. I'd asked you to cover for me in Mrs Enum's class and say I was sick, so I could help Rodney, who was struggling with math. Like, he couldn't afford to fail it. You nodded like you'd understood, but you said nothing to her. The next time we went to class, Mrs Enum said, "Some people think they have the syllabus at their fingertips and don't need to come to class. These people can just teach the class themselves, then."'

'Ah! That's why she said that,' I said.

'It's like, the lights were on, but no one was home. And you became so selfish. After that, I just stopped sharing stuff about Rodney with you.'

What she wasn't saying (maybe because the last time she'd said it we'd stopped talking) was that her dating Rodney happened around the same time as my parents' official divorce. The timing wasn't right. Maybe I wasn't capable of seeing anything else outside of myself. And because of that, our friendship had gone from deep to surface, little by little over the years. I asked her some more about Edward, trying to remedy a slight that had gone on for too long.

'He might be the one, Zainab,' she said.

'Oh wow. Really? How do you know?'

'I feel it. I've heard that when you know, you know. And you, what's new?'

'I had sex,' I blurted out. A thin woman had been approaching with a gift, but my words sent her pirouetting and she headed in the opposite direction.

Here was Densua's chance to tell me it was OK, and to dish on the wild, amazing time she and Edward were having.

'Ei! This is big news. With whom?' is what she asked me.

'He's history, but I'm glad I did it. So how is *he*?' I nudged my elbow in the direction of Edward, where he was surrounded by his friends in their polo shirts and seersucker shorts.

'How is he how?'

'In bed.'

'Oh Zainab, you've become too much,' she said, heading off to stir a giant pot of sauce. 'This Brooklyn place *is* changing you. Or is it that room-mate of yours?'

'I've also heard that if you want to marry a person, you have to make sure the engine works well.'

That's my motto, said Jamila.

I was sure Edward would marry Densua whether or not she was a virgin. Heck, *I* would marry her, just to be taken care of. I was convinced that even with her banking job, she would always have home-cooked meals waiting for her husband.

'Well, if Edward is the one for you, I'd better start saving to buy my maid-of-honour dress. Those things are pricey.'

The elevator door slid open, and in flooded a large group of people. In the mix were Mary Grace and Kweku, Mary Grace in an American Apparel all-black uniform and red hair, Kweku in jeans and a button-down shirt. These were my people. Sort of out of place, just like me.

I went to meet them.

I hugged Mary Grace and introduced Kweku to her.

'We already met,' they chorused.

'At the Angélique Kidjo concert, remember?' said Mary Grace.

'Right,' I said, wagging my forefinger at both of them, as if I had to choose between them, and then I wondered why I was doing that and I curled my finger into a fist and told them to follow me.

When we got to the kitchen, which Densua hadn't left since I'd come into the apartment, she was checking on pieces of chicken baking in the oven.

'Kweku Ansah!' she said, hugging him very enthusiastically. 'Zainab didn't tell me you'd be coming. What a surprise. It's been ages!'

'Wow, I'm surprised you remember me,' said Kweku.

I gave Kweku and Densua the space to catch up while Mary Grace and I explored the apartment, beers in hand.

'Dude, your eyebrows look . . . different?'

'Threading disaster in the 'hood. Lesson learnt. Never doing that again. Is it really bad?'

'You look a bit stunned.'

'Oh no!'

Wrist circled with a delicate gold bracelet, she reached to my face and swiped her finger over my brows. Then she dusted off her hands.

'Just think of people around here sitting on toilets and wear your new look with confidence. We're all human, no? The first time I tried to dye my hair, I looked like Carrot Top.' The image amused me.

We stopped in front of a series of black and white photos, against an exposed brick wall. The apartment exuded masculine energy, and it was clear Densua was still trying to jigsaw herself into this space. I recognised a round vase from her old apartment that now sat atop the surface of a cube-shaped table.

'Stock photos,' Mary Grace said, her brow raised in tickled disdain. A seashore, a close-up of a zebra print, a row of pebbles.

'Why are we such haters?' I asked, satisfied that she wasn't impressed.

'Because I don't like investment bankers. I don't know what your beef is.'

'He's turning my friend into a housewife,' I said. 'And she says he might be the one.'

'Your guy is cuter,' said Mary Grace.

I agree, said Jamila.

It's not a competition, said Zeina.

'In the elevator up, I reintroduced myself as your room-mate and told him he was welcome to our house whenever he wanted to come.'

'No, you didn't!'

'Calm down. I didn't embarrass you. You'll thank me later. I just did half your work for you.'

We went back to Densua, who quickly enlisted my help in serving her guests, so I barely had time to talk to either Mary Grace or Kweku, but having spent more time with Mary Grace these last weeks, I trusted that she and Kweku were fine in each other's company. She wasn't as man-crazy as I'd initially feared.

I switched from beer to a cocktail Edward had mixed. I hated admitting that it was delicious, but after passing around a plate of canapés, I wound my way back to the punch bowl. At one point, just as I was scooping from the bowl, he came over to ask me to get some beers for an older-looking group of people, most likely his bosses. It was the overfamiliarity of his ask, his tone, just who he was that annoyed me. We didn't know each other. Sure, I was his girlfriend's best friend, but he had no right.

'Get them yourself,' I almost shouted.

At this point, I'd drunk more than I'd eaten, but I wasn't in an uncontrollable state. I went into the kitchen, got myself a plate of chicken and chewed three pieces. I was licking my fingers when Kweku came over.

'Nice turn-out for Densua, right?'

I was probably raising my brows like an insane person.

Listen to your friend Mary Grace, said Jamila, so I let go of thinking about my brows and smiled back, picturing Edward trying to push out an extremely hard poo.

'Want some chicken?' I asked.

'I had some. Really tasty. It's so grown-up here. Her man seems cool?'

Before I could stop myself, I said, 'He's a prick.'

'Whoa. What did he do to you? This is the first time I've heard you swear.'

'He's making her shrink. She hasn't left the kitchen since I got here.'

'I'm sure she's in the kitchen because she wants to be in the kitchen, or because she likes cooking.'

'I hope so,' I said. 'She does like cooking.'

'Yup, I wouldn't worry about Densua.'

Mary Grace waved jauntily as she made her way to the cocktail bowl.

'What do you think of *her*?' I asked Kweku.

'She's a riot. I like her. She seems chill.' I was going to tell him about her charging me rent, but his words stopped me. 'She's easy to talk to.'

'I can get you a room. But careful, it might cost you a lot of money.' Why did I say that? What was wrong with me? He looked taken aback, but said nothing. My tongue felt loose and heavy in my mouth. 'I'm sorry. I'm still upset by Densua's man.'

'Let me get you some water.'

He came back, glass of water in hand, and his eyes crinkled and his dimples deepened.

'I'm sorry. That was unnecessary.'

'You're a mean drunk, I see. Well noted.'

'I am . . . was not drunk. I'm not drunk.' I playfully hit him and he caught my hand and held it. We stared at each other and I extricated my hand and saw Edward carrying his beers to his bosses. I clapped inside. At least one victory for the day.

It wouldn't have hurt you to get them for him, said Jamila.

No, you were right to let him do it himself, scowled Zeina.

Fati was a tie-breaker, but sometimes she sided nowhere. So I had an angel-and-devil-on-my-shoulder situation. Or a Good Samaritan and an ancient feminist.

I sent my gaze around the room. Mary Grace had now struck up conversation with a blonde man who didn't seem to be boring her. Densua was in Edward's armpit, being presented to the bosses. She said something and the men burst into belly-emptying laughter. Densua *was* fine. This was her world. She knew how to work it.

As if he'd read my mind, Kweku said, 'See, you don't have to worry about her. How are you feeling?'

'A bit light-headed.'

'Shall we go get some air?'

'Let me tell Mary Grace,' I said, feeling whatever spirits Edward had put in that punch rising up my body. Mary Grace shooed me away, and I admired her for coming into a space where she knew no one and having the ability to grow so comfortable she didn't need me. How did she do it?

Kweku and I took the loft's elevator, and as he pushed the button, I said, 'This is the life. An apartment with direct elevator access. Densua is living the dream, even if her man is horrible.'

'I want a house, I've decided,' Kweku said. 'Or a whole apartment building.'

'Me too! A brownstone, converted inside, with lots of white walls and high ceilings and a big studio for drawing.'

The vapours from the punch began to cloud my vision so I couldn't tell where we were going until we ended up near the Hudson River, where the sound of water revived me. Was it a babbling or a bubbling brook? I don't know why biblical thoughts were flooding my mind. How had I managed to drink so much? We sat on the wooden logs jutting out of the pier and watched families walk up and down.

'I started Columbia and a week later the towers were down.'

At first, I wasn't sure why he had brought up 9/11, but when I followed the direction in which his eyes were trained, I made out the empty space where the twin towers had once stood. 'It changed my whole experience of college. I was lucky we already had our American passports, because my international student friends really suffered.'

'Yes, we're still suffering. Sometimes I feel like a prisoner in this country. Everywhere I go, I'm monitored. But I can't imagine what that was like, seeing two landmarks crumble to dust.'

'I was taking calculus, one of those early-morning classes, and someone got a message on their phone or something. Or maybe it was the professor. We all ran to find a TV, and it was horrendous. You couldn't stop watching it. But New York picked right up.'

'People are nothing if not resilient.'

'Yup, I loved the shrines people set up all over the city.'

He gets points, said Jamila, *for using the right word.*

'I was watching it with my mum,' I said. 'For some reason I wasn't in school. She was in tears. "People should stop hiding behind religion," she said. "These people are killers. Plain and simple. This is not Islam."'

I realised my shoulder was pressing into his. What if I just turned and kissed him? He was squinting, as usual, although this time the sun was out in force. I began to lean in. My shoulder crossed the line that separated us. I was moving in for the kill.

'I want to, Zainab,' he said under his breath. Then quickly added, 'But let's do this when we've not been drinking. Make sure it's what we both want.'

He's right, said Zeina.

Wo yo, this one is too proper, said Jamila.

I'm starting to like him, said Fati.

I nodded, although if I could have dived into the Hudson and stayed hidden in its murky waters I would have. Only thing was, I couldn't swim.

'Shall we head back, then?' I said, trying to save face.

He took my hand and held it as we walked back, and that made me feel less like gutter water.

'Mum's legendary end-of-summer barbecue has a date. She'd love to see you. Bring Densua and Mary Grace, too. Don't worry, I'll remind you about it.'

When I'd sobered up and helped Densua clean up her sparkling new apartment, I asked her what I should do about Mary Grace's not helping out in our apartment.

'People here withhold rent for things like that,' said Densua. 'Or pay her less.'

Don't listen to her, said Zeina. *That's not the way WE do things*.

I wanted to scream at Zeina. *She* was the one who said I hadn't done anything about my constantly cleaning the apartment. Now I was looking for solutions, and she was already bad-mouthing them. Family could be so infuriating. I wanted to scream, but I had to keep my confusion bottled. Was I the only one going through something so insane? Having your family watch your every move was the most exhausting thing I'd experienced in all of my twenty years.

'Or just have a conversation. I hope you had fun!'

'Do you believe our ancestors have the power to come back?' I asked, barely listening to Densua. I was hoping, praying she would say 'I know what you mean.' Even though the psychic I'd seen had been somewhat encouraging with the cards she'd pulled, I still wasn't quite a believer in what I was going through.

'Zainab, you're so random, oh my God!' she said breathlessly. 'What are you talking about?'

'Like, do you believe our ancestors can speak to us?'

'Remember the abiku poem we studied in Mr Vanderpuije's class? Is that what you mean? Like when a child keeps dying and coming back to its parents? And the parents scar it to make it stay. I can never forget that visual after reading that poem. Our traditions can be really backward.'

She's not ready, said Jamila.

She'll never be ready, said Zeina.

Give her time, said Fati. *Already talking about abiku is a start.*

'I could ask my pastor when I finally make my way back to church,' Densua said, and I was inclined to agree with Zeina. 'It was so good, the church in Brooklyn. You should come with me next time.'

Densua had been trying to save my soul since we were thirteen, when she got born-again. Over the years, she'd grown less fanatical, but still tried to get me to church. I dropped the ancestral theme and brought the subject back around to Mary Grace's cleaning habits, but just as I was about to ask her how much to deduct from the rent, Edward appeared and Densua fitted herself back into his armpit.

'Babe,' Edward said. 'Everyone loved your cooking. But next time, not so much oil? I saw the way it was dripping from someone's plate.'

Ah, that one needs a dirty slap, said Fati. She often surprised me.

Why did he speak to Densua that way? If she said he might be the one, I would be supportive, but he was giving me all kinds of wrong energy.

Cook yourself then, I wanted to say to him. Instead, I said my goodbyes and left.

Chapter Twenty-Seven

A Discovery

The next day, I wrote Mary Grace a cheque for $650, slid it into an old bank envelope and placed it on the living room table, as I had with the last rent cheque. I wondered about including an explanatory note, but it would be better if we spoke in person. The grandmothers said they wouldn't use Densua's pay-less approach, but not a single one of them had paid rent in their lifetime. Mma Fati had lived in a house she'd had upgraded from a hut to a compound home. Densua dealt with money. I trusted her. Time to feed the *flâneuse.* It was time for a long walk.

It bothered me that there was absolutely no one I could talk to about the grandmothers. Maybe Mary Grace, but if I shared this with her and she belittled it, living with her would be unbearable. I would just have to wait for my book to make a splash, then people would take me seriously.

I went towards Graham Avenue and turned right, moving deeper into the borough instead of towards Manhattan. I hit a wall at Flushing Avenue, so I took a left. The housing projects on my left gave way to the Boar's Head factory, which manufactured the bacon I bought. I'd first tasted bacon by accident in college, around the time I'd gone through my awakening, and had been hooked on it ever since. The week before my mother had visited, I fried all the bacon I'd bought and spent the week eating BLTs.

The Dobermann dogs I saw patrolling in the factory sent me scurrying to the other side of Flushing Avenue, where the buildings were industrial and ochre-coloured, like Jamila's skin. I continued up past nondescript buildings until around Knickerbocker Avenue, where I saw a ground floor full of clothing. At first I thought it was a wholesaler's factory, but then I saw racks of clothing labelled $1, and I bit the bait. Inside was a second-hand clothing buyer's dream; a starving pre-graduate student's life-saver. Racks of vintage clothing, shoes, bags and belts.

You know someone like me could have worn these things, said Fati as I thumbed a pair of snakeskin pumps. Fati was always fashionable, from what I remember of her. She never wore those boxy old lady sneakers. Like my mother, she matched her shoes with her bags. I was a broken chain in their fashion connection.

I didn't wear shoes, said Jamila.

But more importantly, said Zeina, *you don't know what spirits have passed through these clothes. This place makes my skin crawl.*

'You don't have skin,' I almost retorted.

It's true, agreed Jamila. *See that hair there.* It was blonde and long and sticking out from a sweater. *You don't know who it belonged to.*

And so just like that, my ancestors bequeathed me a fear of vintage clothing and the dead people whose spirits might have been lurking around their old wardrobes, and I slunk out of the warehouse. This would have been so great for my bank account.

When I got back home, before I could tell Mary Grace about my discovery, which I was sure she'd appreciate (if it wasn't American Apparel, it was vintage), she was waving the cheque in my face.

'What is this?' she asked, her large eyes bulging widely. I had never seen her like that. 'Why is there less rent this month?'

'Oh,' I said, trying to be breezy, though my heart was sprinting, 'I wanted to talk to you about that. Um, I want us to discuss how we clean the apartment.'

'Then talk to me, don't underpay me. Do you know how much rent you're supposed to be paying?'

'No,' I squeaked. 'I just got tired of cleaning all the time.'

'I have to say I'm disappointed you'd do this. I wanted to live with you because I thought you were drama-free and sensible and smart. But this . . .'

'You could have told me the apartment building was yours,' I said, finally letting out what had been weighing on me all these weeks.

'How did you know? Did you snoop through my things?' Her voice was rising. I thought her eyeballs would pop out of their sockets.

'Alex told me,' I blurted out. Blame it on the boy who'd dumped me. 'Because his friends had told him.'

'Well, bitch, this apartment should cost you a thousand dollars, so think that through. You owe me fifty.'

I tore up the cheque. That was the last time I would ask Densua for advice. I sheepishly wrote a new one and handed it to Mary Grace.

'We can do a cleaning schedule,' she said, after she read the amount and was satisfied with it. 'I clean, you clean. And I didn't mean to call you a bitch.'

'You were so mean,' I said, in need of a big hug from my mother or some warm older body. My grandmothers were too wizened and invisible for this kind of raw surface wound. They were better for the soul-deep pain. And they *had* warned me. 'Let's never fight again.'

'As for those nosy men downstairs . . . Yes, the building is my family's. My aunt in Queens, remember I told you about her? Well, it's hers, but since I'm here, she's made me the super-slash-manager. But I don't own it. I told her about you and she asked me to charge you full rent, but I begged and pleaded. It's why I am so upset with that stunt you pulled. Aren't we friends?'

I nodded.

'She told me she had really a bad experience with some Togolese tenants, and to make sure I took a deposit and even more.'

'Your aunt is sounding borderline racist, Mary Grace. Yes, Ghana is next to Togo, but it's not the same country.'

'Her generation *is* racist and homophobic. If you knew the names I was called back home because of my skin colour. And if anyone from home found out that I date girls too, glory hallelujah, there would be an inquisition!'

'She shouldn't get a pass, though. Just tell me when she's coming so I avoid her.'

'I swear she's a sweet woman. Just doesn't know any better. But next time, we talk things out before you have your little worker's revolution.'

That was going to be my advice, if only you'd listened, said Zeina. *To talk to her about cleaning the apartment. And Densua also told you to talk to her, but you weren't listening.*

'And just so you know, I pay her rent, too. Because if I lived here for free, I would become her puppet – and I would have no autonomy. So don't think I'm cheating you. Anything else you want to tell me?'

I shook my head, even though I had a long, long list: take your hair out of the bathtub, it clogs the drains; don't drink my milk; keep your shoes off the sofa; turn off your air conditioner when you go out; stop licking the cooking spoon. I could go on, but I said nothing. I didn't want any other explosions.

'By the way,' she said. 'I broke up with Aliya.'

'Ah ha! That's why you're so pissed off,' I worked up the courage to say. 'I'm sorry to hear that. What happened?'

'I don't know . . . She was controlling. Didn't like me for who I am. Would always say things like "Why are you wearing that?" I didn't feel good with her. I attract people who seem to like my free spirit, and then after a while, they want me to be what *they* want me to be.'

'I'm sorry.'

'It's all good. I'd rather start grad school without the baggage. And I've been talking to that guy from your friend's thing.'

'I thought you didn't like bankers.'

'Here's the thing: he's not a *banker's* banker. He and Densua's fiancé—'

'Boyfriend. They aren't engaged.'

'OK, they went to grad school together. This guy was once a journalist at *Vice* magazine. He's quite intriguing.'

I was beginning to think he might be the reason she'd broken up with Aliya.

'Isn't that the magazine that tries to be extra provocative to the point of sleazy? I don't know about this guy, MG.'

'Let me worry about him. Work on Kweku and we'll double-date.'

'I admire the way you're able to bounce back so fast,' I said.

She picked up the furry crocheted throw that was on the sofa and pressed its floral patterns between the pads of her thumb and forefinger. Mary Grace, for all her worldliness, was just an old lady who had found herself in the body of a twenty-something-year-old, what with her collection of blankets and throws. Maybe that was another reason we got along. I could think like an old lady thanks to my grannies.

'I wasn't kidding about what I said about growing up,' said Mary Grace. 'I felt like the ugliest thing around. Even my own mother would tell me to stay out of the sun so I wouldn't get any darker. I don't know how, but one day I saw my face in the mirror, and in spite of what everyone – even my parents – was saying, I liked it. I liked my curly hair, my lips, the dark skin. I found it beautiful. And so I learnt to be confident early, all by my little old self. So now, when I like someone, I go for them, not to make me feel better about myself, but simply because I like them. And unlike your friend Densua, I want to have as many experiences as possible before settling down with someone. I think the worst thing is living with regret.'

'Makes sense,' I said. 'I definitely don't want to marry someone because of pressure.'

You should learn from her, chided Fati.

Or listen to us, said Zeina.

Chapter Twenty-Eight

A Blast

Uncle Ali invited me for lo mein and said he had some news. I also took some of my drawings to show him, because he'd lived with two of the three women who were whispering their ancient wisdom into my ears. Even if I couldn't tell him the truth about them, he might understand my work. And he would certainly know details I could use to improve their renderings. After his feedback, I would finally present Sam with the best drawings I had. We'd sell the comic book for big money, and my face would be splashed on a bus like Carrie Bradshaw.

OK, if all that was too wild a dream, we'd start with grad school. I could picture my first day of class: I would be the wunderkind, the one all the professors had heard about and would jostle to have in their class, the one who would give the speech at graduation. The dream kid from West Africa who had become a comic book sensation, a field where black women were remarkably missing.

I probably had a big Cheshire Cat grin as I turned the bend on 32nd Street, and before I could arrange my face, I met Alex's green-eyed gaze. Time stopped. My heart pumped blood a mile a minute. How was I looking? I was wearing my work trousers – slacks I'd picked up at H&M at the Holyoke Mall – and over those I'd thrown a floral blouse. My hair was in flat twists – not the most flattering hairstyle for me, but quick and easy for work. I looked like nothing. I was carrying two bags: the extra one for my packed lunch, which I'd slowly been mastering, and a Nalgene bottle of water (buying bottled water was eating into my budget faster than a termite on paper). It was a Wednesday. I'd thought it would be an uneventful kind of day.

Keep moving, suggested Zeina. *You don't know him, he doesn't know you. All he did was help you get a head start in life.*

Oh, but he's good-looking, said Jamila. *Let's not run away. Just soak in that beauty for a short spell.*

He's already seen her, said Fati. *But that's why I always tell you to dress nicely. Because you never know. You don't listen.*

'Hey,' I sang, the end of my one-word sentence ringing in my ears.

'Zainab,' said he. He who had made me realise my heart was just a brittle thing pretending to be muscle. 'You work around here?'

'Yes.'

I knew he didn't work there and that he was far from home, but I couldn't dig out the words to make conversation.

'So, how are you?' I managed flatly.

'Good. I'm meeting a friend in Bryant Park. They have movies in the park, and I don't know if I told you just how much I enjoy watching the classics. It's *Charade* with Cary Grant.'

'Never heard of it, and Bryant Park is a long way from here.'

'I get a good parking rate here.' He pointed behind him.

He must have been meeting Stephanie or whatever his girlfriend's name was. Tiffany. Vanessa. One of those names. It wasn't ancestral like mine was. His girlfriend was sure to be two-dimensional; she didn't roll deep like I did. But why did my heart hurt like so? I really wanted something with this kid. A delicious sex-filled summer. Like those French girls experienced in those new-wave French movies in my paapa's VHS collection.

His head is misshapen, volunteered Jamila. It was true that in the light of day, without the flutters of lust clouding my vision, his head was pinched smaller on one side. But it was nitpicking. We all had our flaws. My nostrils were too big.

'I'm gonna be late for this thing, but we should hang out sometime,' he said. 'If you'd like.'

'OK, let me know,' I said, waving and hurriedly heading in the direction of the Manhattan Mall. We were technically going the same way, but I wanted to cling to the hope his words were weaving in my soul. We *could* hang out, couldn't we? If he'd said that, then he was speaking the truth and just needed space or a break. He wasn't necessarily *back* back with his ex-girlfriend, was he? We could hang out, and maybe rewind to the moment just before we'd ended things. He wouldn't have said we should hang out if he were back in a committed relationship, would he? The questions swirled in my head, and a big smile crept back onto my face. It was the pick-me-up I needed. The grandmothers warned me not to fall for it, but I shoved them to the back of my mind.

I went through the revolving doors of the Manhattan Mall entrance, and as I passed by a security guard, she sighed heavily. I wondered what was giving her the blues. I smiled at her, to reassure her: everything will be fine. See, my man came back. Yours will, too.

He's not your man, Zeina snuck in. *Girls really like foolishness. Forget about him.*

And not everyone spends their every minute thinking of men, said Fati. *That woman might have children she's worried about.*

Wo yo. Maybe she's not worrying and just looks that way, said Jamila. *Some people are born looking angry.*

That made me snort as I took the elevator down to the food court. Uncle Ali was already seated, reading a book. I peered at the cover.

'*The Brothers K*,' I said loudly, startling him from what must have been an engrossing scene.

'Zainabou,' he said, getting up to hug me. 'Dostoyevsky can write, my God! Every time I read this book, I spot something I missed before. Especially in Vanya's scenes. Have you read it?'

I shook my head and he placed the book on the table.

'But why have you abandoned us? You could always come and spend weekends with us. The door is wide open. Your cousins would love to see you.'

'Thank you.'

My uncle just liked having everyone squished in by him, I was realising. I couldn't imagine either of those two children uttering any such words. And it was telling that he said nothing about Aunty Emefa. She certainly didn't want me back.

He was always a good child, said Jamila. *It's a pity his father didn't claim him, and now he has a fear of abandonment.*

I took good care of him after his mother died, said Fati. *His father would have squeezed all the goodness out of him. The man was my half-brother, but he was a terrible father. Would have used Ali to make him money if he could have.*

'Well, I've missed my niece. Thank you for meeting me. Let's order?'

Abandonment was exactly what I'd done to him, and now I felt bad. I wasn't sure if I liked knowing things about people that they hadn't shared with me. It made me feel like a voyeur. I tried to quieten down the grandmothers as Uncle Ali and I stood up and went to Wok & Roll with its red and yellow faux-Hanzi script. At least now I knew how we were related. Uncle Ali and my mother shared the same grandfather but had different grandmothers; my mother's grandmother was Zeina, who died before Uncle Ali was born. So he didn't have Jamila's blood. That was why the old ladies said we didn't make boys in our family.

He ordered lo mein and I went for chicken fried rice.

'We can take up your offer to write for us,' he said, leading the way back to the table. 'We enjoyed the sample tremendously. We can't pay a lot. It will be twelve dollars per article.'

If I could wing an article a week, forty-eight dollars every month wouldn't pay my credit card debt, but it could cover my phone bills and give me change for a grocery store item or two. I wouldn't say no.

'Thank you, Uncle! Will people write to me?'

'Let's run a few that you write yourself first, and then I'm sure readers will soon catch on.'

He told me about a funeral he'd been saddled with in the Bronx, and how his children would be starting back at school soon, and how his wife was driving him crazy because she wanted to move into a new place. I wondered what had changed in our relationship that made him confide in me. Did he consider me a true agony aunt?

Tell him to stop being stingy, said Zeina.

'Uncle, but the apartment *is* small,' I said. 'And Dzifa and Ibrahim shouldn't be sharing a room. One of them is a teenager.'

'Zainabou, I keep sending money to build our house in Ghana. If they would all be patient, there's a juicy reward down the line.'

I couldn't see my cousins settling into life in Ghana. New York was their home. He'd have another battle to fight when he dropped that bomb on them.

'I hear you,' I said, 'but if, for now, you can move into a three-bedroom place, your family would be thankful.'

'You're so wise,' he said, chomping on a mouthful of noodles. 'I mean that column you sent. I marvelled. At your age, I don't think such wisdom ever passed through my brain.'

'It runs in the blood,' I said. 'I'm named after a wise woman, after all. Talking of which, I want to show you something I've been working on. But let's finish eating first.'

I didn't want sesame oil smudging my drawings.

After I'd wiped down the tables with the flimsy paper towels we'd been offered, I showed him the sketches of each woman as she'd manifested herself to me, with some pastel shading to bring them to life.

'You've drawn our family,' he said. 'That one, she looks just like Mma Fati. It's uncanny. Wow, I'm so proud to have such a talented niece.' He studied the other drawings and repeated that I had talent. He stared hard at Jamila's picture, then covered his mouth. 'This one looks just like Fati's grandmother. I didn't know there were photographs of her. You are really gifted. Look, I have goose pimples.'

He lifted up his arm to show me.

I didn't say no, there were no photos involved, she revealed herself to me. But the moment was uplifting.

'The one of Mma Fati is yours,' I said. 'I should have framed it.'

'Oh, thank you, Zainabou. I'll frame it myself. I didn't know you could draw like this. Why are you hiding such talent from the world?'

You finally got him his gift, said Zeina.

I hadn't even realised it. Finally!

It's good to keep your word, said Jamila.

Also, calm was settling in the frenzy of a world my mind had become. This wasn't all just a figment of my imagination; I was in true communion with my ancestors.

On the train ride back to Bushwick, I smiled at a baby drooling in a pram across from me. A man hit my head with his briefcase. Break dancers twisting aggressively in the small standing room of the subway car didn't bother me. I grinned through it all. If I could have a concert of angels blowing clarions behind me, it would have been perfect. Not only had my man come back to me, I had a second job, and I now knew I wasn't going crazy. I was a real-life medium who could talk with my ancestors. And I made shrines for them that could make me very wealthy. Did it mean that I had to sacrifice something for this ability?

Your firstborn son, said Zeina.

'Are you serious?' I whispered under my breath.

She's teasing you, said Fati. *Remember we don't make boys*.

Libation every now and then won't hurt, said Jamila. *We get thirsty*.

I got home and Mary Grace was cooking. It actually smelt good. And she was on her own.

'Wow, it smells like a restaurant in here.'

'I've found my cooking mojo,' she said. 'I should only cook when I'm PMS-ing. Things just taste so much better with the hormones or something.'

'What are you making?'

'Stewed chicken with my lola's recipe. Curry leaves make all the difference. Every time I visited the old woman, she would have this cooked just for me. Isn't it amazing how food can revive someone who's long gone?'

One day you can tell her about us, said Jamila. *Just wait till you've been friends for at least six moons.*

I say twelve moons, Zeina cut in. *After seven moons she can still reveal her true self.*

Moons are months, explained Fati.

I was glad for the translation, but the stew smelt too good and left me no room to concentrate on moons and true selves.

'I'll make the rice if you want,' I said, inviting myself to her meal. Why was I becoming a person whose nose went after other people's things?

'Yes please. Without a rice cooker, I'm no good.'

I went to my room, peeled off my clothes and changed into a T-shirt and shorts. How to tell Mary Grace about my day? A new job offer, Alex back! I didn't want her to kill my vibe, but if I couldn't tell her, where was the fun in what I'd experienced? Moments like these were made just for sharing with girlfriends.

Don't forget, you don't know each other that well yet, warned Zeina.

'You wouldn't believe who I saw today,' I launched. It was in sharing news like this that Mary Grace and I would grow closer.

'Alex?' My rocket ship came crashing down.

'How did you know?' I was so ready to play the guessing game with her, but I suppose I was *that* see-through. She passed me a bottle of beer and I took a swig from it. When her back was turned to me, I poured a drop on the floor. I couldn't see how that would benefit my grandmothers, but I remembered from my readings on ancient Egypt that offerings of meat, beer, bread and clothing were given to the gods. It was a practice even more ancient than these women in my head.

'He's the only person who is keeping you from seeing that you have a great man in Kweku. What did the asshole say?'

'He said we should hang out.' She wouldn't ruin my good mood.

'You believe him?'

'I mean . . . he didn't have to say it. He could have just said bye, but *he* was the one who volunteered that we hang.'

'So when are you meeting up?'

'We didn't make plans. Yet.'

Mary Grace was doing what I hadn't allowed my grandmothers to. Poking holes in the cloud of my happiness. But I wouldn't let anyone – alive or dead – rain down on me.

'I will let him know I'm in control of the story now. So how's the not-banker journalist?'

'If the sex wasn't so good, I'd have dumped him a long time ago. But, sweet Mary and Joseph, he knows what buttons to push.'

'I can't wait to have good sex,' I said, and stared at the ceiling. *With Alex.* If anyone was counting, I'd only had sex once. The night I lost my virginity.

I measured out two cups of rice, washed it twice even though the packaging insisted that water simply be added for cooking. My mother's brief presence was still strong in the apartment. Wash it twice, three times for good measure, and then pour in water to the level of your thumb knuckle. It worked, for some strange reason. Whenever I was possessed with an independent spirit and didn't follow her instructions to a T, my rice failed.

Mary Grace's sauce was flavoured with deep spice that started out slightly bitter and then became aromatic and sweet and tangy; my rice was fluffy and each grain could be picked up individually.

'We're getting there,' I said, leading the last forkful to my mouth.

'Only when I PMS, don't forget.'

Chapter Twenty-Nine

The Elevator

Having all my life ducks lined up in a row inspired me. I went to see Sam just before leaving the office for the day. He was typing on his computer and raised a finger till he was done. The bun was of the high kind.

The man is grown-up handsome, said Jamila. *Can't we have them all?*

'How may I help you, Zainab?' he said, and then gestured to the seat across from him. Since I messed up on the Aunt Abbie letter, he seemed to have grown distant. Or maybe it was just my reading of things. At least he still let me type up and edit the letters. Now, I triple-checked them before I gave them back to him.

Just be bold, said Jamila.

Sometimes subtlety works better, said Zeina.

My courage began to take leave of me. The only people who had seen the drawings were my room-mate and my uncle. They were hard-wired to root for me. What if my work was no good? I couldn't quite show him the drawings yet. So I thought hard and fast. Work permit! Visas!

'I was wondering if Altogether Media sponsored visas,' I said.

'I don't know that we do or that we have,' said Sam. 'Lemme check with Donna in HR and I'll get back to you. Do you need a visa now?'

'No, I have my Optional Practical Training, which allows me to work. I was just wondering for afterwards . . . If I came back to work here after graduation, for instance . . .'

'Yeah, I'll definitely have to talk to Donna first.'

'Thank you,' I said, rushing out of his office before my embarrassment would show and heading for the elevator.

He didn't refuse, so chin up, consoled Fati. *But you have to believe you're gifted, because you are.*

I pressed the elevator button, and as the doors slid open, I was reminded of unspooling a can of sardines. The elevator was overflowing. Right in front was Kweku. He waved, and just as the doors were sliding shut, he jumped out.

'What if the next one is even worse, crazy person?' I asked.

'Then we'll squeeze in together. Hi, you. How is your day going?'

'OK,' I said. 'I didn't mess up. Scanned and scanned and scanned. Kind of asked to be hired full-time. Your day?'

'Wow, awesome that you asked for the job. My campaign kicked off today, and I feel like an adult. Celebrations all round.'

'Eh. I don't think they like me enough here. I probably won't get it.'

You're being negative, said Fati.

She's protecting her heart, said Zeina, for once on my side.

Sam was suddenly standing by me. I hadn't seen him approach. The skin in my armpits pricked. Why had I been so loose-lipped? Had he heard me?

'Um, Sam,' I said, 'this is Kweku. And this is my boss.' He couldn't have heard, could he? And I was using my Ghanaian accent; that was what we did, Kweku and I. Although he had more of an American accent than I did, we slipped into our *ohh*s and *enh*s maybe a bit too much.

'Are you going on a date?'

'Oh no,' I said. 'He works in the building too.'

Quiet of the oh-so-awkward kind descended.

'Kweku is working on his first big ad deal,' I said, quickly, shoving in words to push out the silence. But why had Sam asked that question? What was it to him?

Maybe he's interested, said Jamila, screaming in my head.

He is already spoken for was Zeina's response.

Sam and Kweku began to talk about Kweku's work. I heard Sam mention 'iconic ads' and how Kweku had big shoes to fill.

'I know,' said Kweku. 'It's awesome working for a brand that's so established.'

The elevator slid open after what felt like an aeon, and was thankfully half full. We walked in and Sam was going on about how he'd wanted to be an advertising person – his poetry MFA had to make him a natural at writing copy – but had ended up editing comics instead; it was what paid the most at the time. They had a conversation outside of me, until we got downstairs and out of the elevator, where Kweku said, 'Zainab was the best artist in school. You have a good one with you.'

'We sure do,' said Sam, slipping on sunglasses and waving at us. 'Don't worry, Zainab, I'll look into the visa thing for you. And we like you plenty.'

He *had* heard me! I wanted to die. After Sam left, I thanked Kweku for putting in a good word for me, although I was mortified.

'Remind me to stop being embarrassing around you.'

'See, he was nice about it. Why are you worried about not being hired? Or is this just Miss Perfection shining through?'

'I already knew, deep down inside, that they don't sponsor visas. Companies like this one rarely do. It has to be a bank or big pharmacy. So by asking if they sponsor, I'm just pre-empting the whole we-can't-hire-you drama that is going to ensue at the end of the summer.'

'You can't be so sure they won't hire. Look, I'm twenty-two and I got my own account. Sure, I'm not *the* lead on it, but I had to push to become a project manager on the thing. Maybe pitch them something outside of your regular work? Or go above and beyond on the next project they ask you to do. Bosses lap up things like that.'

'Mary Grace says I should do that too, but my project isn't ready yet.'

'Hey, I understand. I'm just like you that way. If something doesn't feel cooked, I take my time, to the point of inertia sometimes.'

Was he talking about us? Why weren't we cooked? Did he know I had feelings for someone else?

'Oh, before I forget,' he interjected, 'there's this thing in your neighbourhood I've been dying to check out. It's called Drink and Draw. I think it's every Wednesday. Would you like to go with me? It's your scene. Or like people say these days, it's totally your jam.'

Wo yo! It took this man so long, said Jamila. *And you see, it wasn't about you at all.*

He shouldn't ask, he should just come and take her, said Zeina. *I thought these modern people believe that real men just do.*

Their men are made differently, said Fati. *More gentle.*

I hoped I would find out one day, but something must have happened to Fati with my grandfather. No one talked about him. Was that why she'd tried to keep me away from men?

'That sounds really nice,' I said, coming back to the present. 'When shall we go?'

'Next week? Whenever you want.'

'Next week! It's a date!'

Was it? Why did I say that? And Alex?

As I sat on the subway, I took out my notebook and drew Kweku and Alex in running clothes, on their marks at the start of the race track. The grandmothers as referees. Jamila puffing on her pipe; Zeina massaging my shoulders; and Fati making sure neither Kweku nor Alex was crossing the starting line.

I was drawing to calm my thoughts. I had a date with a man I sort of liked but was unsure about. I had a non-existent date with a man I adored who had dumped me. What kind of life was this?

Chapter Thirty
Drink and Draw

I spent the afternoon sloughing clean the apartment. Mary Grace had made an effort to clean for the first couple of days after our rent spat, but things had slowly ground back to normal.

I'd learnt a trick from my mother: spray your room with whatever perfume you usually wear, and when people come in, they are not overwhelmed with a new smell but with the smell they already associate with you. The problem was that I didn't have a signature smell, and I just had one bottle of perfume, Shalimar, which I never wore. So I went into Mary Grace's room.

Her bed was unmade. Reddish strands of hair twisted and tangled on the rug by the bed. Even in its undress and mess, it still radiated more adult than my room. Maybe because she had a proper dresser, which was where I now stood. I uncapped her Chanel No. 5, and smelt its expensive timelessness. I sniffed her Bulgari, its bottle alone suggesting that I would not smell like it in the near future. Then there was one that almost made my knees buckle. It had no identifying label but came in a simple green vial. That could be my smell. It was delicate and zesty all at once. If I sprayed it, she wouldn't know, would she?

We are women who use what we own, said Jamila, sobering me up, especially coming from her.

I left Mary Grace's room. Enough of the sneaking around.

I had made a major decision since my last date: I would no longer dress up to please men. I would only dress up for me. Wear what I wanted to flatter my no-curve-having body. I looked good in jeans. That was when I felt my best. I could squat if I wanted to, jump, climb things – although I hadn't had reason to climb anything in a long time. Besides, this thing Kweku and I were going on tonight wasn't a date. It was a thing with my handsome childhood buddy. My new best friend, I'd decided, at least while Alex was still in the picture. So up went the easy-to-slide-on jeans that actually made me look like I had a butt.

If you're thinking like this, you're still trying to please someone, said Zeina.

I ignored her and slipped on a blouse. I was as flat as an adolescent boy, but it was how I was made and I had to learn to like it. The next step was not buying those Victoria's Secret push-up bras that gave my teeny-weeny boobs extra oomph.

At 7 p.m., the buzzer rang and I shot up, startled. After I calmed myself, I let him up. It was the first time Kweku had come to my house. He got to the door and gave me a big smile and hug. He smelt fresh. It was clear he'd showered before coming. Had he gone all the way home first?

Is any of that important? said Zeina. *Give him water.*

'Would you like a drink of water?' I asked.

'Yes please,' he said, stepping into the world of Zainab and Mary Grace, a world that currently smelt like Shalimar, which evoked a golden age, the grace and class on which my mother floated, grace and class that I certainly didn't possess. 'No wonder everyone is moving to Bushwick. You people have space! My apartment in Harlem was a box, and back then I thought it was big. This is palatial.'

'You doth exaggerate a bit,' I said, opening the fridge for a bottle of water.

Kweku laughed as I poured him a glass. 'Which one is yours?' he said, pointing to the doors to our rooms.

I flung open my door and tried to like what I saw. It was simple. My sheets were white. My curtains were beige. My plastic bookcases, as juvenile as they were, added a certain amount of kitsch to what would have honestly been a plain room. And I'd converted my Nepali scarf into a cover for my rack of clothes. At first I did like what I saw, and then all its imperfections began to grow bigger. Like, I'd tried to arrange my clothes in rainbow colours, but what was a white shirt doing between yellow and green? White and black went to the extreme ends of the rainbow.

'Ready?' I asked.

'Your place is nice,' he said, washing his glass in the kitchen sink.

He has good home training,

'You've made a home for yourself. Oh, I almost forgot. We need pencils and sketchbooks. I remembered when I was on my way here. They provide the booze, but not the supplies.'

'I gotchu,' I said.

We left my street, and the last wisps of sunset were being drowned by the black of night. The street lights of Graham Avenue had blinked on, and we walked up to Bushwick Avenue and then took a left onto McKibbin Street.

'Here they are,' said Kweku, squinting up at the buildings. 'The infamous McKibbin lofts.'

I had passed by them a few times, but knew nothing about them.

'Why are they infamous?'

'This is the hipster capital of Brooklyn.'

'I thought that was Williamsburg.'

'These lofts are its core.'

'How do you know so much about this place?'

'I've gotta keep my pulse on what's hip. And these are the people my clients want to be selling to.' He waved from one building to the next. 'In there are the rich kids who really don't want people to know they're loaded.'

'Like Mary Grace.'

'Exactly. But you can tell. Their style is ragged chic. They look messy from a distance, but check out the labels of their clothes.'

'Why pretend?'

Kweku shrugged. 'Because it's what's in vogue now. As an ad

person, I cash in on that. It's just beginning, but this will soon be the cool place to live.'

'Cashing in on their lifestyle sounds cold, if you ask me.'

'These things go in waves. Tomorrow, something else will be the hip thing. You think it's wrong to be aspirational? Who knows, one day the aesthetic will be from Ghana.'

'Our little old country? No! Do you really think so?'

'I'm sure of it.'

I looked at the McKibbin lofts. Box-like, with large windows, hemming both sides of the street. They would probably get a lot of light.

Night cloaked us as we walked higher up the street, where we hit a cul-de-sac, and I wasn't sure if we should go left or right.

'Where's the place?'

'Morgan Avenue.'

'I don't know where that is.'

'I thought this was your 'hood.'

'This part has always seemed too industrial for me. And there's a big garbage or recycling centre somewhere over there. You can even smell it. I love wandering, but some places just don't attract me.'

'Remember when we'd visit each other? I once walked all the way to your house from mine. There was a market and a railway line . . .'

'Wasn't the Odaw River there too?'

'Yup! That glorified gutter. There was a footbridge we went over.'

'The memories,' I said.

We took a left and a right and miraculously landed on Morgan Avenue.

'Now, do we go left or right? These buildings don't even have numbers on them.'

'It's your 'hood, you're in charge.'

We chose to go left, and from nowhere, a loud bell tinkled, the sound cutting through the thick night air. Then a blast of light. We stopped, Kweku pressed his palm against the small of my back and we watched as a train came past, a prehistoric machine, moaning, its overhead lights a sharp beam of other-worldliness. The locomotive engine, something out of the early twentieth century, was trailed by graffitied wagons.

'Far out,' he said. 'I wonder where it's going.' I felt like I was in a movie. 'That was so unexpected.'

We arrived at 3rd Ward, the train long gone, the only reminder of its presence the echo of its bell in the distance. In the reception, as I stretched out my hand with my ten-dollar bill, Kweku said, 'I've got this.'

'I've been living here for over a month and didn't know there was this amazing art space here,' I said, then asked how much membership cost.

'Three hundred a month,' said the receptionist, a tongue ring dashing in and out of her mouth as she spoke. If my head could have popped out of my neck, it would have. No wonder I hadn't heard of it. It certainly didn't have *me* in mind. Well, I would make use of all Kweku's hard-earned dollars.

We climbed up the stairs, and another flight, the large glass rectangles of window black with night outside. The open space we arrived in was packed with bodies. Kweku went to get two chairs left in a far-flung corner of the room. A minibar had been set up with cans of PBR. I got us four cans.

'Good thinking,' Kweku said. 'Of course, they had to get the cheapest beer out there.'

We sat in a sea of mostly white bodies, and I wondered how many of them fitted Kweku's description of pretending to be poor. It was impossible to tell. We all looked like we were struggling. Hair losing its dye; clothes that appeared threadbare; T-shirts with giant holes in them. To be honest, Kweku and I were actually the best-dressed people there.

A man walked in in a bathrobe, and I was excited. While I loved drawing the female form, in college I hoped, just once, to be able to ogle a nice male body. It never happened.

The man, his hair hanging limply down his neck, disrobed. If I'd been looking for the kind of muses Leonardo da Vinci worked with, we were miles away from that. Who could forget David's abs, his muscle tone, the sheer power of his body, even in his resting, pensive state. This man looked like he had drunk a few PBRs too many. His legs and arms were skinny, but his gut pushed out. He sat on a block in the middle of the room.

'OK, everybody,' said a bespectacled woman. 'Welcome to Drink and Draw. We hope you brought your pencils and sketchbooks. David over here . . .'

I chuckled loudly. The irony. Kweku smiled and raised his brows at me.

'Tell you later.'

'. . . is gonna do one-minute poses to warm you up. Then we'll move into shapes he'll hold for longer and longer. The beer is free and unlimited. So let's drink and draw!'

David stood on the block and all my judgement melted away. That was what I loved about drawing. The people in the room, their voices, their bodies faded. The exercise became about observation and science and shapes and nobody gave a rat's arse whether the model was good-looking or not. Where had that come from, 'rat's arse'? Probably one of my college teachers. As David did various stretches, I shaded with my pencil, capturing the essence of his shape. He gave me triangles, curves, negative space, and I drew lines, blocked in those forms. When he took a pause, the chatter in the room grew, and the people came back to life. I peered in Kweku's notebook and laughed.

'Hey,' he said. 'This is a judgement-free zone.'

'I'm sure he'll thank you for making his, um, thing larger than life.'

He covered his sketches with both hands. It was funny how we focused on entirely different things. Then he stretched his neck and looked at my sketches.

'Show-off,' he said. I stuck my tongue out at him.

We spent an hour drawing and downing more cans of PBR,

and when we were done, a woman poked me from behind and gave me a sheet.

'Your neck,' she said.

She'd sketched my hair, up in an afro bun, and the lines of my neck. It was long and slender.

'Thank you,' I said. So I wasn't the only one who drew other people's hair. In my new notebook, I'd continued sketching Sam's hair on days when his ponytail was just out of this world. The more stressed he was, the spikier the bun.

That's my neck, said Jamila. *I gave all of you your delicate bones. In my day, we would wear rings of brass that the blacksmith had made and you should have seen how beautiful we were. Zainab, how beautiful you are. That's what that woman is telling you. That's what Kweku wants to tell you. If you would let him.*

'Every time we're together, I feel like a girl hits on me, no?' I said, trying to ignore Jamila's words. 'She liked me, right? The girl who drew my neck.'

'Ha,' he said. 'Everyone thinks you're wonderful.'

I didn't know what to say to him. Thank you? You too? I said nothing, and as we walked out into the Bushwick night air, now cool and quiet, the silence grew loud.

Just say thank you, barked Zeina.

'That was fun,' I said. 'Thank you.'

'Shall we do it again? When I was living in Harlem for undergrad, I walked everywhere. I got to know pretty much the whole of Manhattan. I would love to discover other corners in your neighbourhood and end up at Drink and Draw.'

'And what about *your* neighbourhood?'

'Houses, houses and more houses. If it's where my parents live, you can imagine how bourgeois it is.'

'You never know what suburbanites might be hiding,' I said.

'What do you want to do now?' he asked.

Should we go out to eat? Should I ask him up for tea? Although the last time I'd suggested such a thing, I'd been rejected.

You can do anything since you're a polygamist, said Zeina.

I almost laughed out loud, but she was right. Alex. What if we had a clear shot this time? It would be unfair to Kweku, whom I clearly also liked. But Alex was there first.

We were passing in front of the McKibbin lofts, and the light from the apartment windows floated down onto the street, warm and square.

'I'm kind of tired,' I said, and stretched my arms to the skies.

'Well then, let me get you home and I'll head back to Montgomery, New Jersey, in my Cinderella coach.'

My heart sank when he said that. But I was doing the right thing. I wasn't going to be a polygamist.

'How are your folks?' Kweku asked.

'*Folks?* You make them sound so serious. There are some Americanisms I refuse to accept, and that is one of them.'

He laughed.

'OK, how are Poppie and Mommie?' He had deepened his voice.

'Much better. They're fine. Saw Paapa at graduation, and Mma came last month.'

'Are they good now? I remember when they split up,' he said. He was looking at me with a furrowed brow, as if the divorce had just happened. 'You were distraught in your letters. You filled them with quotes from obscure poets. I'd never heard of most of them.'

'Really? I've buried all of that. They're fine. Better apart than together.'

'He has other children now – I remember you told me.'

'Yes, my half-siblings are growing up so fast. Every time I see photos, I have to take a step back.'

'Your mum didn't remarry?'

'No. I don't think she wants to.' There was half an inch between our bodies as we walked, our arms almost touching. I could feel the heat radiating from him, and yet we remained separate, too scared to acknowledge our attraction, to bridge the space between us.

It's your fault, said Zeina.

Let's leave them, said Jamila. *Maybe she'll change her mind.*

'Your mother,' continued Kweku. 'She'd stare me down whenever she dropped you off at my house.' He stopped and put his hands on his hips. 'She'd stand there like that and glare at me, not saying a word. After she left, if I wanted to try anything, I would see her eyes all around you.'

I laughed. 'I can see her doing that.'

At my door, he reached forward and hugged me.

'I had a great time,' he said.

'Me too,' I said. 'And hey . . . what would you have tried?'

'Oh, you know, the silly games that little girls and boys play.'

I almost said, 'Do you want to come up and play those games?' A part of me began to wish there was no Alex. I had enjoyed spending time just being with Kweku, which wasn't a thing I could say about Alex. But for now, I would not give the old ladies the satisfaction of calling me a polygamist.

Later, I whispered to them, 'I knew it. It's your eyes that are preventing me from finding true love. You've been doing this since I was a child.'

You are doing it all on your own, said Zeina. *Don't blame anyone else. This boy adores you. You ultimately decide for yourself.*

Chapter Thirty-One

Groundnut Soup

For someone who had expressed such an aversion to her man's lifestyle and profession, Mary Grace was spending a lot of time with her investment banker. That weekend, she was going to the Hamptons with him. Mary Grace never let anyone hold her back – why should I sit around and be miserable? I took my sketchbook and drew Jamila. I wanted only her energy over the weekend.

It's good you're listening to me, said Jamila. *Zainab, we are animals. Your city has erased nature with all this metal and brick. Of all three of us, I've spent more time watching nature. I say you should be like the woman spider.*

'What does the woman spider do?' I drew Jamila smoking her pipe and weaving a web.

It's relentless when it's going after what it wants. Yarn by yarn it weaves a web and gets closer and closer to the male. The male runs, but the woman doesn't stop.

'I wouldn't want a man to be like that around me, so why should I be like that?'

Because in the end, you have more to lose when the two of you lie together. So why not go after what YOU want?

I soaked in her words. If the female spider had two male spiders, she would definitely go after both of them, wouldn't she?

All your home training is going down the drain, said Fati.

'Shh,' I said, and then texted Alex. He said he would be in the city over the weekend and we could definitely hang.

Friday? I'll make dinner, I texted.

She's trying to win him through his stomach, said Fati the practical.

It could work, said Jamila the sweet. *If she's spider-like.*

Or go terribly wrong. But we should let her learn things herself, said Zeina the acerbic.

'Doesn't the female spider eat the male when she's done with him?' I said.

Exactly, rasped Jamila.

Saturday? Friday's no good, buzzed my phone.

My insides itched. Of course, I couldn't have everything go my way, but still, it irked me that I couldn't control this situation, even if I had spun my web. Alex was a slippery male spider.

I drew Jamila's big eyes, her thin eyebrows, her plump lips. Her hair threaded to stand proud and radiate from her head so she resembled the sun or a giant female spider. I took my Conté crayon, the one that was brown and made me think of clay, and shaded her in.

Make groundnut soup for him, she suggested.

'I don't know how,' I said.

It's in your bones; just let your fingers guide you.

On Saturday, I went into the Food Bazaar, where I filled my cart with tomatoes, okra, habanero peppers, onions, ginger and garlic. My mother always threw in an eggplant in her soup, so I grabbed one. I went to the breakfast aisle and reached for a jar of peanut butter. In the frozen aisle, the skin on my arms pocked, and I went for chicken thighs. I wasn't about to suffer through hacking a full chicken. I already had rice.

I took a shot of Mary Grace's whisky – which she had told me I could drink whenever I wanted – and dropped it on the floor as libation for the grannies. Then I cleaned the kitchen, now an ancestral laboratory, and washed the chicken thighs and placed them in the IKEA pot Mary Grace and I had now burnt food in many times. On top of the thoroughly scoured chicken, I threw in roughly chopped vegetables and covered them with water, then let the pot simmer. I scooped peanut butter and mixed it with water and sent my fingers into its slippery smoothness. I pressed out lumps, and thought of the sculpture class I'd taken that had us prepare clay from scratch. Food was sculpture. It was art. Why hadn't I approached it that way all this time? I'd treated it as something to be feared. And yet it was so close to my heart.

When the peanut butter was now looking like a brown solution or a failed chemistry experiment, I heated it slowly, stirring it until a golden yellow separated. I added it to the chicken and took out the whole vegetables and blended them. To strain her vegetables back into soup, my mother used a colander she said *her* mother had given her. I pretended my plastic sieve was Fati's colander. I tasted my soup and it was just like my mother's. This was the first time I'd cooked something I was proud of in that kitchen. I let it sit some more and went about cleaning the apartment.

I changed my sheets, fluffed out my pillows.

Whatever happens, said Zeina, *make the best of the situation.*

You could still tell him not to come, said Fati.

You're living, said Jamila. *Everything you need is already in you. When in doubt, just come into the kitchen and remind yourself of this.*

'Thank you,' I said.

I took a jar of shea butter – one of Mma's gifts – and got to work on untwisting my hair.

When the buzzer rang, I jumped. I couldn't get used to its harsh interruption. I was wearing a denim mini skirt, a T-shirt, no bra. I'd thought about going for romantic, but look what happened the last time I did that. This time I should look effortless.

I thought you weren't dressing for your dates any more, said Zeina.

'I'm not dressing *up*,' I said.

Still, I'd put on mascara to make my eyes pop, and lip gloss. My afro floated around my face. He seemed to take forever to come up. I took one last look at the apartment.

He knocked and I drew open the door. He looked freshly shaved, in a white shirt and jeans and hair cropped close to his scalp. He held a bottle of wine. See, grannies, I wanted to shout. I took the wine and set it on the kitchen counter.

He was studying a small photo on the wall that Mary Grace had taken when she was twelve. It was a black and white close-up of an upside down moth. I always thought of vaginas when I looked at it.

I wrapped my arms around him from the back and he clasped his hands over mine. I wanted to trademark that move as the Zainab Move for Shy Girls ®. It was semi-confident, but because you made the first move, you didn't have to see judgement, surprise or whatever other emotion in the other person's eyes. I pressed my nose into his shirt and inhaled his fragrance, a warm vanilla–tobacco blend. He turned around and my lips met his. We kissed frantically. I undid his buttons, then he pulled off my T-shirt. I was glad I'd gone for no-fuss. He pulled off his trousers and picked me up onto the sofa.

'Your room-mate?' he asked.

'Out of town.'

Up my skirt went and the warmth of his tongue slid in and out of me. I was beginning to learn what all the fuss was about. This was heavenly delicious, even though I worried I hadn't shaved well.

We went into my room, to my stash of condoms. Our bodies twisted and bent around each other. We fell off the bed and onto the parquet, making us break into peals of laughter.

I put my T-shirt back on. It would take me a while to get used to being seen naked by someone. Alex seemed comfortable in his skin.

And yet, was that good sex? A lot of acrobatics, yes.

It wasn't good, said one of the grandmothers. Surely Zeina. I was too drunk in my feelings to care.

'Are you hungry?' I asked after the cuddling was becoming a bit too aggressive and we weren't saying anything.

'I've been hungry. You were the one who jumped me. I came for dinner.'

'Fine,' I said, herding him out of the room. He reached for me and pulled me in for a deep kiss.

I heated and dished out the groundnut soup and served it with balls of rice I'd prepared that morning.

'This must be from my cookbook,' he said.

'No, it's my mum's recipe.'

'So you *can* cook!'

'It's ancestral. But I can make you something from the cookbook tomorrow, if you'd like.'

Aargh. Why did I say that? It was too late to take it back. Can you unscramble his brain, grannies? They ignored me.

After we ate, he went to the bathroom, and the grannies finally resurfaced.

Some of those things looked painful, said Zeina. *Are you all right?*

That was tame, said Jamila. *I had this lover, we would go all day. It was too dark at night, where I lived, so we could only meet during the day. Try and ask this one to go again, he'll say he's exhausted.*

She wants him to stay, said Fati. *Although I don't like that he's here. Maybe ask him to watch a filim with you.*

That surprised me. She'd said 'film' the way all my extended family back home pronounced it. Two syllables. The other grannies probably didn't even know what that was.

He came out of the bathroom fully dressed, with shoes on. He didn't look like a person about to spend the night, and I didn't want to be rejected, so Fati's suggestion would have to wait for another day.

'Thanks for coming,' I said, swallowing the gulp that had filled my throat.

'It was fun,' he said, and smacked my bum. 'We do it again soon?'

'Yes,' I said, tamping down the rising disappointment.

After he left, I slid down the side of the sofa. Why did I feel so empty? If Mary Grace were here, she would baptise it: it was plain and simply a booty call.

Because you need a fence around you, said Fati. *You don't like things open.*

And that is a man who plans to be as wide open as you will let him, said Zeina.

You could keep one for the body, and the other for the heart, suggested Jamila. *But juggling is not for the faint-hearted.*

Chapter Thirty-Two

Jazefa and Poems

Sam called me into his office. I summoned all the positive energy I could. Maybe I could steer the outcome to what I wanted just by being chipper and thinking good thoughts. After almost three months of being in New York, my boy-starved self had calmed down. I was no longer smitten by everyone who came my way. I'd grown used to Sam's face and quirks, and still found him interesting to look at, but he no longer made me hold my breath as he had those first days. He had shaped nicely into the role of boss-friend. A boss I could hang out with.

'So, I spoke to Donna from HR and really tried to put in a good word for you,' he said, untying his ponytail. His black hair hung just past his clavicles. 'But we just don't sponsor.'

My heart ached. For something I had already anticipated, why did it still hurt?

Rejection always hurts, said Zeina.

'The best we can do is you come back for an internship after grad school and maybe something would have changed by then?'

'Thank you,' I said.

'I really wish there was some loophole we could work around,' he said, 'but Donna says since 9/11 things have gotten strict.'

Back at my desk, I wiped away the tears that had made their way out of my eyes and checked my email. Uncle Ali had written. I had my very first non-doctored agony aunt letter to respond to.

Do your work, chided Fati.

I quickly read over the letter:

Dear Aunty Jazefa,

My husband is a respected member of the Ghanaian community. And yet he's having an affair with another woman. I'm at my wits' end. I've tried everything to make him stop straying. And I mean everything – buying lingerie, threatening to leave him or to expose him, visiting the juju man. What should I do? I truly do not want to leave him. We have four children together.

Yours,

Cheated on in the Bronx

How would I advise this woman? I thought as I went about my work. This was a tough one. Grannies?

When we get home, they said.

Sam came to my cubicle, and I started.

'Oops,' he said, holding an envelope. 'Didn't mean to startle you. It's just that I almost forgot. This Friday, I'll be reading some poems. Bring as many peeps as you can. It's only three bucks to get in.'

Maybe if I showed what a team sport I was, Sam would look through all the legalese and find that loophole he'd mentioned.

The bar was named after an infamous Russian intelligence agency, and had been decorated in red and yellow with hammers and sickles. It was surprisingly packed. I didn't know Sam could pull in a crowd like that. But then again, just because we worked together didn't mean I knew a thing about him. My only intel on him was that he had a girlfriend. I wondered who she might be in the row of girls sitting in front. Who was the most eager beaver? If they'd been together for a long time, she probably wouldn't even be interested any more. She would be able to recite all his poems, which she either loved or was sick to death of.

Eish, you're such a cynic, said Fati.

Just like her namesake, said Jamila.

Densua was already there, on her own, not tucked in Edward's armpit.

'Wow, I thought you'd be the last to arrive,' I said, hugging her. 'Where's Edward?'

'All my bosses are away – yes, even him – and so I am breathing,' she said.

'Everything all right with you two?'

'Living together is hard papa. Like, just pick up the clothes and put them on the hook. Anyway, I'm not being discreet. He's fine.'

This was the first time Densua was opening up to me about *any* relationship, and if she was talking about a benign thing, it must have meant there was more going under the surface of her ocean. I had to tread carefully. Say the wrong thing and she would clam up. So I decided to give her the television reporter's calm pursed-lip look. Uh huh, keep going.

'I'll be fine too. I need to learn to let some things go.'

And just like that, the conversation was shut down, placed in a padlocked treasure chest and thrown into the deep murky sea of Densua's mind.

The poets went on stage one by one. At the third poet's turn, I felt a hand on my shoulder. I turned and it was Mary Grace, now blonde. When had she found the time to do that? This morning, she was still red-haired. I had to get used to her face all over again. She looked even darker with the blonde hair and was incredibly striking. I was sure she'd turned many heads on her way to me. She passed me a bottle of beer. I had already downed one. She waved at Densua.

'I need to pee,' I said, passing the bottle back to Mary Grace. 'Be right back.'

I got up and walked through the crowd now spilling into the back. Who knew poetry would have such a draw?

It was almost as if I felt him before I saw him, because every part of me froze, except for my heart, which I could almost hear beating in the cave of my ears. I definitely saw him first, and didn't move until he'd locked eyes with me. He had an arm hooked in another person's arm. A woman's arm. She was even blonder than Mary Grace. There was lipstick on his T-shirt.

There was low lighting in the room, but I could see the lipstick. It was dark and unmissable. How did lipstick end up on a person's shoulder unless planted there intentionally? How did a city of eight million people manage to feel so small? I don't know if I waved first or if he waved first. But hands went up and then went down and then my feet carried me to the bathroom, where I couldn't keep my fingers sturdy enough to open the door, but I managed to still go in there and pee and then somehow I was back with Mary Grace.

'Alex is here with another woman,' I whispered.

'No way,' she said. 'What an asshole. Did you talk to him?'

'I think . . .'

Sam was about to go on. I really wanted to see him, but I didn't feel good, like the beer in my stomach would come up. I hadn't eaten, had I? Sam was on stage. He clutched the microphone and lowered his head so his mouth was close to the foam.

'Wow! Give it up for Richard, Amara and Janet! Hard acts to follow. I just want to say a big thank you to our hosts for tonight . . .'

He thanked an eternal list of people and my belly churned and I wanted to leave, but I had to see him perform at least one poem. That one poem opened the floodgates. I couldn't even tell if it was good or not. It just made me feel sicker.

'The day we met, a string of birds stroked the sky. There was one, a straggler like me. You were at the head, pulling, commanding the shapes of the other birds. Except for me. I couldn't keep up. But it was why, you told me later, it was why you liked me. I moved to my own rhythm. You went for me because you couldn't control me . . .'

It was saccharine.

'I think I'm going to throw up,' I said to Mary Grace. I couldn't take any more. That Alex was in the same room as me but that another woman was in the space I thought was mine was suffocating.

'Let's get some air,' said Mary Grace.

'What's going on?' asked Densua. Mary Grace must have

signalled to her, because all three of us went outside and up the stairs into the pale orange light of evening.

'I stuck a middle finger up at the asshole,' said Mary Grace.

'Can someone please tell me what is going on?' said Densua. 'I'm so lost.'

'The guy Zainab was seeing is here with another woman.'

I couldn't look up. I was studying my feet.

'Men are awful,' said Densua, and then I raised my head and saw her look at me with what I was sure was sympathy or love.

'Let's walk,' said Mary Grace, and the two of them took my arms. I felt cocooned and safe and taken care of, and yet I still wanted to cry and crawl into my bed. At least I had friends who loved me.

'Fries?' said Mary Grace as we walked in front of the Belgian fry place where I'd gone with her, Seth and his friends earlier in the summer.

'I'll vomit,' I said.

'Ah ah, Zainab! That was unnecessarily graphic,' chided Densua.

'I need to sit,' I said. I didn't know what to do with myself. Every pore in my body burnt with rage and sadness.

We walked till we were at a small park I'd never visited, and there we sat on a bench and watched people walking their dogs, others pushing shopping carts containing their entire lives, and couples kissing. My heart hurt.

'Where are we?' I asked, in spite of how I was feeling. The *flâneuse* in me still wanted to know exactly where I was in the city.

'Tompkins Square Park,' said Mary Grace.

'Listen,' said Densua. 'It hurts now, and let yourself cry. Tomorrow you start again and find the right person for you.'

What did *she* know about heartache? She'd never shared. But I nodded.

'I love you guys,' I said, and burst into tears.

Chapter Thirty-Three

Ladies' Night

Densua and Mary Grace got me home and into bed. They went out of the room, then Densua came back in to hug me.

'We're going out tomorrow, all three of us. Dancing.'

'I don't want to.'

'It's not optional.'

'Okaaay,' I said, and buried my head under my pillow.

I heard the door shut and then I was left with myself.

Except I wasn't.

Get rest, Jamila said.

I closed my eyes and all I could see was Alex holding that other woman's arm. The lipstick on his T-shirt. Him kissing me right here on this bed. They were so comfortable with each other, he and the woman. Was *I* the other woman? If they were out at a poetry show, she was the accepted, visible one. He had come here to hide. We hadn't gone anywhere; in fact he had been all too enthusiastic about coming here and me cooking for him. It was beginning to add up. Had he used me? Or had he felt sorry for me? Or did he like me and was simply torn between two people? The questions wouldn't stop. I had wanted to have him for his body – was that what Jamila had suggested? Well, I didn't know how to separate the heart from the body. It just hurt so badly.

The grannies hummed me a song. One my mother had sung when I was little. Their voices, a mix of gravelly, sweet and a huskiness that poured from Zeina, were balm to my itching heart. I thought I wouldn't be going through this again soon, but it was my own fault. I'd had to learn the hard way.

I slept and woke up and the light forced my eyelids open. My body felt heavy on the bed and I understood the full weight of the expression 'hit by a truck'. How could something so emotional have such a physical effect?

Outside my room, the apartment smelt like bacon frying.

'Your favourite thing in the world,' said Mary Grace. 'I have to go in to the restaurant now, but when I come back, we're doing happy hour with Densua and then dancing, OK? But eat this in the meantime.'

'I don't feel like eating, I don't feel like dancing.'

Mary Grace's blonde hair brushed past her shoulders down to her back.

'Why did you change your hair?'

'Because I love Marilyn Monroe.' This didn't surprise me. 'She wasn't a blonde, but she became one. I love people who choose to design their lives. Freddie Mercury. Prince. I could go on. But more than just the surface stuff. When Ella Fitzgerald wasn't being allowed into clubs because of her skin colour, Marilyn said if they'd let Ella sing, she'd come and sit in the front row. She was badass. So what's stopping you from creating your own life?'

'Because my ancestors are heavy on my back,' I said. 'They would talk the nonsense right out of me.'

'We all have those.'

'Trust me, not like I do.'

'OK, I'll help you shed some of that weight.'

We aren't easy to throw away, oh, said Fati.

'Tell me. What's the craziest thing you've ever wanted to do?'

'I don't know . . . Murder Alex?'

'That I'll do for you. But seriously, tell me . . .'

'Bungee jump?'

'You should do it!'

'I don't have insurance yet.'

'OK, something within reason.'

I thought of my dream of tagging a wall in New York City with my work, but it reminded me of Alex. Ugh. I needed to think of something else.

'Maybe getting high?'

'Done!' said Mary Grace. 'OK, so let's change plans. You and Densua come pick me up at the restaurant, and Jay will hook us up. I'm so excited to pop your smoking cherry. Then we'll go dancing. I'm like your virginity midwife or something.'

That made me laugh.

I took the plate of bacon she'd extended and tried to eat it, but my mind–body connection was too powerful. I had barely even put a piece in my mouth and I was already gagging.

'I'll try later,' I said.

I managed to eat the bacon later that day, mixed with fried eggs and leftover white rice. I cleared away the mountain of dishes in the dish rack. I scrubbed the rack clean, including the corners where slimy black gunk had accumulated. I scoured the work surface of the kitchen, trying to rid my mind of thoughts and grandmothers' opinions. I moved over to the bathroom, the drain clogged with Mary Grace's new blonde hair. When every bit of the apartment was clean, and the evening began to swallow the light of day, I willed myself to take a bath. I filled the tub with water and plopped in globs of shower gel. I dipped my body into the lukewarm water and felt myself finally relax. I thought of the future I'd begun to paint with Alex and what a silly little girl I'd been. The doorbell rang, forcing me to slosh out of the tub. I stared ruefully at the water, wishing I could have just stayed in it all evening.

Densua came up dressed in a floral summer dress. Her hair hung down to her shoulders.

'You know I'm not going anywhere,' I told her, wrapping my towel tightly around my body.

'Trust me, we all need this outing. Or at least I do. I have to go in to work tomorrow. Sunday work annoys me the most. I need to dance my butt off. For me?'

I would do it for Densua. If I couldn't summon the energy to do it for myself, I would try to do it for my friend. I put on a pair of jeans and a T-shirt and Densua sent me right back to my room to change. I wouldn't remove my jeans and there was nothing she could say about that, but I switched into an asymmetrical blouse that showed off my shoulders.

It took immense kilowatts of energy to push myself out of the house and onto the G. We got off at Mary Grace's restaurant and I had a sudden appreciation for Mary Grace. She was a child of privilege, but she was still working in an unglamorous job and making enough money to maintain her independence. We stepped inside the restaurant, buzzing with patrons, and I spotted her talking to a couple in the back.

'We're friends of Mary Grace,' said Densua to the barista.

'Ah yes, she told me you'd be coming. Is the bar OK?'

Densua nodded but hummed under her breath, 'Are we not good enough for a table?'

'I like sitting at bars,' I said. 'I want to get drunk at the bar. Cry my sorrows away to the bartender.'

The bar in question was simple, with modern light fixtures and metallic design. We sat across from a bartender who looked like a teenage boy, and I wondered if he, like me, had found way to cheat the system. If I poured my heart out to him, he looked like he'd start crying with me.

'Mary Grace's friends!' he croaked. 'I'm Jay. What can I start you with?'

'Red wine, please,' I said, unsure who was going to be footing the bill. Densua? Mary Grace? In any case, I could nurse a glass of wine the whole night. My skills had grown impeccable.

'Please make that two.' Densua stretched out her card.

Jay shook his head. 'First round is on us.'

'Thank you,' I said. 'Alcoholic healing, here we come.'

'I'm moving back to Tudor City,' Densua said. Her tone was flat, matter-of-fact, as if she were continuing a conversation we'd started.

'Oh,' I said. 'What happened?'

'You inspired me,' she said.

How had heartbroken little me been able to do such a thing? I wanted to hear more, but I knew how easily Densua retreated into that hard snail shell of hers. One had to go molo molo, like my art teacher used to say.

'You've been here only a summer, and you're already living more than I ever have,' she went on. 'You're not letting old ideas of who you should be stop you from doing what your heart wants. Like, I admire how you're hurting not because you've lost a potential future husband but because you just wanted to have good sex.'

My eyes were ready to pop out of my head. Had I said something the other day? Did sadness intoxicate the way alcohol did?

'Wait, what?' I said. 'Did I actually say those words to you?'

'Mary Grace told me.'

I looked behind me at my big-mouthed fake-blonde-haired traitor of a room-mate. There were parts of myself that Mary Grace knew about that I couldn't reveal to Densua, as much as I wanted to. But why divide myself into compartments? A year or so before, I had read a book that talked about the horcrux as a way to achieve immortality, by hacking one's soul into pieces that would eventually be stored in different objects. I was one fragmented person: the way my parents saw me was definitely not the way I saw myself; the way I presented myself to Mary Grace was worlds away from how I'd made myself appear to Densua. Did we all do this? Or were there people who were integral, wholly, truly their own selves regardless of who they were presenting themselves to? Mary Grace tried, but I'd seen her in that store at the beginning of the summer, with her mother's friend. She was a saint when she was with fellow Filipinos. Could I be that person who was truly herself no matter what? Who was that person anyway? I was only beginning to learn. And then add in my grandmothers!

'You weren't shocked to hear that?' I finally said.

'At first I was. You know your room-mate has no filter. She didn't even say sex. She dropped the F bomb. So that threw me off. I can't imagine you even using the word.'

'Yes, that was a hundred per cent Mary Grace.'

Jay, the young bartender, set out a dish before us plated with olives, wedges of cheese and chunks of chorizo. At first I didn't even want to touch them, but my hands had more control over me than I realised, because before I knew it, the wood of a toothpick was firmly squashed between my fingers, and then a piece of cured meat was heading into my mouth. I savoured the heat of the chorizo and took another. My finger–mouth connection was proving stronger than my mind–body connection.

'So anyway,' Densua said, pushing a piece of cheese between her teeth and then talking with her mouth full, 'I kept hearing my mother's voice saying, "You girls should get married oh. Don't do book long and end up alone." '

'But Aunty Jane has been saying that since even before we got our periods.'

'She wasn't joking. So when Edward came along, he seemed to check all the boxes. I was ready for him to pop the question, even though I'm only twenty-two, to the point that I was willing to ignore the warning signs. Not long after we started dating, he cussed out a waiter because he thought the man had pocketed his change. Turns out *he*, Edward, was in the wrong. His apology was flippant, but I was all in love, so I didn't even call him out on it. Then just last week, I had a different opinion from him on General Motors stock, and the man threw a plate at me – just because I didn't agree with him.'

I gasped out loud. 'No, Densua.'

She nodded, then choked on her words. 'He missed. And don't worry, I'm not going to be the woman who stays till it's too late. I won't be that woman you hear about on the local news. You know I didn't have a TV at Tudor City, so I never watched local news, but now that I'm at Edward's, on rare late nights I turn on the TV, and it's so gruesome. It makes New York sound scary.'

'Yes, Uncle Ali's wife was always watching that stuff. I'm so sorry to hear this, Densua.'

'I don't know why women do this to themselves and to their

daughters. Absorb all this pressure. Maybe it's a lot more complicated for some. I see my mother, and she would be much happier without my father, who just lords it over her. And yet I was about to make the same mistake. Let's promise each other we are going to live our lives fully and not depend on men to complete us.'

'Here's to not repeating the mistakes of our ancestors,' I said, raising my glass.

'You and this ancestor business,' said Densua. 'The ancestors lived. Now, it's our turn. Our world is nothing like theirs.'

This one doesn't know anything, said Zeina.

You really should learn from us, said Fati.

Oh, they are right, said Jamila. *The sweet girls.*

She sounded drunk. When I offered them libation, I suspected Jamila was the one who lapped it all up. I was sure Mma Fati didn't touch a drop of it.

Mary Grace appeared with a plate.

'Everyone in the kitchen knows my friends are here, so you people are getting spoilt rotten. Here's a Spanish tortilla, some padrón peppers and Iberian jamón.'

I took the peppers, and their seared heat woke me up.

'This is really good,' I said to Mary Grace.

'I told you, every night we run out. That's why I never have leftovers. *Buen provecho!*'

'*Gracias!*' I said.

Jay the bartender poured us another glass of wine each. Mary Grace brought us more little plates of food. We ate different types of open-faced sandwiches, each with layers of flavour and cured meats.

'I'm just going to take my things quietly and move out,' Densua said. 'He doesn't even deserve to know I'm leaving. I'm still friends with the management at Tudor City. Today, I put down the deposit for a studio.'

'You don't think he'll find you?'

She shook her head.

'Silly question,' I said. 'What did you do with all your stuff?

Like your bed? It seems like a lot of work to be moving back and forth.'

'Girl, the place in Tudor City already had a bed. When I moved to New York, one of the Mount Holyoke seniors told me, your first two years as an analyst, focus one hundred per cent on work. She said, find a furnished apartment right next to work, even if it costs a bit of money. You work hard, you'll get a huge bonus that will buy you all the furniture you need later in life.'

'Gotcha,' I said. It must have been nice to be able to afford such luxury.

'The guy is most certainly an alcoholic,' Densua was now saying. I had wound open a tap that didn't want to be closed. 'Says his job is stressful. Who doesn't have a stressful job? Every day downing shots of whisky . . . and then getting aggressive for next to nothing. But you, Zainab, thank you. I was doing something that went against everything I stand for and believe in, just to please people back home, traditions, I don't know what. I have to go back to being true to me.' She reached forward and planted a kiss on my forehead.

Her words were beginning to roll together. I would have to slow down my drinking. At least one of us had to be sober. It would be horrible for Mary Grace to find us both sloshed.

Densua grew even more confessional, revealing how she would send her mother money to help her run her business back in Ghana because her father was too stingy. It was why she worked even harder than the average investment banking analyst. She couldn't afford not to make her bonus. Suddenly, me and my lack of responsibilities were given a reality check. There was Mary Grace, whose family could take care of her and yet she held a job; and there was Densua, who was supporting her family. I could do better on all fronts.

By the time Mary Grace sat down with us and tucked into her dinner, it was well past midnight.

'Sorry, ladies,' she said. 'I thought tonight's shift would end earlier, but as you saw, a lot of people turned up.'

'This,' slurred Densua, 'is better than some random bar or club. Your restaurant is amazing. Zainab, this place is nice papa. We have to come back.'

We were served a plate of mini flan, an almond cake and the creamiest crème brûlée I had ever tasted. I said so.

'Crema catalana,' corrected Mary Grace. 'We're a Spanish restaurant.'

Densua opened her purse and began to rummage through it. Mary Grace put her hand on Densua's.

'My treat.'

'Then let me at least tip this handsome gentleman,' said Densua.

'I'll tip too,' I said, resolutely reaching for a ten-dollar bill. This wasn't the slow reach I'd been doing all summer long.

'You are too kind,' said Jay, ruffling his hair.

'Ah, before I forget,' Mary Grace said, dipping into her apron pocket. 'Thanks to Jay over here . . .' She spun a thick joint between her fingers, quickly waved it at me, then slipped it back into the pocket.

'I'm fine,' I said, shaking my head. 'Maybe one day, but today you guys have given me all the healing I needed. Thank you.'

'We can still go dancing,' Densua piped up, oblivious to what we were talking about.

'Let's go home,' I said. 'Tomorrow I'll introduce you to cuchifritos, the best hangover breakfast in the world.'

Mary Grace hailed a cab and the three of us got into its belly.

'Good evening,' said the driver, and from the inflections of his greeting, I knew right away he was one of mine. Do I be true or do I pretend?

'*Ete sen?*' I asked him.

'Oh, fine, fine! Thank you! The body is fine, ohemaa.' I couldn't see his eyes, not even in the rear-view mirror, as dark as it was, but he was beaming from the inside out. 'And your sister, she's OK?'

'Yes, just a little tired.' I rested Densua's head on my shoulder.

'I'm also from Ghana,' said Mary Grace, forcing a Ghanaian accent out of her throat. The driver guffawed.

'Then I have three Ghanaian queens in my car,' he said. 'I am a very lucky man.'

We arrived at our apartment and I changed Densua into a T-shirt and tucked her into bed. Mary Grace was already in her room. I sat on the sofa and soaked. The night had been unexpected. Magical, almost. Energising. I sketched down ideas for the book about Zainab and her ancestors, and drew the scene involving Alex and his girlfriend. It teased back my sadness and I curled into myself. Had I liked him that much? Or was my ego bruised and smarting from being rejected? It was somewhat worse than being rejected. I'd been strung along like a rag doll in the dirt. If I could squeeze myself into a knot of flesh, maybe I could force out the pain like a bubble. Pop.

Zeina has something to say to you, whispered Jamila.

'What?' I said.

Zeina was quiet. All I heard was the train rumbling a few blocks away. Zeina stayed mum.

Chapter Thirty-Four

Zeina's Story

Tell her, insisted Jamila.

There are some things the past should keep buried, said Zeina.

Even I don't know what they are talking about, said Fati.

Take your pencil, Zeina said.

They quietened down, and after a long silence, Zeina had me sketch her village. An oasis in a sea of brown sand. I drew two girls in a room, sitting on a thin mat, staring at each other. I couldn't tell who was who, but I was sure one of them was my relation from the shape of her long bones. I sketched them holding each other's hands, tears running down their faces. I took another sheet. One reached out and wiped the tears off the other's face.

Zeina had me draw sheet after sheet, until I had a few drawings done. I went back to the beginning and she filled in the dialogue.

'Go to Mopti,' said the one who did the wiping. 'It's better this way. Go with him. We'll always have each other in here.' She pressed her hand to her heart.

Fati was born in Burkina Faso, so that couldn't be Zeina who was going away to Mopti, in Mali. She was the one speaking. She looked almost like me. Very slim, with tightly coiled hair combed out in an afro.

'We can't keep sneaking away and doing this. I'm now married and you should get married too,' she continued.

'We love each other,' said the other girl, speaking for the first time.

'Love is not enough. I don't want you to stay. Take the man's dowry and go with him to Mopti. Go!'

The other girl left Zeina sitting alone in the hut, and when Zeina was sure the girl was not coming back, her shoulders quaked and she broke down in tears.

'I'm confused,' I said.

Zeina and this girl were lovers for a long time, said Jamila, after Zeina didn't respond. *She didn't know I had seen them, but they did everything together. It was more than friendship. It was two people who never wanted to be apart. Even after Zeina got married, they kept their friendship. When the girl was offered kola nuts by another family, she told Zeina she would turn them down. She wanted to remain free. But for some reason, Zeina wouldn't have it. And that's what happened – what you saw. After the other girl left, Zeina didn't eat for days.*

Every time I saw them go into a hut, I did everything to make sure no one else knew they were there. The times were already changing. In my childhood, they would have been left alone, but I knew if the men in the village got a sniff of what they were doing, they would be deeply embarrassed or even hurt.

'Zeina?'

I don't want to talk about it, she said. *I moved on. Gave birth to Fati.*

I didn't know this about my own mother, said Fati.

When the other girl died – in childbirth a few years later – the news came back to our village, said Jamila. *Not long after that, we lost Zeina, too. Some people are just born to follow each other. And not everyone gets to have a love like that.*

I didn't want to know how Zeina had died. I was too scared to hear that she had taken her own life. I wondered what my mother would make of this story. She would think me entirely batty if I told her I knew the secrets of my grandmothers. What were they trying to tell me with this story? If I compared the two men in my life, neither of them had given me the kind of bond Zeina and her friend had had. Or at least not yet. Alex was nowhere close to giving me that kind of friendship. But Kweku and I, we already had a bit of that.

'What are you telling me?' I asked out loud.

Many things. One of them is that the sadness and loneliness you sometimes feel came from a long time ago, said Jamila. *We keep passing on these things, unless we wake up and stop sending them down.*

I also think my mother and grandmother are telling you that you came to this city to be free, said Fati.

And you'll know a good thing when it's in front of you, concluded Zeina.

Their words were a lot to think about. Instead, I picked up the still unanswered agony letter for Uncle Ali's paper. Zeina said the woman whose husband was cheating on her should cut the man's organ. Jamila said she should start seeing another person. Fati said our societies were polygamous, so she should just accept things the way they were or tell her husband to marry the other woman.

None of their answers was satisfactory, but they had given me a bone . . . Sometimes, one just needed to talk.

Dear Cheated on in the Bronx,

I am so sorry to hear your dear husband is straying from your marriage. After being married for so long, sometimes feelings fade and one party looks outside the marriage for a spark or for excitement. In everything you tried, you didn't mention that you have talked to him. The first step is to open up lines of communication. Tell him how you feel. Then do some work on yourself – you might have to shape the way your marriage is differently. Either you are both allowed to go outside the marriage, you go your separate ways (amicably or otherwise) or you work your way into finding each other again. Should you decide on the last method, several marriage counsellors are available in New York City.

Yours,
Aunty Jazefa

Chapter Thirty-Five

Pitching the Grandmothers

Kweku rode down in the elevator and came to my desk. He was standing in the spot usually reserved for Sam, and at first, I was embarrassed, because our office didn't exude the bright sunshiny finish of his office upstairs. But then, I thought, so what?

'Long time no see,' he said, adjusting the cap on his head. 'I'm beginning to think I have bad breath or BO or something you didn't want to tell me about. Like maybe you don't like that I wear caps.' He tilted the peak forward.

'Oh no, Kweku,' I said. 'Was just dealing with drama.'

'Not drama with Mary Grace, I hope.'

'No. Let's just call it growing pains.'

He looked at me and my belly dipped. Why hadn't I made space for him all summer long?

'Well, if there's any way I can help, let me know.'

'That's kind, thank you. To what do I owe this visit?'

'Mum's legendary barbecue is this weekend, and she asked me to personally deliver the invitation. Since I let it slip that we've been hanging out, she hasn't given me any peace. I've been told I'm picking you up from the train station.'

'It sounds like this is an invitation I can't turn down.'

'Nope. And if you don't come to the Princeton train station, I'm sure she'll send me all the way to your doorstep to come get you. You know she's always liked you better than her own children. "Zainab Sekyi is so well brought up" and Zainab Sekyi that. I liked you, but it was too much being compared to you all the time.'

All my good training paid off, beamed Fati.

'Please invite Densua and Mary Grace.'

No, whispered Zeina. *This one is for you alone.*

'OK,' I said. I would decide for myself later.

That brief interaction with Kweku left me feeling warm – not flushed like with Alex, but a good warmth. Similar to the sun in Accra – always there, yes, sometimes a bit too hot, but reliable. Alex's heat was like New York's heat. Short, intense and totally unbearable.

I thought of Kweku's words: *I liked you* . . . Why did he use past tense?

I took my sketchbook and studied the drawings I had worked on over the weekend. I had drawn the scene in the poetry bar. Sam was on stage, with a bubble of his poetry, and my avatar was standing across from Alex, his lipstick-smacked T-shirt and his girlfriend. My eyes were welling over. My grandmothers appeared in the next frame, their fists covered in boxing gloves and wearing high-waisted shorts.

'When he goes into the bathroom, POW, we'll knock him out,' read the speech bubble coming from their collective mouths.

'Better yet,' said Zeina in the next frame, 'a hex on his descendants. No more beautiful children after this Alex boy. They will all suffer bad skin.'

'We can't do that,' said Fati, her boxing gloves on her hips.

'She was just trying,' said Jamila, a glove scratching the scalp under her star-shaped head wrap. 'What can we do?'

'Cloak our girl in love.'

The grandmothers surrounded my avatar. In the next slide, Zeina stuck a leg out and tripped Alex as he and his woman left the bar. Alex stood up and looked around at the empty air around him.

I closed the sketchbook, got off my seat and knocked on Sam's door.

'Zainab!' he said. 'Did you like my show?'

'It was dope,' I said. *Dope?* What did that even mean, and from whom had I picked it up?

Alex, volunteered Zeina.

'Can I show you something, Sam?'

'Sure!'

'So, I have an idea for a graphic novel. Um, it's about a girl called Zainab who comes to New York City, and her baggage is literally her ancestors. Her grandmother, great-grandmother and great-great-grandmother help her navigate New York's dating scene. Like this is one of them.'

I showed him the frames.

'Did this really happen?' Sam asked. 'Or is it imagined?'

'Which part? My ancestors protecting me? Or the douchebag?'

'That you got treated badly at my show?'

'I'm over it. And it was my own fault. I should have listened to the signs. They were there all along.'

'I'm so sorry, Zainab. Welcome to New York City's dating nightmare.'

'Tell me about it. Listen, I know Altogether Media can't sponsor my visa, but maybe when I finish this, you can buy my work or something?'

'The conceit is amazing. I love the grandmothers – they are so realistic, and we can tell they're Zainab's family. You could be on to something big. I think the way you deliver the story could do with some honing, but you're definitely on the right track.'

'Yes, this is just a draft.'

'Like, after the one grandmother trips the asshole, the other could kick him in the butt. Play up the absurdity and stretch things out. They could have a whole scuffle. Then in the next slide, there's no one by him and the girl is looking at him like he's lost his mind, because he's saying someone pushed him and hit him. "There's no one here," she'll say. The cool thing about the graphic novel is you can do so much with it. Don't even think in frames and panels. Tell you what: keep at it in grad school; that's why you're going there. Refine your art, work on it over and over again and come back to me. Don't go to the next guy. I mean it, Zainab, you can email or call whenever to show me your progress. When it's good and ready, we'll get it out there.'

'Thank you, Sam,' I said. 'Don't pretend you don't know me when I call you in three months.'

I clutched my book to my heart. I had finally done it.

Good girl, said the grandmothers.

My phone buzzed when I went back to my seat.

I'm so sorry about the poetry show. It was a big misunderstanding. I'd like to make it up to you. Tell me when I can call you.

Throw his number away, ordered Zeina.

I did just that. Delete. Then I wished I hadn't been so hasty. I should first have texted him, 'Get lost', with a bunch of expletives, Mary Grace style, before deleting the number. But it was too late. In any case, I felt good. I had taken back control of my life.

Chapter Thirty-Six
Quiet

I sat in a car of the New Jersey Transit train, the smell of its faux-leather seats invading my nostrils. In the tunnel heading out, I didn't know what I'd see on the other side. Living in New York for the summer had felt like an entire lifetime. Apart from going to IKEA, this was my first trip outside since arriving. The train groaned on its tracks and I looked out the window. Across from me was an older black woman. I'd chosen to sit there because she looked nice and she reminded me of my drawing of Jamila.

'Honey,' she said. 'Your skin is gorgeous. Oooh chile!'

'Thank you,' I said.

'My mother had skin like that and people made her feel bad for it. I mean, the world is upside down. She had the skin of a queen, and yet . . .'

I was beginning to regret my choice. I looked about me. A few others were scattered in the car. Why was I suddenly uncomfortable?

Even though she's a stranger, be kind to her, said Jamila. *I lost family who ended up in this land. A lot of people like her are lonely because of things that happened a long, long time ago. We are one and the same family. It's the same blood. Listen to her.*

'. . . she did everything to make sure we could be lighter,' said the woman. 'To be able to get into places. If our hair was coiled too tightly, she would press the kinky right on out of there.' She wiped her eyes.

'I'm sorry,' I said. 'I'm sorry we did this to you. To each other.'

'Aww, sweet baby girl, don't be sorry. Just wear your skin and your hair proud as you already are.'

She looked outside the window. Narrow towers shooting smog and industrial roofing zigzagged by; the drab brick walls and soot-covered windows of factories shot past, and yet patches of green still managed to push through the blight. The woman got off at the first stop and was replaced by two white men in football jerseys, their basketball caps turned backwards. I missed the woman already.

Dude, dude, dude, they peppered every single one of their sentences. It hurt me that America watered these two and did everything to pluck out the other woman as a weed. This woman or her ancestors was the very reason I could be sitting in a car like this and was being ignored by the two dudes. Only some decades before, it would have been dangerous for me. These were the sobering thoughts with which I arrived at the Princeton train station, where Kweku was waiting for me in a shiny black Mercedes. My heart did a flip. Bright thoughts swept away the sad ones. I was genuinely happy to see him.

His parents' house was colonnaded and at the end of a U-shaped driveway. It was palatial – the same word he'd used to describe my apartment. This was what my Uncle Ali wished he could have had. Now I understood why Kweku still lived at home.

'I would never move out of here either.' I shoved Kweku as the wheels of his mum's car ground to a stop.

'I'm actually planning on getting a place in Brooklyn, or back in Harlem. You just saw how long it takes to get here. The commute is killing me.'

'You're crazy, I would suck it up and keep living here.'

'Says the person who moved from the Bronx because of the long-ass train ride?'

'It was my crazy cousins that broke me.'

We got out and the aroma of grilled meat welcomed us. The faint sound of voices wafted over. We went into a large living room, where highlife blasted in from the outside, which was a large well-shorn lawn on which garden chairs had been arranged.

'You could even have a pool if you wanted,' I whispered.

Some uncles and aunties were sitting around in the living room, Ghana-style, waiting to be served.

'Kweku,' an aunt called. 'My Guinness must be cold by now.'

'Yes, Aunty,' he said and signalled at me to follow him. We went through a white door into a steaming kitchen. 'Mum, look who is here.'

'Ohhh, my darling,' said Kweku's mother, wrapping me in the folds of her boubou. She didn't look like she had aged one bit since the days she would pull up in the school's cramped driveway to pick him up in her Audi. 'But you're a woman now. And so beautiful. No wonder this one is so smitten.'

'Mum,' Kweku groaned, and opened the fridge. He took out a bottle of Guinness.

'Ei, you'd better put that thing on a tray with a napkin or Aunty Sophie will be sending you back,' his mother said. 'How's your mother?'

'She is well, Aunty Kim. She came to visit last month.'

'I would have loved to see her. But do you ever put on weight?!' she asked, hands on my hips. Ghanaians adored commenting on the flesh on people's bones.

She went back to stirring a giant pot of jollof and my mouth watered. I hadn't eaten breakfast because I came prepared to stuff my belly.

'Anyway, enjoy your body now,' she concluded. 'When you have children, everything will fill out.'

Kweku came back in and rolled his eyes,

'Uncle Mante also wants a Guinness.'

'He likes it straight from the bottle,' said Aunty Kim.

It was fascinating how Kweku's mother, a big deal of a lawyer – probably why they were able to live in this place – still had the brain space to know exactly how each of her family members liked their drinks. I was really in awe of how mothers managed to keep it all together. I liked that Kweku was the one going up and down doing the serving, not his little sister.

'What are you drinking?' Aunty Kim asked me.

'Juice, please.'

'We have apple, pineapple or guava.'

'Guava, please.'

I was sure by the end of the day I'd have said so many pleases that my stock of the word would have diminished. Kweku came back in and led me by the arm out of the kitchen onto the lawn. I liked his skin next to mine.

'Pops knows you're coming, but let's see if he'll recognise you. I swear the man is losing his memory.'

I wasn't sure I'd remember Kweku's father either. It was always Aunty Kim who showed up at school. She would come for all the PTA events, and I only saw Kweku's father when I went to their house, and that was only if I stayed late.

A group of men had gathered by the giant barbecue, on which pieces of chicken, slabs of meat and sausages were crackling. The man in the apron with the close-cropped salt-and-pepper hair I was sure was Kweku's father, Uncle Dominic. He had an oblong face, strong teeth, a long nose and those same dimples that dappled Kweku's cheeks. I had probably never given him much mental space because Aunty Kim was so full of life that her husband had no choice but to live in her shadow.

'Pops,' said Kweku, breaking through the conversation the men were having.

'Oh hello,' said Pops and gave me a blank stare.

'Zainab from—'

'Good heavens,' said Pops. 'But of course. Well, you've all blossomed into these formidable young men and women.'

I almost laughed. Of course Pops wouldn't have changed either. I could now remember being in such awe of his vocabulary back then. And he had a lilt to his voice, probably from his days at Cambridge University.

Kweku took me to other side of the lawn, where his younger

siblings were gathered. They I would have met in the street and passed right on by. They were babies when Kweku and his family left Ghana.

'So Uncle Dominic totally didn't recognise me,' I told him.

'It'll come back to him later. Abena and Kojo, remember Zainab?'

'Your first girlfriend,' teased Abena. Even as a child she was feisty, like her mother. That hadn't changed. 'He still loooves you! You're all he's been talking about. Zainab this. Zainab that.'

Kweku shoved his sister playfully.

'Kweeeku,' shouted his father.

'Back in a second,' he said, and left me with his siblings, who were surrounded by their friends. I wondered if I was the only friend Kweku had invited over. Granted, he told me to come with Densua and Mary Grace, but I'd chosen not to. These young ones spoke rapidly, their accents now inflected with the rolling American Rs instead of our Ghanaian way of swallowing them. I tried to get in on what they were talking about: the new Will Ferrell movie. Since the movie date with Alex had gone sour, I hadn't really felt like walking into a cinema.

Kweku came back with a plate of grilled chicken. I pounced on it and chewed in what must have so unladylike a manner that he just gawked at me.

'I didn't eat breakfast, what?'

He laughed and said he'd get me more.

'No, I'm waiting for that jollof I saw your mother cooking.'

'And she's making kelewele.'

'Can I just marry your mother?'

'Don't worry, she taught me well,' Kweku said, and I could tell he had spoken too quickly. His dimples showed and hid. Then he went off to the barbecue station, before I could say anything. What would I have said?

I noticed for the first time that I hadn't heard a word from the grandmothers since arriving at Kweku's. Hello, I said in my head. Radio silence. It was nicely quiet, but at the same time, kind of lonely. Just like the way they'd appeared, their disappearance was troubling.

The lawn filled up with people. The music grew louder and the DJ slipped on his headphones. Kweku was back at my side.

'Your mother is not playing with this barbecue at all.' I pointed at the music station.

'Yup, he's one of the famous Ghanaian DJs from the Bronx.'

'I like it,' I said, as the DJ played Daddy Lumba's 'Aben Wo Aha'.

'This brings back memories of Accra I didn't even know I had! Let's dance?'

'We'll be the only ones.'

'So what? Someone has to start. Let's go!'

I liked this side of Kweku I hadn't seen. Confident. Then again, this was his home turf and it would be a problem if he couldn't be confident here. He took my hand and we went to the middle of the grass, shuffling left to right and wringing our hands in the air as if we held handkerchiefs, the basic highlife step. Aunty Kim rushed out with her dish towel and pulled a woman sitting in a garden seat to join her. After her friend's initial shyness, they both shimmied their waists and took over. All eyes were on them. Would I ever grow to exude such ease? For some reason, I was convinced that even in middle age I would always wear a delicate shell around my body. But I wanted to be like these two aunties, so sure of themselves. I couldn't wait to become an aunty, with that kind of confidence, ease and familiarity.

Kweku was right. More people joined us, and the DJ kept us dancing with hit after hit. Amakye Dede, Tic Tac, Ofori Amponsah, Obrafour. Songs that transported me right back to my mother's kitchen in Accra. One good thing that came after my parents' divorce was music. There was music again.

Now, the lawn was teeming with people. I helped Kweku carry plates to the older guests, and when we finally sat down to eat, I wolfed down my kelewele and jollof rice. It tasted just like home. Since Mma's visit, I'd deprived myself of good jollof for so long, because I just couldn't get it right and I didn't want to go up to the Bronx. Even if things were fine with Uncle Ali, going up there would bring back memories of those first lonely days in New York.

Kweku and I danced so much we were the last ones on the floor. The DJ was playing Boyz II Men and it took me right back to when the two of us were children.

'We kissed to this song,' Kweku said, smiling.

'Wait. Hold up. We kissed?' How had I buried such an important memory?

'OK, it was a quick peck.' He stopped, looked off into the distance and broke into belly-holding laughter, then covered his mouth. 'Here I was thinking you were my first kiss, and you don't even remember it.'

'How did I react?'

'It was so long ago, I can't remember. All I know is I held onto it for days, weeks, months. It was the bravest thing I'd ever done. Kissing Zainab Sekyi.'

'And we never spoke about it?'

'We were best friends, but you scared me to death. I didn't want to ruin the moment, so I just left it where it was.'

'I scared you to death?'

'You were one tough cookie. Like there were ten thousand more of you that would hold you down no matter what.'

'Why do I not know this about myself?' I said. It amazed me, my interior life versus what I projected. It was totally cognitively dissonant. 'I scared you, huh? Do I still scare you?'

'Not a chance.'

I pushed him playfully. This felt right, and I wanted to stretch being here with him for as long as I could, but it was getting late and Brooklyn was a long way from here.

'Shouldn't I be heading back to the train?'

'They don't shut down. These trains are heading to the city that never sleeps. It's in their best interest to stay open. Have dinner with us?'

Words I wanted to hear.

The dinner table was decorated with candles and covered with a spread of leftovers. A few other guests still straggled, so I didn't feel like I was overstaying. Chatter echoed about the table and Kweku's mother's laughter rang out high every so often. I sat next to Kweku, our feet touching under the table, and after dessert was served I leant over and whispered that I should probably get going.

'Mum has prepared a room for you.'

'Oh, really?'

I thought of my mother in Accra and what she would say. Probably 'Go home now.' Grannies?

Nothing. I tried to imagine what they would tell me to do. Jamila would tell me to stay. Fati would say I should go home right away. Zeina would probably say nothing. Why were they so silent?

One of them had said something about being in the estuary. We were far from the New York estuary now. Maybe I only heard them in the New York area! I wanted to laugh. If I'd known this all summer long. All I had to do was to leave the city. Even IKEA wasn't far enough. It was like the granny phone connection was only viable in the New York City metropolis.

Grannies? I tried again. They were truly silent.

'First thing tomorrow morning, I need to get to the station,' I said, smug that I was finally able to do something without my ancestors giving me their run-down and commentary.

'For church?' he said, furrowing the skin on his brow.

'Jokes,' I said.

Staying in Jersey tnite, I texted Mary Grace, in case she got worried.

Pls don't tell me ur at Alex's was the instant reply.

I had totally forgotten that Alex lived in this very same state. But probably not in such a neighbourhood. For Alex, I would conjure up a neighbourhood with a car wash with yellow plastic triangles, and banged-up storefronts, and the worst kind of decay.

The grandmothers, probably Jamila, would ask me to wish him well. Fine, I wished Alex well. Good luck to him and his life.

No, I responded. Kweku's mum's. Tell u more l8r.

I felt bad that I hadn't invited her or Densua, but when I saw my room, I was glad. If they had come with me, we'd be on our way back to New York by now. The bed was neatly made with pink and grey sheets, and a photo of a bouquet of roses above. I sank into the bed. Someone's guest room bed was more comfortable than my everyday bed.

As I revelled in the comfort supporting my weight, I tried to call on the grandmothers again, then I stopped. It was time to enjoy the quiet of my mind. I looked about the room. This was the American dream for many. And while owning such a house was nice, I didn't see this for myself in my future – living in the suburbs. I wanted to stay in New York, but I'd have to be very wealthy to have this kind of life, and it might mean hearing my ancestors for the rest of my life. But maybe there were other cures for that.

A soft knock rapped at the door, interrupting my dreams. I let Kweku in, and wordlessly we slipped under the sheets and our lips met. I managed to grin through our kisses, and my heart grew full. He touched my shoulders and his eyes didn't leave mine, and it was magical.

'This, my friend,' I said, 'is our first kiss.'

'It's yours. I'm sticking to my story.'

'Your parents' bedroom is how far from here?' I asked.

'Next door.'

'Oh my God, Kweku! Out!' I pushed him out of the bed. 'Go!'

'Goodnight,' he said. 'You made the barbecue extra special.'

'Goodnight. No, wait, one last question.'

'Shoot?'

'Why did it take you so long, Kweku Ansah?'

'I wasn't sure you liked me in the same way,' he said. 'I wanted to be sure.'

'I tried to kiss you way back when – at Densua's party.'

'You'd been drinking. You've heard of beer goggles? I was scared you'd sober up and think you'd made a mistake. But now, I'm sure.'

'And when did that happen?'

'Drink and Draw.'

'But you still did nothing.'

'I was waiting for you to make up your damn mind.'

'Wo yo,' I said out loud.

'What?'

'Something one of my grandmothers would say to totally crazy behaviour. OK, go, go, before we get caught!'

He kissed me and tiptoed out and I was sure my body was glowing in pink and green and all kinds of happy fluorescence in the dark of the room.

The grandmothers had been going on and on about how blind I was with Kweku. Zeina's words, *you'll know a good thing*, echoed in my mind's chamber. I could finally see it, all by myself. Kweku was a good thing.

Acknowledgements

This book came to me in 2020, when everything seemed like it was falling apart. I wanted to write a feel-good story; I wanted to write a love letter to New York City, a city that has my heart; I wanted to write a book about friendship.

And now *Zainab Takes New York* is out in the world, with huge thanks to: Jess Whitlum-Cooper at Headline Accent, for giving Zainab a home; Maria Cardona Serra, Anna Soler-Pont and the Pontas Agency family, for fighting hard for me; Jori, Nansu and Ciku, for the feedback and for becoming my sister scribes; Fawzia, for swimming classes with Emile; to the Popenguine family, thank you for fête after fête; Monsieur, Nana, Rahma, Pierre and Emile, for being the best family a girl could ask for. For my ride-or-dies, Efua, Michelle, Melissa, Kuorkor, Pearl, Valerie, Irene, Linda, Baafra, Mammie, Tracy, Taryn, Yaba, Dufie, Iyore, Biiftu, Matti, Anna-Lisa, Asantewa, Christine, Eugene, Chloe, Heather, Alia, Lollise, Najiyah, Rama, Zain, Jessica, Denise, Elissa, Liz, Jacqui N., Nii, Anissa (who always says yes to me), Makena, Sia, Nana-Ama, Jackie K., Kweku, Nana D., Nana E., and Bisi: this one is for us.

KEEP IN TOUCH WITH AYESHA HARRUNA ATTAH

© Pierre Poncelet

@ayeshahattah

/AyeshaHarrunaAttah